THE PERSIAN GIRL

Abigail said, 'The girl must be disciplined. As the aggrieved party, you shall be the witness to it, Sir.' She turned on Hope. 'Assume the position, you naughty girl!'

Hope bent over the little pull-down table. Abigail threw the chit's skirts and petticoats up over her head and pulled her drawers down to her ankles.

I blinked at a ripe, rounded and neatly divided little bottom.

The 'governess' swished a schoolmaster's cane, the kind with a curled handle. 'A dozen, do you think, Reverend?'

I made a noise in my throat.

'Quite right, she deserves twice that for her clumsiness.' Abigail pushed her sleeves up to her elbows and swung with a will.

Hope emitted muffled shrieks, shook her legs and wriggled her bum as Abigail's weapon drew line after fiery line across the pink firmness of her charming target. I, of course, reacted. By the time Abigail had counted to twenty, my staff had risen and was projecting before me, well beyond my shirt-tails.

Abigail grinned at my wagging stalk. 'Perhaps,' she suggested, 'if Hope were to assuage the need I see you suffer from, Reverend, you might be moved to forgive her transgression?'

I nodded.

'Her maidenhead must be preserved against her nuptials, but . . .' She took me in hand and directed my cock's head into the burning cleft in Hope's bottom.

THE PERSIAN GIRL

Felix Baron

This book is a work of fiction.
In real life, make sure you practise safe, sane and consensual sex.

Published by Nexus 2008

2 4 6 8 10 9 7 5 3 1

First published in Great Britain in 2008 by

Nexus
Virgin Books
Random House
20 Vauxhall Bridge Road
London SW1V 2SA
www.rbooks.co.uk

Addresses for companies within The Random House Group Limited can be found at: www.randomhouse.co.uk/offices.htm

Distributed in the USA by Macmillan, 175 Fifth Avenue, New York, NY 10010, USA

The Random House Group Limited Reg. No. 954009
A CIP catalogue record for this book
is available from the British Library

ISBN 978 0 3523 4501 1

The Random House Group Limited supports The Forest Stewardship Council [FSC], the leading international forest certification organisation. All our titles that are printed on Greenpeace approved FSC certified paper carry the FSC logo. Our paper procurement policy can be found at www.rbooks.co.uk/environment

Typeset by TW Typesetting, Plymouth, Devon
Printed and bound in Great Britain by CPI Bookmarque Ltd, Croydon, CR0 4TD

Symbols key

 Corporal Punishment

 Female Domination

 Institution

 Medical

 Period Setting

 Restraint/Bondage

 Rubber/Leather

 Spanking

 Transvestism

 Underwear

 Uniforms

Foreword

Sir Richard Francis Burton; as edited by Felix Baron

The catalogue read: *Lot#217. A tin trunk, circa 1860, containing a number of esoteric volumes, many with curious woodcuts, all in poor condition.*

To me, 'esoteric volumes, with curious woodcuts' means only one thing – ancient erotica. 'In poor condition' was a fair warning but we collectors can't help but dream of discovering a lost Cleland or something naughty that Mark Twain hadn't dared to publish. I instructed my agent to bid up to £200 pounds. He secured it for £165.

The first thing I saw when I opened the trunk was a mummified baby mouse. From the look of the poor creature's bed, the trunk had been immersed at some time and it wasn't waterproof. The copy of de Sade's *Justine, ou Les Malheurs de la Vertu* might have been worth something – it was a second edition – but water had welded the pages into a solid lump.

Adeline Greaves' *Flogging, a Treatise*, had fared better. It was legible, if one wanted to read a book in which the first twenty-eight pages are devoted to the preparation of the brine in which one plans to soak one's birch twigs.

I'd unpacked eleven more texts in various stages of disintegration before I came to a large parcel wrapped in butcher's paper, tied with twine and sealed with red sealing wax. Someone had taken the trouble to protect the contents, which raised my hopes of a 'find'.

Opening it disappointed me, at first. It contained manuscript pages, stained and tattered and in an illiterate hand. I was about to dismiss it as yet another amateur attempt at the novelist's craft, when a line on the title page leapt out at me.

Dictated in his declining years by Sir Richard Francis Burton, to Brigit Makepeace, his felatrice and amanuensis.

It made sense, in a way. Burton's wife, Isabel, was a true Victorian – prudish outside but perverse within. She was reputed to have privately condoned the sexual exploits of the translator of *The Arabian Nights* and *The Kama Sutra*, even to the extent of enthusiastically participating in his debauchery. In public, she presented herself as prim and proper. She edited many of Burton's works, deleting the more shocking passages. When he died, she destroyed all of his unpublished manuscripts.

Isabel might well have indulged an ageing Burton with the services of an orally adept whore. He might equally well have taken advantage of that privilege to produce and protect manuscripts he knew would burn if Isabel found them.

I have no provenance for this work. It doesn't bear his signature. Nevertheless, I have pieced together torn pages, examined stained ones by ultraviolet and simply made educated guesses where passages were missing. I've corrected and modernised Brigit Makepeace's colloquial and phonetic language. I accept that, where Burton spoke of events at which he wasn't present, he relied on reports that he considered accurate.

Here, then, is my best restoration of Sir Richard Francis Burton's recounting of *The Persian Girl*.

Post Scriptum: In these chapters, Burton mentions his prowess with a sabre from time to time. He does not exaggerate his skill. Modern fencing experts have ranked him as the best swordsman of all time, with Cyrano de Bergerac coming in second.

One

My wife, Isabel, is publicly a prude, privately a wanton. On my previous birthday she had woken me by taking my left testicle into the wet warmth of her mouth. That delightful reveille had been followed by an extensive and intrusive tongue-bath that lasted a full two hours and climaxed with my spending copiously into the navel that indents my wife's soft white belly. So it was that I lay abed on that nineteenth day of March, pleasantly anticipating another cleverly devised erotic treat.

Maude, Isabel's personal maid, threw the drapes apart and announced, 'Madam says to tell you your bath is ready and breakfast will be served in the morning room in half an hour, Sir.'

I cracked an eye enough to squint at the girl's silhouette. It was somehow different that morning; less restrained. Maude is a saucy little snip who enjoys a much more intimate relationship with her mistress than society condones. I don't object. Isabel is lascivious by nature, else I'd never have married her. If, when I was away on my Country's business, my wife assuaged her passions by taking a servant's face between her thighs, I'd rather it be Maude who 'tipped her velvet' than that Isabel rutted with one of our footmen.

Isabel and Maude ride a common hobby-horse. Maude is pleasantly contoured but she aspires to the unnatural shape that current fashion decrees is most feminine – the wasp waist. Isabel encourages her in this. Most days, Maude goes tightly cinched about her middle, corseted down to seventeen abnormal inches. On the anniversary of my natal day, unless I was mistaken, she was relaxed to her natural shape, perhaps twenty-two inches around her waist.

As I bathed and shaved and trimmed my moustache, I wondered how and if this unlacing was to play a part in whatever sensual delights my wife had planned for me. I dressed in a fresh sleeping suit; a newly fashionable garb, akin to the Eastern *pyjamas*, that was rapidly replacing the nightshirt. I toed into Moorish slippers and belted on a Chinese-style dressing robe. How cosmopolitan society had become! I'd not yet broken my fast and yet I was already arrayed in garments inspired by three different cultures.

Isabel was waiting in the morning room with a brocade robe over her own gauzy sleeping suit. Her lips had been touched with colour and she was perfumed, something blending lavender with vanilla. A wicked grin twitched her lips. My cock stirred in anticipation.

She greeted me with, 'Happy birthday, Richard!'

My gift from her lay across the breakfast table. I made myself inspect and admire the ornate scabbard before unsheathing a prime example of the sword maker's craft. The sabre's blade had been forged from the finest Sheffield steel. Its full length was inlaid with silver filigree and engraved. On one side, The Lord's Prayer had been etched and on the other, an invocation to Allah, in Arabic script. The heft and balance were perfect.

'Isabel! It's magnificent! I can hardly wait to try it.' I folded my dear wife to my bosom.

She murmured, 'In sport, not in earnest, I pray.'

As I hugged her, I felt her long fingers slide beneath my robe and explore my turgid length through the silk of my pantaloons. 'Does the scabbard please you, my husband?'

'I shall have to sheath my weapon to test its fit,' I responded.

'And so you shall, to the hilt, later.'

Breakfast was served by Maude, a departure from our custom, further proof that she and Isabel had been scheming. I was regaled with coddled eggs, devilled kidneys and

2

two heaped servings of kedgeree. Replete, I pushed back from the table.

'After that feast, I think a nap is in order,' I announced. 'You'll join me, Isabel?'

'Richard, if it isn't an imposition, young Maude has need of your expertise in Eastern medicine.'

'She's sick?' I looked at the girl, who appeared remarkably well and, for some reason, was removing the pinafore that had protected her Jacquard blouse and bombazine skirt while she'd served us.

Isabel grinned. 'It's a strange malady that has defeated the finest minds of Harley Street. She – we – hope that your experience in arcane medical practices might provide some clue as to its treatment.'

I suppressed a chuckle and put on a playful frown. 'Poor girl. Tell me, Maude, what are the symptoms of your unfortunate condition?'

Maude bobbed a little curtsey. Fighting to keep a straight face, she told me, 'An ache, Sir, a real bad *throbbing* ache and a fever.'

'And where on your person are you afflicted?'

She looked at the floor. 'I'm 'shamed to say, Sir.'

Isabel interrupted with a brusque, 'It's her pudenda, Richard.'

Maude mumbled, 'Yes, Sir, my cunny, as I calls it, me being but a simple girl.'

'He'll have to examine the affected area,' Isabel said.

I nodded gravely. 'No diagnosis is possible without a detailed inspection of the afflicted parts.'

In a mockery of modesty, Maude stepped closer, hands folded before the junction of her thighs, swaying her hips. I looked at her ankle-length black skirt and raised an eyebrow at Isabel.

'Silly girl! You'll have to remove your skirt,' my wife told Maude.

'Yes, Madam.' She unhooked the loop at her waist and let her skirt fall. Maude was wearing no chemise, just her drawers. A lady's drawers are made in two parts, joined at the waist with an opening from front to back, to facilitate

3

natural functions. I could easily have parted hers to make my inspection but I signalled with a finger and said, 'And your undergarment, Maude.'

Her drawers fell. Maude's cap was modestly set upon her curls. Her upper body was demurely concealed by a high-necked, leg-o'-mutton-sleeved starched blouse. From her waist down, she was nude except for the silk hose that were gartered just above her knees. The contrast of innocence with salaciousness was delicious.

Maude's belly was a sweet curve, deeply dimpled by her navel. Her mound was alabaster, with but a token wisp of down. Its slit was neat and tight.

I wet a fingertip and drew it down the crease of Maude's groin, from the point of her hip to within an inch of her pudenda. The girl shivered at my touch. A muscle in her belly twitched.

I repeated the caress, down her other groin's crease. Maude moaned and made tight little fists.

'Part your thighs,' I told her.

'Can you tell what ails the girl?' Isabel asked.

'I'm not sure yet.' My finger traced the line of Maude's slit with as light a touch as I was capable of. With each slow teasing caress, the girl became more agitated. Presently, her lower lips parted a fraction. The ball of my finger became slick with her dew. When I applied the slightest pressure, she parted and I was stroking the sensitive inner edges of her outer labia.

Maude groaned.

'She'll die of anticipation, Richard,' Isabel complained. 'For God's sake, stick it in!'

I thrust, just one finger. Inside, the girl was dripping with the liquor of her lust. My finger slid through clinging sponginess that did, indeed, seem uncommon warm.

'Is she fevered?' Isabel asked.

'She's hot, but I'm not sure that it's an *unnatural* heat,' I told her. Slyly, I added, 'Perhaps if I had some means of making a comparison?'

Isabel grinned wickedly. 'The sacrifices I make for my servants,' she sighed. Her robe was already unfastened –

something she'd doubtless taken care of while my attentions had been elsewhere. She threw it aside, revealing the fine gauze of her *pyjamas*. The trousers of her sleeping suit fastened with a drawstring and were open at the front. My dear wife tugged the slit wide to expose her own *mons veneris*. She came close and thrust her hips at me. 'There. Make your comparison, Richard.'

I assumed a thoughtful expression and wormed a finger into Isabel's female parts. Frowning in concentration, I explored both of the lovelies' cunnies, rotating, rubbing, delving deeply.

'Well?' Isabel asked, with a slight hitch in her voice.

'Truth be told, I do believe that you are both fevered. Could it be that the complaint is contagious and has passed from one of you to the other? Isabel, can you recall any occasions when your private parts came into close contact with those of your maid, Maude?'

Maude coughed. Isabel was unable to suppress a giggle. 'I believe that there might have been such an occasion,' she confessed.

My fingers worked a little harder, with a little more urgency, inspired by the lewd images my wife's admission conjured up. 'And we enjoyed connubial congress not two nights past,' I mused. 'I also could be afflicted. If this is the sickness I believe it to be, in the male it leads to a priapic state.'

'Please, Sir, what's that?' Maude asked.

'A stiff cock,' my wife explained. Her use of such language betrayed her. Isabel, in the drawing room, blushes at the slightest innuendo. When aroused, though, her language becomes that of the gutter. She gives the lie to the cockney expression, 'She's such a lady she won't say "cock" even if her mouth's full of it.'

'Is it, Sir?' the cheeky maid asked. 'Is it stiff?'

'We shall see for ourselves,' Isabel announced. She flipped my robe open, exposing my engorged condition, for it had escaped my *pyjamas* and stood, jutting from my loins like a lance *couchant*.

Maude gasped, 'It's a rare big one, Madam.'

'The questions were, is it hard and is it hot?' Isabel touched me with the backs of her fingers. 'It feels fevered to me,' she said. 'What do you think, Maude?'

The maid wrapped my shaft in her cool fist. 'I believe you're right, Madam.' She squirmed a little as she spoke, for I had introduced a second finger into her cunny and was testing that narrow channel for elasticity.

Isabel, being more mature, was already accommodating three of my fingers without showing any outward sign. 'Richard,' she said, 'you must prescribe for yourself. What may we do to alleviate your condition?'

'It must run its course,' I explained, 'but the symptoms may be treated by cooling the affected area.'

'Cold compresses?' she asked.

'It would not be wise for me to pause in my treatment of you and your maid while they were fetched, so perhaps you could improvise some way of dampening my distended part without leaving my side?'

'Maude,' Isabel said, 'spit on your Master's member.'

'Yes, Madam.' She leaned over and spat.

'I doubt that will suffice,' Isabel said. 'More like this.' She, in turn, leaned over my lap. Her mouth worked. Spittle appeared at her lips and drooled down in a long string, which she aimed precisely into the eye of my cock. 'Does that help, dearest?' she asked me.

'More, I think.'

Maude took a turn, imitating her Mistress.

'I think the full length should be wetted,' Isabel decided. She knotted a fist in Maude's hair, knocking the girl's cap to the floor. Isabel pressed down, not that Maude seemed reluctant. The girl's lips parted, formed an 'O' and slithered down half the length of my shaft.

'All the way,' Isabel told her.

Maude's head shook. Isabel drew her back up. 'Can't,' Maude explained.

'Of course you can! It's simply a matter of breathing through your nose. Watch me!'

My dear wife swooped, not pausing until her lips brushed my pubic hair. ''E 'at?' she asked.

6

Maude tried again, with great diligence. By the time Isabel had demonstrated her technique a dozen times, with Maude doing her utmost to imitate her, the maid achieved her goal. It seemed that swallowing cock induces salivation, for both were drooling – running at the mouth. I, of course, was feeling remarkably lustful but, as pleasant as the exercise was, the alternating of their mouths slowed things down. I was sure I wouldn't achieve release that way.

'There is a theory,' I croaked, 'of the healing powers of opposites. Light dispels darkness. Water douses fire. Yin heals yang.'

'Yin is the female essence, and yang the male, no?' Isabel asked. 'How would you apply this theory, in such a case as this?'

'By the close juxtaposition of the male and female parts,' I explained.

'I see. Maude, mount your Master.'

'Yes, Madam,' was the chit's eager response. Facing me, she threw a leg across my lap. Isabel steered my shaft. Maude lowered herself. My dome sank into her. She twisted her hips and pushed down. My stem began to disappear but when it still had half its length to go, the maid paused. 'That's as much as I can take, Madam,' she explained. 'The Master is too big.'

It was clear to me that she was lying. She was delightfully tight, but I've known tighter. Her maidenhead wasn't the problem. I'd felt no trace of the barrier that had likely been rent when she was of a much more tender age. No, this pretence was part of their scheming, the sweet vixens!

'I shall assist you,' Isabel announced. She removed the jacket of her sleeping suit, baring the beauty of her mature breasts. My cock twitched inside Maude in response. I've examined every inch of my dear wife's body, in detail and often. Even so, her nakedness never fails to stir me.

Isabel marched to the sideboard and bent at her waist to open the lowest drawer. I sucked a breath. Her bosom is never more attractive than when pendant and the trousers of her *pyjamas* rode low on her shapely hips. Her position threatened to dislodge them entirely.

She returned with one of my riding crops. 'Bend forward,' she told Maude.

The girl gave me an apologetic look and leaned to rest her cheek on my shoulder. Isabel inspected the raised curves of her maid's young bottom.

'So you think you can't take any more?' she asked.

The crop whistled and landed with a resounding crack. Maude gasped and jerked at me. Another inch of my flesh sank into hers. Six more blows had her pubes pressed to mine but Isabel wasn't content, and nor was I. Each time the crop landed, Maude gyrated. Her internal muscles clenched and relaxed. She juddered. My neck grew wet with her tears and slobbering. I was beginning to feel sorry for the girl when she convulsed, contracted fiercely, and yelped.

Now that it had become obvious that pain had been the source of her pleasure, I let myself release. I was still jetting when Maude slithered off me.

Isabel is a firm believer in, 'Spill not thy seed upon the ground.' Her mouth ensured that mine wasn't allowed to.

Two

I was informed that a gentleman had left his card but no message. When I examined the pasteboard I understood why. The name on it was spurious and the address fictitious. Her Majesty's Confidential Office is fond of such games. Sir George Armbruster, the secretary of that office, calls such messages his 'surreptitious summonses'.

As I had been instructed, though it seemed like foolishness to me, I took a hansom to Burlington Arcade. Strolling up it, I made sure I wasn't being followed.

It was quite irritating. I've danced with Dervishes; taught as a Sufi; entered the Holy of Holies as a hajji, and walked the breadth of Sind in the guise of a Buddhist monk. I *certainly* needed no instruction on how to cross London discreetly.

Nevertheless, I took another cab, to Jermyn Street, disappeared down back alleys and finally emerged in Lavender Square. A secret knock on the door to the servants' quarters of number 47 gained me access to a panelled room, where I flirted with a pretty young maid until Sir George deigned to see me.

'Richard,' he boomed, 'what do you know about a fellow called Pasha Benim ben Midras?'

'Educated Balliol, honours in ancient languages; sixth degree Scottish Rite Freemason; scion of a cadet branch of the Imperial House of Osman and a man of considerable influence in the Province of Van, in South Eastern Turkey.'

'Oh? Y'heard of the man, then. Reliable, would you say?'

'Hates Russia, so our faithful ally in that regard. He'd put Turkish interests before ours, of course.'

'Quite, quite. He sent you a message.'

'Oh?' I waited.

'Peculiar, really.'

I waited some more.

'Wouldn't have paid much mind to it, 'cept for what happened to our man in Paris.'

Questions never get much out of Sir George, so I said nothing in the hope that my silence would draw him out.

'This Pasha chappy, sent packages with his note.' Sir George rose, went to the next room and returned draped in silvery mottled fur. 'Recognise this?'

'Siberian wolf.' I took it from him and held it up. The pelt was better than seven feet long, not counting the tail. 'I didn't know they grew that big,' I remarked.

'Your Pasha claims he shot it.'

'He was in Siberia? That doesn't sound like him. He's a man as likes his creature comforts.'

'No. He claims he killed the beast not a bowshot from his palace.'

'There are wolves in Turkey, but not Siberian and especially, not of such a size.'

'What d'ye think he meant, then?'

'Siberian wolf? A threat from Russia, most likely.'

'Then why the deuce didn't he say so?'

I wasn't about to explain the workings of subtle oriental minds to as obtuse an Englishman as Sir George. I simply shrugged. 'You mentioned "packages"?'

'A thousand guineas, in gold.'

'And sent to me, by name?'

'Mm.'

'It seems that Pasha Ben Midras perceives a threat, from Russia, and is willing to finance a visit from me to help him with it. Does Her Majesty's Confidential Office concur?'

'Yes.'

'Then I'll set off for Turkey post-haste. By the way, you mentioned something happening to an agent of yours, in Paris. What was it?'

'He was taking an early stroll in the Bois de Boulogne when he was attacked and mauled to death by an enormous wild dog.'

I packed my new sabre, my 'Dragoon' Colt .44, a change of clothes, and the thousand guineas into my trunk. My 'Arkansas Toothpick', a blade similar to that made famous by Colonel James Bowie, my linen and my toiletries, went into a carpetbag. I dressed in black broadcloth, suitable for the American clergyman I'd decided to travel as. There was a concealed pocket in my jacket for my two-shot .25 calibre Derringer. I carried a swordstick with a spring-release sheath and a twenty-inch blade, 'As furnished to discerning gentlemen, world-wide, by Smith and Smith, of High Holborn.' It had a brass ferule and a heavy knob, shaped like a ram's head, so it was a fair weapon even without its secret. The handle concealed a compartment, just big enough to hold five gold guineas.

My preparations were as complete as I could make them.

Isabel bade me a tearful farewell and I was off in a hired growler, heading for Leigh-on-Sea. My chartered steam yacht picked me up at midnight, at high tide, from behind cockle shed number seven. It took me across the North Sea, through the Northern Canal and into Amsterdam.

Two hours after I'd disembarked, a porter was stowing my baggage in one of a steam train's luxurious private carriages. I had four berths to choose from, two above two, on opposite sides of the door, running width-wise. The upper berths were no more than five feet above the floor, leaving little headroom in the lower ones, so I decided I'd sleep higher rather than lower. A sturdy pull-down table was fixed to the outer wall, below a window, with two plain chairs tucked under it.

After another hour we pulled away. I composed myself for a tedious journey, for at least as far as Breslau, in Silesia.

As it happened, my tedium was delightfully relieved by the time we reached Liège.

Three

The dining car was only half-full that evening but Abigail Smythe asked if she and her two pretty charges might join me at my table. 'These European trains are so full of foreigners and you, being an American and a man of the cloth, well, you Americans aren't really *foreign*, are you. You being a large person, and all. We'd feel safer in your company, wouldn't we, girls?'

Her 'girls' agreed, enthusiastically.

I kept a grin off my face. Abigail presented herself as a governess, escorting her young pupils, Hope and Grace. She gave their ages as fifteen and sixteen. For the duration of that meal, I doubt a single true word passed her lips. I'd never heard of an English governess who wasn't of good family but in reduced circumstances. Abigail's manner of speech denied any 'good family' in her background. Had I been the American clergyman I feigned to be, I might have been fooled but I'd been raised in a class where governesses were as commonplace as scullery maids. I'd tupped more than my share, in my youth. Besides, young Hope had an uncommonly wide mouth and a turned-up button nose, features I found erotic but hardly indicative of a refined bloodline.

Both girls' faces had been artfully painted to make them seem more youthful. The dusting of powder failed to conceal the subtle creases at the corners of their eyes. By the appearance of their hands, I judged them to be in their early twenties.

I had no doubt but that I was being set up for some cunning swindle. Its nature would no doubt reveal itself in due course. Meanwhile, all three girls were pretty and I had no other amusement to hand.

The meal passed without incident. No mention was made of an inheritance that it would require my aid, and a small investment on my part, to secure. No decks of marked cards emerged from the oversized matching reticules the three carried. Those bags confirmed my suspicions. Although they were capacious, they seemed to be empty, or close to it. I've never known a woman to carry a bag that wasn't so stuffed she had to commandeer her escort's pockets to accommodate extra gewgaws.

Breakfast was much the same, except for a pretty and well-rehearsed little squabble between the 'girls' as to which of them would sit by my side. I did my best to look pleasantly abashed by the compliment.

At lunch, Abigail asked my advice about the safest way a lady, or a gentleman, might conceal any valuables while travelling in foreign parts. I affected ignorance. Hope made some suggestions that a more sophisticated man than 'Reverend Longfellow' might have taken for risqué innuendo. He, of course, being so naive, simply looked blank.

Perhaps because of my obvious 'innocence', or because I'd revealed that my purse wasn't cleverly concealed, the vixens moved in on their prey that very evening.

'Bratwurst with sauerkraut,' Abigail sneered. 'Perhaps a little wine would make our supper more palatable. What say you, Reverend?'

'Wine?' I blinked from Hope to Grace like an owl.

'Their parents allow the girls a thimbleful, on special occasions.'

'In that case, by all means. "Take a little wine, for thy stomach's sake." May I seek your advice on the choice, Miss Abigail? We don't see a lot of European wines back in Kalamazoo. Something mild, if you please?'

Abigail suggested a port. As the Reverend Longfellow, I affected not to know the difference between fortified and unfortified wine. Hope, the younger girl, sitting beside me, made sure to keep my glass topped up.

As myself, I can down a full bottle of port, followed by a couple of large brandies, and still shoot the pip out of an ace of spades at thirty paces. As the Reverend Longfellow, two glasses had me slurring my words. After three, my eyes were unfocused and I swayed with the train.

Abigail, sitting opposite me, exclaimed, 'What on Earth is that!' and leaned to peer from the window.

I turned my head but maintained watch on the table via its reflection in the glass. Hope, deliberately and with precision, took the bottle of port and poured a generous measure directly into my lap.

We all four exploded from the table, the girls squealing and I staggering. Hope begged my pardon.

Abigail reproached Hope with, 'Clumsy little fool!'

The girl burst into crocodile tears. All three tugged at me. I was drawn in a flurry of female consternation, looking foolish and bewildered, to their carriage. There, confused, I suffered my boots and stockings to be pulled off, followed by my wine-soaked trousers and sticky drawers. Grace disappeared with both garments and a muttered, 'Find a valet.'

It had been nicely executed. I had to admire their efficiency. In a matter of minutes, two of them had their clerical guest seemingly helpless and compromised, while the third made off with his keys, headed without a doubt, for his carriage.

But their charade was not yet done.

Abigail said, 'The girl must be disciplined. As the aggrieved party, you shall be the witness to it, Sir.' She turned on Hope. 'Assume the position, you naughty girl!'

Hope bent over the little pull-down table. Abigail threw the chit's skirts and petticoats up over her head and pulled her drawers down to her ankles.

I blinked at a ripe, rounded and neatly divided little bottom.

The 'governess' swished a schoolmaster's cane, the kind with a curled handle. 'A dozen, do you think, Reverend?'

I made a noise in my throat.

14

'Quite right, she deserves twice that for her clumsiness.' Abigail pushed her sleeves up to her elbows and swung with a will.

Hope emitted muffled shrieks, shook her legs and wriggled her bum as Abigail's weapon drew line after fiery line across the pink firmness of her charming target. I, of course, reacted. By the time Abigail had counted to twenty, my staff had risen and was projecting before me, well beyond my shirt-tails.

Abigail grinned at my wagging stalk. 'Perhaps,' she suggested, 'if Hope were to assuage the need I see you suffer from, Reverend, you might be moved to forgive her transgression?'

I nodded.

'Her maidenhead must be preserved against her nuptials, but . . .' She took me in hand and directed my cock's head into the burning cleft in Hope's bottom.

The girl's rear passage resisted some, but not as a virgin bum would have.

Hope squealed, 'I am undone!' and rotated her hips to further enhance her undoing.

I thrust with a will and was still at it when the door opened. Grace had returned with her reticule bulging and her free hand behind her. The girl was squirming with suppressed excitement. She tossed her bag on to the lower berth to the left. It chinked.

I half-turned, bearing the impaled Hope with me. 'What's in your bag, Grace?' I demanded. 'Open it up and show me.'

Instead, she showed me what was in her other hand – my revolver. A loaded Dragoon is a heavy beast. It took both of her hands to hold it trained on me.

'Silly girl!' I said. A smart thrust of my hips propelled Hope off my cock and into her 'sister'. Reaching over the sprawling girl, I plucked my pistol from Grace's fingers.

'You have to cock it,' I told her.

'You can't peach on us,' Abigail claimed. 'How's a Reverend gentleman to explain being robbed while distracted on account of he was buggering an innocent young girl? You shop us and we'll shop you.'

In my natural voice, I said, 'You might shop me, by all means. Consider, though. I'm no Yankee clergyman. I'm an officer and an English gentleman with credentials that are verifiable at any British embassy or consulate, and I'm wealthy, to boot. You three, on the other hand, are whores and swindlers, likely known to the constabulary. As you have discovered, I have the means to pay bribes and fines. I doubt you do.'

Abigail changed her tactics. 'Look, Mister, whoever you are and whatever your game is, we was just having a bit of a lark with you. We didn't mean no 'arm.'

'And no harm has been done,' I assured her.

'What then?' she asked. 'Forgive and forget?'

I looked down at Hope, sprawled on the floor with a nice display of limbs even though her bottom was now covered. 'This girl and I have unfinished business.'

Abigail grinned. 'And you still horny as a rhinoceros in Spring, ain't you? Well, my Hope don't never lift her skirts 'less there's a bob or two in it for her.'

'Come now! I doubt there's a depravity known to man that the three of you haven't enjoyed, just for wicked pleasure of it. Own up that you're a lascivious trio of trollops and I'm sure we'll come to terms.'

'Well . . .'

Grace interrupted. 'And if we 'fess up to being three right randy sluts, what then?'

'I propose a fête. We won't reach Breslau for three full days. At the next halt, we'll stock up on provisions – a ham perhaps, or a roast fowl and some sweetmeats for you girls, plus a dozen bottles of bubbly. We'll lock the door and gorge our carnal appetites for three days and three nights. What do you say?'

Hope rolled over and looked up at Abigail. 'Can we, Abby? Can we?'

Grace asked, 'Will there be chocolates?'

'Chocolates, Turkish Delight, caramels, liquorice comfits, all the bon-bons you could wish for, if they're available. Abigail,' I said, 'I am a generous man if a woman pleases me.'

16

She spat into her palm and offered it to me to shake. 'And if *three* saucy girls pleases you?'

'Then they will be suitably rewarded.'

Hope, most ungainly, sitting on the floor with her knees up and her naked cunny peeping up at me from the shadows of her underskirts, winked. 'It's at least half an hour till the next halt. As you said, Sir, you and I have unfinished business.'

'You have a taste for being sodomised?' I asked her.

She put on such a simpering look that I might have taken her for the tender age she feigned, and on her wedding night. 'I dote on it, Sir. I beg you indulge me.'

What a clever little harlot she was! I was still randy, as a man who has been interrupted while buggering a pretty girl would be, but hearing the wench plead for a continuance of the depravity elevated my lust marvellously. I pulled the girl to her feet. She turned to lean over the table again but I had other ideas. I have deft fingers when it comes to unbuttoning and loosening laces. My hands turned her this way and that, each twist disposing of a fastening, until she stood naked but for her high-button boots and silk hose. I lifted her slight weight bodily and set her boots' toes on the lower of the pair of berths, facing the beds.

'Hold fast,' I commanded.

With her standing on the berth below, gripping the one above, I manipulated her body, hollowing her back and protruding her bottom. Once more, my cock's head nuzzled the tight purse of her back passage. With my hands lightly on her hips, I said, 'If you dote on it, then show me. Impale yourself, little nymph, and dance the sodomites' polka.'

'While you "poke her",' Abigail jested.

Hope wriggled and pressed down. Once more, her rear opened for me. I simply held fast, allowing her the freedom to skewer herself, which she did with a squeal of delight.

'Grace,' she exclaimed, 'I do declare our Reverend's a veritable Priapus incarnate.' Her pronunciation of the god's name was inaccurate. No doubt it was a word she had read in a penny-dreadful but had never heard used.

Hope swivelled her hips slowly and lasciviously. 'He stirs me in ways, and places, no man has ever stirred me before.'

17

I was not so innocent as to take her praise at face value. It is a common trick among practised whores to compliment their clients extravagantly. It can accelerate the transaction and perhaps earn a slut half a crown above her usual fee. In this case there was no agreed fee and we had three full days in which to indulge ourselves, but a skilled worker cannot but do his, or her, best.

I took Hope's warm soft hips in my hands and stilled her gyrations. My feet moved me closer, so that I stood immediately beneath her. Leaning back, I thrust straight upwards. The impact of my thighs on the backs of hers was such that I lifted her feet off the berth and bounced the girl, 'in my lap' as it were.

A great gasp escaped her lips, followed by rhythmic grunts as I pounded up into her, penetrating 'even unto the seventh rib' as a Roman poet once wrote. As Hope jounced, her 'sister' Grace laid a tender hand on her shoulder. 'Well done!' she exclaimed. I wasn't sure if the praise was aimed at me or Hope. 'Hold tight, or this great stallion will surely throw you to the floor.'

I took Grace by her wrist and guided her hand down to Hope's cunny, which by then was running wet. 'Diddle her!' I commanded.

Grace's fingers slapped Hope's slit. I pounded into the girl's arse. Abigail watched, grinning.

'I'm . . .' Hope began. 'I'm . . . I *am undone!*' She juddered, went limp and swooned back into my arms.

I set her down on the berth opposite and turned back to the other two harlots. Both stared at my rampant member with rounded eyes.

Abigail drawled, 'And yet it stands!'

Both of them were still fully dressed. I'd sooner have stripped one, or both, but we were closing on the train's next stop. My arms scooped Grace up and seated her on the little table. I took an ankle in each hand and raised them, tumbling her skirts and petticoats about her waist. Her drawers were split from fore to aft. Without further ado, I pistoned into her, holding nothing back. It was a rude assault, but she was a sturdy girl and took it well. Still rutting into her, I turned to Abigail and told her, 'Fetch me clean trousers from my compartment so that you and I may go shopping.'

She returned; the train's brakes squealed, and I filled Grace's pretty little cunny to overflowing, all within a few breaths.

Four

The platform had been transformed into a fantastic bazaar by bright oil lamps and dazzling gas lights. Merchants clamoured for the passengers' business. Unfortunately, there was an ample quantity but little choice of victuals. Abigail and I failed to procure even one roast but we did manage to purchase several boxes of Belgian chocolates and French peppermint sticks, plus three pork pies, two game pies, a cherry tart and a tray of *Dampfnudeln* that were seasoned with brandied damsons. The wine merchant could only produce three magnums of an indifferent champagne so I added half a dozen bottles of Slivovitz and four of a very potable Hungarian red wine, *Egri Bikaver*, sometimes called 'Bull's Blood'. With three hot harlots to service, I'd need all the bullish help I could find.

I sent a porter back to the carriage with our purchases and dallied, doing my best to charm Abigail. She was obviously the leader of the trio and I'd usurped her, in a way, by turning the tables on their plot. If I didn't want to spend the rest of the journey watching my back, I'd best befriend the woman.

There was a stall that offered ladies' dainties. I treated the girls to combs for their hair and two pairs of silk hose each.

'Stockings become Hope's pretty legs,' I remarked.

'Grace's likewise.'

'I look forward to watching your girls try these on, don't you?'

Abigail looked me in the eyes and told me, 'I do, very much.'

I'd hinted, and it had been candidly confirmed, that Abigail was more 'Tom' than tart.

'I hope I will acquit myself well with your girls,' I told her. 'Perhaps I can persuade you to assist me in pleasuring them? A man has his limits. However copious a pot, it can run dry.'

She nodded. 'But our bargain encompassed the three of us, did it not?'

'I thought your preference was for . . .'

'Indeed it is, but not to the exclusion of your gender, Reverend Sir.' She gave me a quizzical look. 'Which do you favour, oysters or stewed eels?'

'Oysters.'

'Me too, but after I've slurped down a dozen or three, sucking the liquor from a nice long piece of stewed eel makes a very pleasant change.'

I gave her my warmest smile. 'Then please consider our three-day orgy your personal buffet, Abigail. If a dish appeals to you, sample it, but no one is going to expect anything from you that it doesn't suit you to offer.'

She tucked her arm through mine. 'Reverend, I do declare, this holiday promises to be as memorable as a Christmas Day orgy in Brighton's best brothel!'

We'd supped before Hope had anointed my privates with port and by the time we returned to the girls' compartment it was well past midnight. 'You may sample the chocolates and open one bottle of the plum brandy,' I told them. 'Our true celebrations will commence in the morning. Hope, put a robe on. We'll divide, two and two. You'll come with me.'

In my compartment, I put Hope in one upper berth and secured her wrists to a handle with a cravat from my chest before taking the other upper berth. She made no objection. Doubtless she'd been tied before, with amorous intent. My reason was less erotic. I'd made friends with the trio of trollops, as best I could, but they were ramp-artists and thieves, first, and they knew I carried a fortune in gold. I'd have been a fool not to take precautions.

Lulled by my swaying carriage and the 'clickety-dee, clickety-dah' of iron wheels, I slept the sleep of a righteous man who'd fucked one girl and buggered another that very day, and looked forward to a morrow filled with similar activities.

Five

The porter who brought hot water for my morning ablutions raised a bushy brow at the length of lovely limb that was exposed in the upper berth occupied by Hope. A pair of golden guineas smoothed his forehead and sent him after another pitcher. I was being profligate with Ben Midras' funds, but the Pasha tithed the salt trade in the south-eastern reaches of the Ottoman Empire. It'd be easier to dry up the Atlantic Ocean with a bath sponge than to deplete his coffers.

When Hope and I arrived at the girls' compartment, Grace was kneeling in a Seitz bath, soaping her privates with unladylike vigour. Abigail, in nothing but her drawers, was standing with her shapely back towards us, encouraging Grace with, 'Spend for me, my pigeon, my pet! Frig with a will, darling dolly-mop! Polish your pearl for Abigail!'

Grace's eyes widened at our appearance. Abigail turned. She might have been the Tom in their *ménage à trois* but she had by far the most womanly form. Hope and Grace were sylphs, almost boyish at their hips and with half-lemon breasts set on narrow chests. Abigail had curves. Her hips flared; her waist was a reed; her bosom a pair of succulently ripe fruits that swayed and wobbled but didn't sag.

'Please carry on,' I invited. My hand gestured towards Abigail's, which was still gently mobile inside the slit in the front of her drawers.

She gave me a sweet smile. 'It wasn't our intent to start without you, Reverend, but anticipation overcame us.'

I didn't correct her for calling me 'Reverend' after I'd set that guise aside. She persisted, I assumed, because an orgy with a man of the cloth would be far more sinful than one with a layman. For some people, if not all, the greater the transgression, the more intense the thrill.

A knock announced the arrival of coffee. Hope and I crowded the doorway as I took the tray from our porter, so that his sensibilities would not be further offended. By the time we had the steaming pots on the table, Grace had rinsed herself and had knotted a Turkish towel low about her hips. I produced my Bowie knife and cut a game pie into four. My blade impressed the ladies, or so they professed. The game in the pie was mostly hare, which occasioned a number of ribald remarks. For lack of milk or sugar, I laced our cups with plum brandy. By the time the last crumbs of pie had been dabbed up and the coffee pots drained, we were as jolly and companionable a quartet as you might wish to encounter.

I stood and announced, 'Champagne!'

Hope said, 'We lack glasses.'

'You've heard of gentlemen toasting their ladies by drinking champagne from their slippers?'

She nodded, frowning.

I continued, 'For want of slippers, we'll use a glove – Venus' glove.'

Hope still looked blank until Abigail explained, 'It's an old expression, you silly goose. Your "Venus glove" is your cunny, pussikin, twat, or how you like it.' Abigail looked at me and shrugged. 'Young whores today – no education.'

'Then we must school them,' I said. I tugged the cord at her waist. Her sole garment slid down to the *rondeur* of her hips. Her eyes on mine, her face expressionless, Abigail rippled her abdomen. Her drawers slithered to her feet.

I wrapped her thighs with my hands and hoisted her on to the upper berth. There, she submitted to my disposition of her limbs, which I arranged as spread as the cramped quarters allowed. I folded a pillow in half and tucked it under her bottom to tilt her hips.

The younger girls watched and giggled as I stripped the foil from a magnum and plucked out its cork. Two fingers of my left hand parted the fleshy outer lips of Abigail's cunny. I tilted the bottle slowly, taking careful aim. Wine dribbled on to her mound. I directed it lower, so that it trickled and foamed directly on to the barely-exposed head of her clit.

Abigail shivered. 'That's cold!'

'We'll warm you anon,' I told her. The wine coursed through her convoluted channel and pooled where her pussy's lips joined into a tiny soft cup. Stooping, I sucked and lapped and probed, working upwards until I was giving the 'feathery flick' to her hard little bud.

As soon as her soft moans and twitching hips told me she was responding, I lifted my head, boosted Hope up to stand on the lower level, pulled her face close to Abigail's cunny, and poured again. The girl buried her face between Abigail's thighs, slurping and snuffling. Abigail clutched Hope's head and humped at her face. I found the uninhibited debauchery so fascinating that I was hardly aware that Grace had taken the bottle from me. I felt her warm softness brush against me as she settled into the lower berth. When I glanced down, she had the bottle tilted to her lips but she wasn't swallowing. Her free hand took my stalk and guided it to her lips. Her mouth, full of foaming champagne, engulfed my knob. I almost expected to feel tiny bubbles bursting on my dome, but the sensations were too subtle to discern. I did, however, enjoy the swishing of her tongue and the vigorous bobbing of her head. When the wine was gone, the minx took my cock from between her lips and poured champagne over it, to slurp off with avid little sucks.

Abigail arched and grunted. Hope turned to me with a triumphant grin. Her face was glossy, partly with wine, mainly with Abigail's spending. I gave her cheek one long lascivious lick before plunging my tongue into her soft wet mouth. Her flavour, part wine, part spittle, part woman-essence, was more intoxicating than the juice of the poppy.

Our kiss was interrupted by Abigail, who eased off the berth feet first, descending between Hope's body and mine. Her legs spread wide, encircling my chest, and slithered down my torso, smearing the wet open mouth of her cunny

24

over my breastbone. A twitch of her shoulders flicked an engorged nipple across my lips. With her back towards the berths, arms spread across the upper one, Abigail worked her way lower down my body, ending Grace's champagne games, until her knees bracketed my hips and the soft lips of her sex parted over the hard knob of my stem.

'Put it in for me, Grace,' she hissed.

Two hands manipulated me, pulling my shaft down against its will, then letting it up to nestle its head just inside Abigail's humid portal.

I raised an eyebrow at Abigail. She'd declared her taste to be more for the weaker gender than for mine, and yet, despite 'the little death' she'd recently enjoyed, she was coming at me like a vixen in heat.

Her eyes blazed into mine. 'I'm going to *fuck* you,' she declared, as if it were a dire threat.

I understood. I was a challenge to her domination over her girls. She had to defeat me, sexually, or lose status. She wasn't to know that I have been a Sufi and a Yogi and have followed the Tantric path. Had I wished to compete with her, I could have gone the three days denying myself any release at all, or I could have internalised my climaxes, enjoying a multitude of orgasms without ejaculation. Either way, I'd have been indefatigable.

I decided to be magnanimous. Winning was vital to her. I would have let a bright child beat me at chess. I'd allow Abigail to defeat me in love's lists, but not too easily.

I braced myself. My feet were set flat and wide apart. My knees were bent and turned outwards. My hands gripped the edge of the upper berth. In my mind, I became a stone statue, immobile, unmovable.

Abigail lowered herself until her cunny embraced both the head of my cock and a little of its shaft. Her legs moved, finding purchase. Her knees were hooked over my hips and her ankles were crossed behind me. With her eyes intent on mine, she raised herself until her soft slippery petals held my dome in only a tentative grip, then gradually lowered herself again. Slowly and steadily, up and down, the slippery vestibule of her sex slathered my helmet. I was supposed to find the partial penetrations unbearable and be moved to thrust into her depths, galloping to a climax. Well, she'd be rewarded with my orgasm, in due course. First, I intended to put her through her paces.

From her waist up, Abigail was rigid. Her hips rotated as she drew herself closer to me. My shaft spiralled into her. She bent at her knees, pressing her mound against my pubic bone. A small grunt escaped her as she ground down with all the force she could muster, forcing my flesh deeper into hers. Holding that position, she clenched and relaxed on me, massaging me with her powerful internal muscles.

Her belly twitched. A bead of sweat appeared on her upper lip. Her forehead creased in concentration.

I gave Abigail my most beatific smile.

Fingers caressed my scrotum. I'd almost forgotten that Grace was in the lower berth, behind Abigail. The points of Hope's nails traced lines down my back. Her mouth was wet on my shoulder.

So – it was to be three against one. 'Kiss me, Hope,' I invited.

She raised herself up with one foot on the lower berth and one on the opposite one. Her tongue worked into the crook of my neck. Below me, Grace weighed the contents of my sac on her palm.

Abigail grinned. She retracted her right leg from behind me and with an impressive display of flexibility, folded it close to her body. Her toes trailed up my chest until she could hook her foot behind my neck. Her left leg followed the same path. Abigail crossed her ankles behind my neck. Hanging thus, the flexing of her thighs alternately moved her cunny from side to side and up and down.

From her navel down, she writhed. My cock became a stiff pestle in the yielding mortar of her sex. She swivelled and churned. Her internal muscles milked at me. Hope stretched in from the side to suck on my lower lip. Grace toyed with as much of my shaft as was exposed from time to time and smoothed a wet fingertip over the pucker of my anus.

I sensed some desperation in Abigail. To her mind, my self control should have disappeared long since. Despite herself, or perhaps she wasn't aware, her focus shifted. She became less intent on stimulating the head of my cock and more on grinding her tender bead against my hardness. Her mouth slackened. Her eyes misted. A droplet of sweat ran down the valley of her breasts.

Her hips lifted and smacked down, splattering aromatic dew with the impact. Abigail gurgled. She screwed at me, lifted up and paused, rigid.

I knew that her joy was upon her. For the first time in the half hour or so she'd been riding me, I moved. My hips drew back. I lanced into her, slapping belly on belly, and at the exact moment I felt her scalding flood bathe my shaft, I let my jism squirt.

Abigail slithered down me, toppling back into the lower berth, tumbling Grace aside. I allowed myself to stagger backwards across the narrow aisle until the edge of the opposite berth caught me behind my knees.

My breath rasping, I told Abigail, 'You are a remarkably fine fuck, young lady.'

She panted for a while before squeezing out, 'Likewise, Reverend.'

Grace complained, 'I'm horny!'

Abigail said, 'Hope, attend to her. Get head-to-tail, you two, while the Reverend and I gather ourselves. We'll join you anon, I promise, right, Reverend?'

And we did.

Six

At Breslau I left the wanton trio with the best part of a pork pie, a third of a bottle of plum brandy, all the coconut-centred chocolates and a hundred and fifty gold guineas. My reckoning was fifty for the sport, fifty for depriving them of other business and fifty for them ignoring the knife I'd left on the table. They'd had ample opportunity to put it to my throat or into my back but they'd abided by our agreement. They were swindlers and whores, but they were honourable ones.

I took away some treasured memories – a droplet of sweat falling from the tip of Abigail's nipple into Hope's waiting mouth – three giggling girls, squirming like eels to find a position in which each could tongue another's ring – Hope licking a smear of my jism off Grace's heaving belly.

By luck, I fell in with a band of gypsies. I speak Rom and have a certain cast to my features. They took me for one of their own, likely a fugitive, and made a space for me in one of their caravans for the next hundred miles of my journey. When our paths divided, I purchased a donkey and cart from them at an exorbitant price and so made my way to the magnificent new railway station at Prague. Before entering that great city, I packed my western garb in my trunk, rubbed walnut juice into my skin and donned the robes and burnoose of a Berber.

Five *filler* bought me the right to tie my trunk to the fishnet that was stretched over the roof of the second of a train's two creaking carriages, and to cling to it from Prague to Pest, changing trains at Vienna. From there, by various means, I reached The Bosphorus. I decided to work my passage across the Black Sea as far as Trabzon on a tramp steamer. I was carrying enough funds to have bought the rusty scow ten times over but the closer I got to my destination the less conspicuous I wanted to be.

Barges regularly ply the rivers south of Trabzon, many of them laden with contraband. Being large, of an unsavoury appearance, and feigning to be mute, I was soon hired as a deckhand.

On the fourth morning it drizzled till midday. In the afternoon, steam rose from both land and water. There was a fecund smell from the mud banks, like a fat woman's unwashed armpits. The air felt like warm whore's milk on my skin. I made my bed on deck, sacks of onions under me, a canvas for my coverlet.

When I woke, I threw off the canvas. It had become a stifling shroud. The sky was a sheet of white-hot metal, just too high to reach up and touch. I took a deep breath. The hairs in my nostrils shrivelled. There was no colour, just glaring shades of white, and I had to squint so as not to be dazzled by the sun's brilliance.

It felt like the East.

It felt like *home*.

That night, Venus was bright near the moon's crescent. It seemed auspicious. I stripped and packed my robes into my trunk. The water was an oily chiaroscuro. It accepted my luggage and then me without a single plash. I swam, pushing my floating trunk ahead of me and into an opening in a forest of reeds.

In Mus, at an inn, I encountered Nesip Pelin, a camel merchant who was heading to Talvan and needed a guard. From Talvan I took the ferry across Lake Van to what I thought was my final destination.

For my first night, I lodged with a wizened one-toothed widow who offered me my choice of bed mate – her, her daughter or either of her sons. I opted to spread my solitary bed on her roof, where there were fewer fleas.

I woke with the Muezzin, prayed, performed my ablutions

and made my way to Ben Midras' Palace. There I waited with the crowd that sought audience until a guard accepted my bribe and presented me to the Pasha.

In Turkish, speaking softly, I told him, 'We'll spell it. Shall I begin?'

His eyes lit up at this secret sign that I wasn't what I purported to be. He peered closer and broke into a grin. 'It's *you*!' he exclaimed. He glanced left and right before whispering, 'Thank you for coming, my friend.' A crook of his finger brought a servant scurrying. I was led to a private chamber.

An hour later my hands and feet had been bathed by a veiled houri and the Pasha and I were chatting over mint-tea and honeyed pastries.

'Tell me about shooting that wolf,' I asked.

'Is that what they told you? That wasn't my message. I wrote that I'd shot a man who was *wearing* that pelt, not that I'd slain the actual beast.'

I sat back and sucked my sticky fingers. 'That makes better sense. I know there are wolves in Turkey, but *Siberian* ones?'

He frowned. 'Unfortunately, it seems that there *are* Siberian wolves here. Our native wolves have been found savaged, throats ripped out. Lambs and kids have disappeared.'

'You haven't asked me here to hunt wild animals.'

'Of course not. I need your help on a much more sinister, but related matter. There's talk in the bazaars about a new sect – a wolf-cult. Such blasphemies come and go. I pay them little heed, apart from beheading their leaders if they look to become troublesome.' He leaned forward. '*This* cult bothers me. If some of my people are foolish enough to take wolves as totems, so be it, but why take *Russian* wolves, unless the sect has its roots in the East?'

I nodded and selected a pastry that was thickly crusted with toasted almonds. 'It's a Russian plot, you think.'

'Am I wrong to be alarmed?'

'Not in the least. Religion and politics make a vile brew. If the Czar is subverting your people through this sect, you have every right to be concerned, as will Her Majesty's Foreign Office be when I inform them.' I paused. 'Chingis Khan claimed to be descended from Siberian wolves, you know. That might be significant. What else have you discovered about this sect, Benim?'

'Typical animalism,' he said. 'Its devotees are promised invulnerability and the power to transform themselves.'

'*Loup garou*,' I mused. 'Lycanthropy. That's clever – the incorporation of old established superstitions into a new cult. The Christian church has long used the same technique, with considerable effect. Do you have any of these wolf-worshippers in your hands, Benim?'

'Not yet, but perhaps soon. That's where the matter becomes delicate.' He sipped his tea as he composed his thoughts. 'I have guests from Persia – an old friend, Datis Zahed, and his brother's widow, Mahbanov, and his aptly named daughter, Asal, or "Honey" in English. Mahbanov serves as Asal's duenna, but not very well it seems. With the widow's connivance, Asal has become friendlier than is seemly with one of my gardeners, a lad named Bora. Bora, my spies tell me, has connections with the wolf-cult. An eavesdropper in my employ overheard Bora promise Asal that she would be initiated into the pack – the wolf-pack presumably – very soon. She seemed eager to join. I'm torn, Richard. I should report this to Datis, but if I do he'll whisk his daughter away. If I don't, she might lead me to the cult.'

'You have no choice,' I told him. 'It's unfortunate, but this threat is more important than protecting the honour of a girl who likely has none. How may I help?'

Benim rubbed his chin. 'If you will, bide with me awhile. My spies will keep watch on both the girl and her lover. Soon, I suspect within the week as the moon is waxing, he will steal her away. I ask that you lead a band of my men and follow the couple. Once you locate the wolf-pack, fall upon it, taking as many prisoners as you can. I will put them to the question and we'll tear up this weed before it roots too deeply.'

I shook my head. 'Benim, you ask me to track two youngsters to the cult's lair, with a band of bravos beside

31

me? It'd never work. Best inform me as soon as they steal away and I'll track them single-handed.'

'But there could be a score of fanatics waiting,' he protested.

I smiled. 'I'll go alone, but not unarmed. Let your men follow at a distance.'

Benim sighed. 'It shall be as you say. Thank you, Richard.' He glanced at the crumbs in the dish beside me. 'More?'

'Thank you, no.'

'I am a poor host,' he said. 'You've had a long and arduous journey. There is another matter I'd value your advice on, but it will wait till tomorrow. A bath and a bed await you, Richard. I trust you are not so fatigued that you won't be able to enjoy them both, *fully*.'

I raised an eyebrow. 'Fully?'

He grinned. 'Nothing strenuous, Richard, I promise. The entertainment I've arranged for you will be relaxing and help you sleep.'

'You are too generous, Benim.'

He clapped. A shapely woman, voluminously clad and doe-eyed above her veil, led me to my bath and, to my surprise, left me to perform my ablutions alone.

The water was so hot that I had to descend into it with caution. It smelled of roses and was slippery between my fingers. There was a basket floating in the middle of the pool that was about the same size as my entire tub back in England. It was piled with soaps in a dozen colours; loofahs, sea sponges, brushes and scrapers, plus a dozen flagons of variously tinted liquids. By trial and error, I found shampoo, which was a blessing after my travels. I soaped and scrubbed and scoured. Tingling with cleanliness, I climbed out to be greeted by a quartet of towel-bearing sylphs. They were delicate little things, barely tall enough to reach my shoulders and softly slender. Their eyelids were gilded and their long black tresses were oiled and perfumed. Each wore nothing but a gauzy yashmak, so fine that I could clearly discern which one's lips were pursed, which one's parted just enough to afford glimpses of tiny perfect teeth, which one displayed the pink tip of her tongue and which one's were blatantly lascivious.

I was dabbed and patted dry, with no squeals or giggles, not even a word. Delicate fingers took mine. I was led into a candle-lit chamber that was dominated by a raised dais, not strewn with cushions as I might have expected, but thickly padded and covered in textured cotton. Signs and tugs directed me to recline, on my back, arms and legs spread wide. One fetched hot towels and aromatic unguents. My face was lotioned, covered, kneaded through cotton, then bared for the ministrations of a cut-throat razor. The girl's strokes were so sure and delicate that it felt as if she were caressing my skin with a goose-feather rather than with a sharp blade.

When she was done, my steaming towels were renewed, but this time only covering my eyes. I was so warm and comfortable that despite the presence of four delightful nymphs, I had almost drifted off to sleep before I became aware that my smallest fingers and toes were being subtly manipulated. The tugs started gently but became stronger, until the joints 'cracked' and the ministering fingers moved on to the adjoining toes and fingers.

Their coordination impressed me. Without a pause, the massage moved from finger to finger, toe to toe, until both of my great toes and both of my thumbs 'popped' simultaneously.

Strong little fingers dug into my palms and the soles of my feet. It seemed as if each and every one of the bones in those appendages was isolated and manipulated before the probing fingers moved on. My wrists and ankles were deeply massaged, then my forearms and calves. When the girls started on my knees and elbows, I became aware that my digits were being revisited. This time, the girls were using their lips. Again, the sweet treatment progressed from smallest to largest. Each finger and toe was licked and then sucked upon, as if it were a miniature cock being fellated.

The slow progression was incredibly tantalising but I was happy to surrender to the teasing. It was simultaneously stimulating and relaxing to have ten fingertips fondling each of the creases between my thighs and my torso and caressing my armpits while four soft wet mouths and sinuous tongues played behind my raised knees and on the insides of my elbows.

My erection became almost painful. Gentle lips nuzzled both sides of my neck. There were tongues slithering the lengths of my groins. Fingers brushed my nipples and danced down the arches of my ribs. The two girls who attended to me above my waist were straddling my arms. I lifted my hands to stroke the softness of their bellies. As if in response, all four humped higher upon me. Four mounds bore down. A girlish cunny spread its hot wet lips on each of my insteps. Two more impaled themselves on my fingers. All four lithe lovelies writhed, stimulating themselves as well as me.

A tongue tickled at each corner of my mouth. I turned my head to the left, to suck the sweetness from one eager mouth, then to the right, to sample and compare the other nymph's oral nectar.

The back of a hand lifted my scrotum. The perineum, called *Hui Yin* in Taoism, is a Chakra, a centre of spiritual power. It is as sensitive as a lip. The caress I was subjected to was so subtle that for a while I wasn't sure of its source. Then I realised. The girls were giving me 'butterfly' kisses – fluttering their eyelashes on my skin. The sensation was almost unbearably exquisite. I reached a stage when it seemed my climax would be inevitable even though my shaft had not yet been touched unless I delayed it by an effort of will, when all four withdrew.

I shook my head, throwing off the cloth that covered my eyes, and started to sit up to protest, but I was not being left unsatisfied. Their ministrations paused for no longer than it took for them to rearrange their positions, and mine.

Gentle hands pressed my shoulders back. Three of the girls, with a, 'Please to allow,' lifted my legs, doubling them up and back towards my waist, while the fourth worked a wedge-shaped leather cushion under the base of my spine. When I was tilted to their satisfaction, they returned to their delightful play. Crowding together, their lovely faces descended upon my private parts. A girl rested her cheek on my abdomen. Her lips engulfed the helmet of my cock and, to my surprise, because everything they'd done until then had been restrained and gentle, gobbled on me, slobbering and slurping in a most obscene manner. Another's mouth opened and took as much of my left testicle in as it could, to tickle my short hairs with its tongue.

The third girl trilled on my perineum, her tongue alternately poking with amazing strength and lapping at my taut skin. The last of the houris somehow worked her face into the cramped space below the other three. Her gentle palms eased the cheeks of my bottom apart. She snuggled in, her lips kissing the ring of my anus as if it were a tiny mouth, then pressing closer. I relaxed that tight sphincter to allow the girl easier access. Wet, hot, stiff and strong, her tongue wormed into me.

All four worked with a will, gobbling, sucking, nibbling, licking and stabbing, all making little squeals and cooing with pleasure, as if they had fasted for a week and my private parts were a delicious banquet. I have that ability that I could have revelled in the delights from dusk till dawn but they were so *eager* in their carnality, those nymphs, that I hadn't the heart to make them wait.

I let my essence flow. The girl I'd blessed with it turned her face and extended her coated tongue. My seed was passed from girl to girl, mouth to mouth, until it disappeared. The wedge beneath me was removed. All four climbed upon me, draping me with their slight bodies. Warm beneath four exquisite, satin-skinned blankets, I slept.

Seven

Benim and I sprawled on low divans, three broad marble steps up from the floor of what he designated his 'Chamber of Justice'. He was attended by three of his palest, prettiest and youngest concubines, as befitted both his taste and his rank. My sole attendant was a lush-bodied odalisque, a Hindu, I guessed. She was of mature years and dark as a cocoa bean. I was content. After three nights of sport with my quartet of girlish sylphs, breasts that were made for suckling and voluptuous fertile hips made a pleasant change. Selin's eyelids were so heavy it was a wonder she could hold them open. Her fleshy lips were sullen – the sort of lips that are made to be bruised by brutal kisses and ravaged by the thrusts of a good hard cock, preferably mine.

She knelt on cushions beside me, tending to the brazier that heated thick black Turkish coffee. On a side table was a tray of honey-baked green figs, each slathered in slightly sour clotted goat's cream. With each titbit I sampled, Selin took my hand and licked the sweetness from my fingers while looking up at me with smouldering eyes.

I let my hand drop. My fingertips brushed a turgid nipple that was set in a halo the size of a saucer. Selin shivered and sucked air through a suddenly slack mouth. She seemed to be what an ancient Hindu text I'd read called, '*Nari dhire dhire khaulana simasimana*', or 'a simmering woman'.

The only furnishings on the chamber's lower level were a single short wooden pillar, surmounted by a camel's saddle, and a rack bearing canes, straps, whips and the like. To our right, a dozen or so of Benin's chattering concubines draped themselves on the satin pillows and silken rugs that softened the steps. Behind and above them, an ornate pierced wooden screen shielded his wives from male eyes while allowing the ladies to watch the proceedings. To our left, more sedate than the concubines, stood or sat two score of odalisques, servants and slaves.

The first miscreant to be called was a boy of about six years.

Selin beckoned me to bend to her. 'He's the Pasha's seventeenth son,' she whispered. 'By Eda, one of his concubines, a favourite of his for some reason. She's skinny as a corn-stalk and lively as a dead frog.'

Benin's Major Domo announced, 'Ayhan, of this House, is accused thus: That he did wilfully spit a mouthful of couscous on to the person of his nursemaid, Mrs Caruthers.'

Benim sat up and frowned. 'Is this true, Ayhan?'

The boy nodded.

'This is a very serious matter.' Echoing parents since Adam and Eve, Benim added, 'There are starving children in China who would crawl naked through thorns for a single mouthful of delicious nourishing couscous. You must learn to like couscous, Ayhan. Perhaps if it is forbidden to you . . .? My sentence is that you be denied the sweet taste of couscous for a full month. No stealing it from other children's dishes! Do you promise?'

Ayhan nodded eagerly and was led away grinning.

The next case was of a pot-washer who was accused of slovenly work. Benim demoted the man from washing the 'above the salt' pots to scouring those in which servants' food had been prepared. The miscreant backed out weeping as he salaamed.

And so the morning passed. Benim passed judgment on those who had committed petty crimes and adjudicated minor disputes. At midday, slaves brought platters laden with vine-wrapped packages of steaming herbed rice and shredded lamb – the Turkish equivalent of sandwiches.

Selin moved closer and dared rest a hennaed palm on the silk that covered my thigh. I stroked the nape of her neck with the backs of my fingers. She arched and sighed.

With the informal meal done, the concubines, odalisques and servants started to leave, except for Selin and Benim's personal attendants.

I asked Benim, 'Is your court done?'

'By no means, Richard. In the morning, I try petty crimes. Now is the time for me to consider the fates of more serious offenders. My justice is sure and swift, my friend. It is better not witnessed by those of tender sensibilities.' He paused. 'Richard, I told you that I needed your advice. I have but two serious cases to judge, today. I want you to help me decide the second offender's punishment, if you would.'

'Of course,' I said, puzzled, for my friend was much more versed in the infliction of corporal discipline than I.

Benim clapped. His Major Domo led in a woman of about twenty, with swaying pear-shaped breasts and lean haunches. Her wrists and ankles were tethered by silken ropes so I judged her rank to be that of concubine. An odalisque would have been in chains.

The charge was read – that she, Onur, had stolen two golden bangles from a chest in the seraglio. I shuddered. The prescribed penalty for theft is to lose a hand. For a girl like this, that would amount to a death sentence. Her beauty marred, she'd be cast out and would be forced to turn to prostitution to feed herself. A one-handed whore would have to sell herself cheaply and indiscriminately. One might last as little as a year, or perhaps as long as five, but certainly no longer.

She pleaded guilty. I braced myself, expecting an executioner to draw a scimitar. It came as a considerable relief when I heard Benim pronounce, 'Twenty strokes with the cane.'

Selin's fingers dug into my leg. She licked her lips. Her body moved with languorous grace as she rearranged the way she was kneeling so that one hard heel dug into the softness of her sex. I scooped a blob of cream from the fig dish and smeared it on Selin's right nipple. Looking into my eyes, she raised her breast in her fist, craned her neck down, and sucked at her own teat so hard that it was drawn deeply into her mouth.

The Major Domo led his prisoner, Onur, to the raised saddle and heaved her up on to it, on to her lower belly. As the Major secured the poor woman's wrists and ankles to rings set in the post, Benim left his divan and went to make a selection from the rack of instruments. So, my salacious friend meted out his own sentences, and doubtless enjoyed doing so. Perhaps that was the real reason the crafty beggar'd 'cleared the court'. With the less debauched members of his household out of the way, the afternoon session looked likely to turn into an orgy. I gazed down at the sumptuousness of Selin's dusky breasts, one indented by her own teeth, and their strawberry-shaped, chocolate-coloured nipples. She caught my eye and husked, '*Hum ho gaye aap ke*', – Hindi for 'I am yours'.

Benim slashed at the air with a five-foot length of thin rattan. I pulled Selin to me by her hair, so that my erection pressed against the back of her neck. She rocked her head from side to side.

Onur's bottom was uppermost. Her body was stretched taut, immobile. Benim brought his cane down across the fleshiest part of her cheeks. My fingers found Selin's nipple and rolled it, testing its resilience.

The rattan cracked again.

Selin wriggled, moving up towards my head but turning her face towards my feet so that I had to reach under her arm to continue toying with her rigid peak. When her cheek squirmed on my abdomen the reason for her movement became apparent. It put her mouth not more than an inch from where silk strained over my staff's bulbous head. Each breath she exhaled was a humid caress.

Onur whimpered. Her bottom had blossomed bright pink, with livid stripes. Selin lapped at my dome through the silk. I realised that I'd been seeping and she now had the savour of my essence on her thick tongue. She must have approved of the flavour because I felt her teeth grip my dome, gently, and her tongue slither over it. When I reached down to touch the corner of her mouth, she was drooling.

Without putting his rattan aside, Benim fondled the burning skin of Onur's slender bottom. His caresses became rougher, more forceful, until he was crushing handfuls of her inflamed flesh between his fingers. The woman writhed and sobbed but he was merciless. At last, his fist released her and he delivered the final two strokes of her prescribed punishment.

I realised that watching Benim's cruelty had tightened my fingers on Selin's nipple. I was squeezing it almost flat. She hadn't protested. Her lips were still mumbling on my silk-covered cock's head, pumping it in and out of her mouth with hard little sucks.

Benim stood back as his Major Domo released Onur and helped her limp away.

The next miscreant sauntered in unescorted and stark naked, hips swaying, belly undulating, licking her lips salaciously. She was just a girl but the look on her face was as old as Lilith, the first seductress. She strode up to Benim, her Lord and Master, the man who controlled her destiny, he who could inundate her with riches or with torments at his whim, stuck her tongue out at him and 'blew him a raspberry'.

Benim looked at me, shrugging. 'You see, my friend? What am I to do with her? In the bedchamber, she begs me to do things to her that any of my wives would weep to contemplate. I call her "python" but not because of her shape. She has the tongue and throat of a snake, if you understand me.'

I nodded. The girl, his 'python', preened.

'She is my favourite,' Benim continued, 'when she's in my bed. Out of it . . .' He threw up both arms in despair. '. . . she's impossible.'

Without being commanded, the girl took two quick strides and launched herself like a prima ballerina to land face down on the saddle. She stretched down to grasp the rings. Her toes pointed as she spread her legs wide. In Persian, she announced, 'I'm ready!'

Benim appealed to me. 'I've used the strap, the cane, the taws and the birch, Richard. I wouldn't wish to spoil her beauty but she's taken fifty hard strokes with an English riding crop and had to sleep on her stomach for two full weeks after, and *still* she doesn't learn. Is she untameable? Richard, if you know of some punishment I might impose that would humble this minx without damaging her, tell me of it, I beg you.'

The girl on the saddle wriggled her bottom at Benim, as if impatient for her chastisement to begin.

I suppressed a chuckle. The girl's nature was obvious to me, but then I wasn't enamoured of her, as Benim seemed to be. Lust can blind the cleverest men. With some reluctance, I lifted Selin's face from my lap and descended the steps to join Benim. Drawing him aside, I whispered, 'Friend, do you remember that fag, Arnold-something, at prep school? The one who was always so clumsy and always getting beaten for it?'

Benim nodded, looking thoughtful. 'We decided, later, that he actually liked to get slippered on his fat little bum, right?'

'So?' I prompted.

His eyebrows lifted. 'You mean?'

'The girl vexes you deliberately, to provoke punishment. Pain excites her, as does attention. Bound and naked, having her bottom whipped in front of a dozen people – she's in her idea of paradise.'

'Then how do I discipline a girl who dotes on pain and humiliation?'

'Simple. Deny them to her.'

'Deny her?'

'She's been disrespectful. For her punishment, condemn her to wear a burqa at all times. Deny her your couch and command her to spend four hours a day standing, facing into a corner, totally ignored.'

'For how long?'

'Ten days?'

'That would be a great sacrifice for me, Richard. She knows tricks . . .'

'Be strong, Benim. Think of the passionate reunion, once her sentence has been served.'

'But what if she disobeys? What if she throws off her burqa?'

'Any infraction should result in a extension of her sentence. If, however, she accepts her lot, meekly and with due diligence, you should reward her.'

'How?'

'A trinket, perhaps, or a pair of silk stockings from Paris, but mainly, with a public beating. For her, the cane is a reward, so use it as one. If she is good, she gets beaten. If she is bad, she is denied all that she craves; pain, being allowed to display herself in public, and the delights of your bed.'

I left my friend to explain her punishment to his favourite. My wisdom, I felt, had earned me a reward, and Selin awaited, writhing with impatience. No sooner had I stretched my length on the divan than she rose with voluptuous elegance and bestrode my shins. I doubt any other woman of Benim's court would have been so bold but once a 'simmering woman' is aroused, she knows no caution. Her eyes burned my shaft through the silk of my pantaloons. The look on her face proclaimed her determination. Selin would not be denied, not that I intended to thwart her. Her trembling fingers loosened my sash. An inch at a time, she drew my pantaloons lower, until the purple head of my weapon was exposed, then she snatched the silk down to my thighs as if the sight of my dome had made her desperate to view its shaft.

Her eyes lifted to meet mine, beseeching. I nodded. Reverently, she raised my rigid column in both hands and planted a delicate kiss on the eye of its head. Without lifting her head, she pressed, using my hard knob to force her own lips apart. Her mouth widened but never relaxed its warm wet pressure. Her strong tongue pressed upwards, squeezing me against the roof of her mouth. Arching her back over my loins, Selin pushed down, forcing my cock deeper and deeper until its helmet butted the back of her throat. Not content, she reared up, as if about to perform a head-stand, and thrust down hard. I felt her throat close on my cock's head. She made a little gargling noise that mutated into a deep purr. The warm liquor of her mouth drooled and trickled down over my scrotum.

For once, I was at a loss. I certainly didn't want her to choke on my bulb but neither did I wish to reject her astounding performance. For want of another reaction, I stroked her hair and made approving sounds. That seemed to content her. She raised her head and gave me a triumphant grin. When I smiled back, she inspected my cock and, seeming satisfied that it was as engorged as it was likely to get, in one swift move lifted her feet up to bracket my hips, raised herself and squatted down until my weapon's head was but an inch from her spread thighs' juncture.

Selin's dense black bush was gashed by livid pink. A deeper pink nubbin, the size and shape of an acorn, protruded from where her lips met. She cocked her head at me, questioningly. I nodded. Her mouth widened in glee as she lowered herself far enough to engulf my dome between flaccid lips, then simply dropped.

Suddenly, I was deep inside her. She'd made no pretence of her passage being too narrow to accommodate my girth. She was a woman, not a girl. Nevertheless, I felt clinging walls of what felt like molten silk close upon me. Inside, she seethed and pulsated. Selin's hips churned, then ground down, then undulated at me. After a few thrusts, she leaned far to her left, folding her vagina, or trying to. My shaft kept it straight but the sensations were exquisite.

She bent right, and gyrated. She leaned back and raised herself so that just half of my shaft still impaled her and its head was pressed hard against the spongy mass behind her pubic bone. In Egypt, I had learned to please a woman by massaging her there. Selin was taking care of her own pleasure in such a manner as to also delight me. I reached down and inserted my thumb, ball up, between us. Selin swivelled and pressed. My thumb crushed her pink acorn while my dome rubbed against the sensitive area deep inside her. Selin began to pant. Her insides milked at me. I sensed that her *petite mort* was close and wondered what I might do to hasten her release.

As if reading my mind, Selin took my free wrist and lifted my hands to the swaying mass of one lovely breast. 'Pinch!' she demanded.

I compressed her rubbery nipple, palpitating it in an accelerating rhythm. With each squeeze, Selin sucked a breath. By instinct, my fingers crushed, unrelenting, inexorable. Her head stretched back. There was a pulse in the side of her neck. She swallowed hard. Tendons stood out along the length of her throat. I felt, rather than heard, a deep grunt forming low in her belly. As the growl erupted, her insides convulsed. Nectar scalded my cock.

Selin toppled forward on to my chest and lay there, inert.

Several long minutes later, during which I'd amused myself by listening to the squeals and giggles that came from Benim's divan, I felt Selin stir. Her cunny gave my cock an exploratory little squeeze and discovered it was still as stiff as ever. She pushed up on to her hands and gave me a quizzical look. Coming to a decision, she swung her leg from over me to dismount, turned her back to me and swung her other leg over me. Once more, she impaled herself, this time leaning forward and grasping my ankles. As she worked, the glorious globes of her buttocks parted. Selin's anus, I saw, was a tiny pierced cone. The way it opened and closed with her gyrations, I knew it was no more virginal than her cunny. I wet a finger and worked it into the tight sleeve of her rectum.

The lascivious odalisque laughed aloud, let forth a 'whoop', and redoubled her efforts. I felt a warm rush of affection for her. I appreciate the unbridled sexuality of a 'simmering woman'. I dote on women who are fierce in their love-making. Best of all, though, is a woman who, although consumed by urgent desire, can take joy in its expression.

I've been told that the natives of the Arctic call the act of love, 'laughing' with a woman. I find that description an apt one, if the coupling is done right.

Selin and I 'laughed' until the moon was high so I slept most of the next day, conserving myself for more sport, but it wasn't making love that occupied my time that night.

Eight

Asal – 'Honey' in English – asked her uncle's widow, 'Will it be terrible, Auntie?'

Mahbanov nodded and slapped a handful of cold lotion on to her niece's warm smooth belly.

'In what way – terrible?'

Mahbanov's fingers spread the creamy preparation in widening circles. 'I've told you,' she teased.

'Tell me again!'

'Your innocence, what there is left of it, will be violated in ways that even your evil little mind can't imagine.' She looked at the expression on her niece's face and added, 'Or perhaps you can.' Almost reciting, for she was repeating what Honey'd demanded she retell a hundred times before, she said, 'You are to be the thirteenth, the last and least in the wolf-pack. As the newest bitch, you will be powerless. Any dog-wolf or bitch-wolf who wants you will take you, by your leave or not. You will do for any of them as they demand, no matter how degrading or painful it might be. In the pack, you will be less than a slave. You will have no rights. They will be cruel and you will thank them for it. The least of them may abuse and debase you, with absolute impunity.' Mahbanov, who was massaging the lotion into Honey's *mons*, slapped that shapely mound for emphasis. 'They won't damage you permanently, of course, but short of that . . .'

'They're going to *rape* me,' Honey said, savouring the words.

'Hardly. You can't be raped when you are eager for the coupling, but don't forget, a wolf-bitch won't allow herself to be mounted until she's been mastered. You must struggle until you feel his teeth on your throat or nape.'

'But they *will* abuse me, debase me, debauch me, won't they?'

'To your vile little heart's content, I promise.'

'There will be marks left on my body?'

'Of course, but none that won't swiftly heal. It's your soul that will never recover from the ordeal. After tonight, you will be damned forever.' Mahbanov cupped Honey's pubes in front and her bottom from the rear, an ointment-covered finger slithering in and out of each of her *sharmgah* – her private forbidden parts.

'More, my Aunt, please? Harder and faster?'

Mahbanov wiped her fingers on her own naked thighs. 'You'll get enough of that before morning. My Honey's honey pot will be filled to overflowing, as will her *culo* and *boca*.' She dried her fingers on a scrap of silk and reached for the two coarse black cotton burqas that hung on the wall. 'We must make haste, lest the salve transport you before the appointed time, Honey.'

Mahbanov led her charge into the palace gardens and through a dense privet maze until they came to a narrow door set in the outer wall. Honey's lover, Bora, had left the exit barred but unlocked. Beyond the walls, coarse cobblestones bruised Honey's delicate toes through her thin slippers but she didn't feel the pain. The salve was working. It felt as if her flesh was numb to a depth of about an inch, but even as it was immune to being hurt, it tingled, like powerfully erotic 'pins and needles'. Honey's nipples, her vulva and especially her clitoris, throbbed in a demanding rhythm. Each breath of air that penetrated her burqa stroked her skin with exciting caresses.

Honey was totally aware but she felt somehow detached and incredibly *powerful*. *Nothing* could harm her. Her invulnerability demanded to be tested. She craved to feel the bite of the cane. She yearned to feel cruel teeth sinking into her flesh. *Any* pain that could penetrate her numbness would surely bring ecstasy.

In her haste to reach the depraved torments she'd been promised, Honey dragged her Aunt by the hand, with, '*Ajale*, Aunt. Hurry, for I am so *hashiri* my *concha* is on fire.'

'My sweet *nekbat*, my horniest of sluts, your flame shall be quenched, I promise.' She grinned. 'Doused in man-milk.' Mahbanov stopped abruptly and said, 'In here.'

'Here' was a walled yard, noxious with vats of night-soil, just big enough to allow its only occupant, a mangy donkey of advanced years, to turn around.

Mahbanov helped her niece up to sit side-saddle on the beast's sway back and led them out and on, to the edge of town and beyond. A brilliant orange sun was low on the horizon but a full moon was rising. The donkey trudged through sifting sands that were stirred by the night-breeze that always followed sunset. Colour disappeared. The landscape turned to silver and sable, bright but deceptive. When the trio had passed between a pair of dunes that hissed softly with the tumble of individual grains down their sides, Mahbanov halted and helped Honey down.

'From here you go on foot. Keep your eyes on *Dhuruva*, the constant star. You will be met by a guide who will lead you to the appointed place.'

The Aunt took her niece's place on the animal's bony back and turned its head back towards town. Honey dragged her feet through loose sand, almost hypnotised by the star she followed. After a while, she became aware that she wasn't alone. A great silvery wolf was padding along beside her. As they mounted a wind-carved dune, Honey knotted her fingers in the beast's shaggy coat and allowed it to help her struggle up the shifting slope. At the ridge of the dune, she looked down on the ruins of an ancient village. Walls that had been built from sun-baked bricks were now crumbled and ragged, most no more than shoulder-high, many just stubs, like rotted teeth. The wolf guided Honey down and between those walls, threading left and right as they followed streets and alleys that used to be but were no more. Eventually, the grey beast led Honey to a steep slope of rubble that descended between the remnants of walls. The wolf loped; Honey scrambled, down, into what had once been a cellar that opened into another cellar, and yet another, until she saw a door that was whole and new and was outlined by a dull red glimmer. She paused. There was a murmur and a dull thumping from within. The wolf nudged the small of Honey's back with its great head. She stumbled forward. The door opened.

For a long moment, the impressions that assaulted Honey confused her. The ruddy light was from copper braziers, set on the floor and standing no higher than her slender ankles. Charcoal glowed in each one but was dimmed by layers of smouldering herbs that wreathed the air with languid swirls of dense white smoke. Honey inhaled frankincense and bhang. Above her, through the swirling veil, the stars still shone, but in diminished numbers. She blinked, trying to focus on the revellers – the pack that she would soon belong to.

A man whose bare body gleamed with sweat was pouring arrack into a bronze bowl for a gigantic she-wolf to lap up. A creature – seemingly wolf from his waist up but human male below – was buggering a naked youth who crouched on all fours. The sodomite had four lupine paws instead of hands and feet. Many of the orgiasts seemed part wolf, or were wearing garments made from pelts or perhaps were part-way through magical transformations. A bitch-wolf whose flaccid human breasts hung through slits in her furry skin seemed to be fellating a dog-wolf who was up on his hind legs and had the pale pink pizzle of a human male.

Hands took Honey's shoulders. Blades slit through her burqa. She watched, bemused, as shreds of her only garment fell to her feet. She felt a twinge of regret when she saw that her slippers were ruined. The iridescent sequins that hadn't been torn away had been dulled by abrading sand. A blotch of blood stained the woven silk close to her left little toe but she wasn't aware of having been wounded.

A hand took Honey's left arm. Fangs closed firmly but gently on her right wrist. Belatedly, she remembered to struggle. Honey was pulled to a low platform that was strewn with pelts. Sprawled spread-eagle, she gladly suffered licks from several tongues. One, she could see now that it was close, projected from a human mouth beneath a lupine half-mask. She tugged against restraining hands, though not too hard. Excitement thudded in her breast. The defilement she'd hungered for was close at hand.

A fur-clad form clambered on to the platform between her feet. An indistinct shape loomed above her. Paws, or gloved hands, parted Honey's young thighs. The animalistic figure descended upon her. She twisted and squirmed, as she'd been instructed to do. The great shaggy head came lower. Honey froze as if either in terror or in an ecstasy of anticipation. Sharp teeth bracketed her throat and closed on it, just firmly enough to threaten. Something hard, hot and wet, nuzzled her sex.

Honey, convinced that her moment was upon her, lifted up her loins to receive her pack-leader. He tensed for his first thrust . . .

There was a splintering crash from above. Something enormous dropped to the cellar's floor.

Nine

A hand shook my shoulder. I covered it with my own, ready to pull Selin down but a more delicate voice than her earthy tones said, 'Effendi! My Master bids me tell you that the time has come.'

The female form was cloaked in a burqa, so I guessed who she was. I blinked back to sensibility and swung my feet to the floor. My quartet of slender bed-mates were standing ready with Reverend Longfellow's clothes. Western garb was more suited to combat than Arab robes. Two sylphs knelt to lace my hobnailed double-soled black parson's boots tightly around my ankles. Another daubed my face with kohl while the fourth handed me my belt, with my .44 holstered on the right, my sabre in its sheath to the left and my Bowie clipped behind.

Two mounted men awaited me outside, with a third steed ready saddled.

'The widow and her niece are being trailed,' one told me. 'We will ride with you for part of the way, if the effendi permits?'

'Just so we don't get close enough to be detected.'

'As you command, effendi.'

Our horses made very little sound in the soft sand. I was led to tracks that were already filling in.

'They have a donkey,' one of my companions told me, 'but they can't mean to travel much further. It's a beast I wouldn't feed to my dogs.'

'Then I should proceed on foot,' I said.

'Effendi! Look!'

A lone figure on a tired-looking donkey was trudging towards us from out of the desert. The rider's head lifted. The rider pulled hard on the reins and kicked the poor beast with its heels. The animal shuffled off at right angles at its best speed.

'That must be the Aunt,' I said. I dropped from my mount and tossed the reins to one of my companions. 'Catch her and return to wait here for me, unless you hear gunfire. If you do, I'd appreciate your speedy help.'

My escort wheeled and broke into a gallop, towing my steed. I marched on, on foot. The donkey's trail, reinforced now by having been made twice, led me directly towards the North Star. When the hoof prints came to an end, I simply navigated by the constant star that has guided mariners since time immemorial. Sinbad must have followed that same small bright light, though I couldn't recall reading any such account.

Sand dragged at my feet but a determined man, well shod and with sturdy limbs, is hard to slow down. My calves had hardly started to ache when I crested a rise and looked down on what I presumed to be my destination, a ruined village. I descended into a labyrinth of broken and eroded walls. There was no visible sign of life but the air conveyed traces of aromatic smoke to my twitching nostrils. As a military man, I knew to take the high ground, so I explored by striding along the tops of crumbled and uneven walls. Ere long, I discerned a faint glow and made for it.

Someone had fabricated a crude roof to the cellar beneath me. It consisted of nothing more substantial than criss-crossed wands overlain with a scattering of reeds. I stooped to see what I could make out in the dim red light below. Directly beneath me, a small but shapely female form lay pinned on a crude bed, held down by four fur-clad, or furry, beasts. A fifth figure was arched above the girl in a position I knew well. There was no doubt in my mind. The victim had to be Honey and in a few short seconds I would be too late to save whatever honour remained to her. Without a further thought, I drew my sabre and my revolver – and leaped.

I landed in a shower of debris, stiff-ankled, at the foot of the platform the girl lay on. My right arm thrust but the creature who had been about to penetrate Honey rolled aside before my blade reached him. I turned my thrust into a slash that took half the hand off another of the girl's captors. He didn't seem to feel the wound but leaped at me, teeth bared and snarling. The guard of my sabre came up under his chin, snapping his head back and toppling him into the press.

My left hand squeezed off three quick deafening shots, more to spread confusion than anything, but I was gratified to see two creatures spin and drop. My iron-shod heel crunched naked toes. An enormous wolf leaped at me. He was met by my cold steel and skewered his own throat. I shook the beast off my blade and whirled, slashing low and severing both an Achilles tendon and a femoral artery. One man-beast backed away from me and tripped on a low brazier, scattering hot coals. In a moment, the rushes on the sandy floor were smouldering. The chamber filled with choking smoke and the stench of burning wolf-pelts. A fleeing female in a wolf-skin cloak brushed past me but I gutted the man who tried to follow her with a *moulinet*, a tight twisting cut that carved a neat circle from the flesh of his belly and let his guts spill into a pool at his feet.

A she-wolf lunged for my thigh. I took a standing backwards jump on to the dais and thrust down, penetrating the animal's nape and severing its spine. Something hit me behind my knees. My feet shot from under me. I landed on the base of my spine with a painful jolt and had no sooner shaken the stars from my eyes when an enormous thud to the back of my head rendered me unconscious.

Ten

My head was filled with roaring white light. The rim of a delicate bowl brushed my lips.

'For the pain,' Benim's voice told me.

I sipped the hot bitter brew gratefully. A familiar musk told me that the satin pillows beneath my face were Selin's smooth thighs. 'The girl?' I asked.

'Gone. Abducted or escaped.'

'My weapons?'

'I have them safe.'

'Tell me?'

'You slew three men and two wolves. My men took three prisoners, not counting the treacherous widow, Mahbanov. The rest escaped.'

'Five of them, I think. Tell me, the ones I killed – did they die from my gunshots or by my blade?'

'One run through, one disembowelled and one bled to death from a wound in his thigh. Why do you ask, Richard?'

'I shot at least two. Werewolves – silver? My sabre is chased with it. My bullets are simple lead.'

Benim snorted. 'That's just superstition, my friend.'

I shrugged and regretted moving my head. 'I've seen things, Benim . . .'

'I shall have silver bullets cast,' he offered, 'if it will comfort you.'

'Crosses carved into the tips of my leaden ones will serve.' I sipped more of the medicinal tea. 'I'm sorry, Benim. I failed you.'

'Nonsense! No man could have done more, and anyway, the game is still afoot. We have the three men we took and Mahbanov. They are being put to the question even as we speak. Unless my persuaders have lost their touch, we'll discover the fleeing couple's destination before morning. As for the other survivors, Satan take them but they'll have gone to ground by now.'

He proved right, though all his torturers were able to elicit from their prisoners was an address, 'At the Sign of the Alembic, Street of Silken Veils, Baghdad.'

'An apothecary,' I surmised.

'A disreputable one, no doubt,' Benim added, 'for it is located in a notorious street of whores. No doubt its primary business is the dispensing of abortifacients and simples against the pox.'

'The Czar's agents utilise a system of "cells",' I offered. 'Each group of spies knows how to contact only one member of one other group, as a precaution. I have no doubt but that the Baghdad group will disperse as soon as it learns the cell here has been destroyed. I must move swiftly, Benim, or the trail will end.'

'I have fifty horsemen awaiting your command, Richard, but first you must heal.'

'My skull is thick. I'm healed enough. I don't think much of my chances of leading a small army through the mountains of Kurdistan, though. Better, Benim, I should go alone. If I travel fast enough, perhaps I will catch up with Honey and her abductors before they reach Baghdad.'

Datis, Honey's father, interrupted with, 'Bring me back my dearest child, Richard, and I will heap untold riches upon your head.'

Benim gave the man a wry look and asked, 'Untold, Datis?'

'A talent, by volume, of gold coins – two talents if she is still pure.'

'The coins will be English guineas,' Benim insisted.

Datis hesitated before mumbling, 'Of course.'

No doubt he'd had it in mind to reward me in some debased currency, half lead and half gold. I dismissed the

'two talents' as impossible to collect, but even one talent –
by volume – was a tidy fortune. A cubic foot of gold wasn't
to be sneered at.

I've never been a mercenary, exactly, but when, in the
course of doing my duty, a few ownerless baubles have
presented themselves to me, I haven't been so foolish as to
ignore them. I see no harm in accepting rewards, even for
deeds I'd have performed without the spur of avarice. The
Koran allows a warrior *anfal* – spoils of war.

Benim provided me with a fine pair of mounts. They
weren't racing camels – thoroughbreds haven't the legs for
the mountains – but they were magnificent beasts, none the
less. I'd got as far as the foothills of Mount Nemrut before
I felt a familiar chill at the base of my skull. With slow and
deliberately overt movements, I drew a Whitney Percussion
'Good and Serviceable' .58 calibre rifle from its sheath at my
side and loaded it. Being very careful to keep the muzzle
pointed at the sky, I fired.

The echoes were still rolling back from the hillsides when
my watchers revealed themselves. There were five of them,
small, wiry, swarthy, tough as hobnailed boots. Each
cradled a long-barrelled flintlock, with the lock cocked. As
soon as the one who seemed their leader was close enough,
I tossed my rifle to him. He snatched it from the air
one-handed and inspected it with the carefully blank face of
a man who is impressed but refuses to show it.

'I bring gifts,' I told him in Turkish.

'Why?'

'I ask leave to pass through your lands. I'm headed for
Baghdad.'

At the word 'Baghdad' he hawked and spat.

'To kill some men,' I added.

His face brightened at the mention of his favourite topic.
'Why?'

'Vendetta. A matter of honour.'

He nodded. 'A woman?'

'A girl – dishonoured.'

'By Persians?'

'Persians, and some Turks.' Kurds hate both Turks and

Persians. I hoped that my talk of killing men of both races should ingratiate me a little.

'You come from Turkey.'

'I am Egyptian,' I lied. To a Kurd, Egypt was likely as distant a land as he'd heard of. Turkey was on the brink of war with Egypt and Kurds believe in 'my enemy's enemy is my friend'. I continued, 'I come fresh from killing Turks in Turkey. Now I go to Persia, to kill Persians.'

He sat motionless for perhaps a quarter of an hour. I kept still, except for the trickle of cold sweat down my spine. My life depended on his deliberations. I reckoned my chances at about six to five in my favour. I'd have preferred better odds.

At last, he asked, 'Gifts?'

I sucked air. 'Six rifles. A case of ammunition. A small purse – all the treasure I have,' I lied again. 'I expect to die in Baghdad.'

'Purse?'

I tossed him a leather pouch containing a handful of coins. A Kurdish bandit wasn't going to leave me with any cash, no matter how sympathetic to my cause he might be. 'And a camel,' I added.

He nodded. One of his companions strode to my mount's flank and drew a short, very sharp, knife. I held my breath. To my relief, he used his blade to shear a pattern into my beast's woolly pelt – a peak and three wavy lines. When he stepped back, done, the leader told me, 'Free passage.'

I loosened the reins that connected the animal I was riding to my second camel and rode away slowly, although my every instinct demanded I spur into a gallop.

It took me a week to pass through the mountains. I was watched the entire way. Sometimes I glimpsed a solitary figure on a crest. Mainly, it was the chill on the back of my neck that told me I wasn't alone.

The Kurd was more than true to his word. I was close to descending into Persia when a water-hole I was seeking proved to be no more than a puddle of mud. I'd have died of thirst if it hadn't been for the goatskin of fresh water that lay close by, on a rock. Truly grateful, I salaamed to the cardinal points before I took the lifesaver up and put it to my dry lips.

I joined the Tigris at Mosul. From there it was grassy plain with patches of marshland as far as Baghdad. I pressed on as quickly as my camel would take me but to no avail. The fugitives had to be moving at least as fast as I was.

In Baghdad, a leering beggar directed me to the Street of Silken Veils. The apothecary was no more than a shack, sagging between a tavern to the left and a brothel to the right. The entrance was so low I had to bend almost double to pass within. I wasn't given time to straighten up. Two cudgels struck my skull, one from each side. The floor smacked my face and I remember no more.

Eleven

It was dark except for a low glimmer some twenty feet from where I lay on a pile of rugs. There were dusty rafters no more than a yard above me. Somewhere close, pigeons cooed. I tried to move. My wrists and neck were bound with leather thongs to a sturdy pole I wore like a yoke. My ankles were similarly confined, apart but immobile. I was naked. There was pain in my head that I suppressed with a Sufi technique I'd mastered a decade before.

The air reeked of sex. A girlish voice demanded, 'Again, Bora!'

Bora groaned. As my eyes adjusted I was just able to make out Honey's slender form, its hips moving urgently, astride her supine lover.

'Leave me rest, Honey,' the lad moaned.

'When I am sated.'

'Your yoni is a Manticore, Honey; a magical beast with an insatiable appetite for the flesh of men.'

The girl lifted up and turned round, presenting her sex to her lover's face, and his to hers. I was put in mind of some Venetian paper silhouettes I'd seen in the collection of a noble gentleman I won't name. There is something very erotic about only being able to see outlines. It leaves it to the viewer's fancy to provide the details. My imagination had no hesitation in conjuring up images of things the lack of light concealed, not that my creativity was put to much of a test. A hand-held shaft and a bobbing head, even if rendered in black and grey, paint a vivid enough picture. Add lascivious wet noises and the portrait of lust is painted.

58

Honey lifted her head and complained, 'You called my yoni "sweet" and "precious flower" but three nights ago, Bora. Remember the tale of how Princess Golpar and the hummingbird fell in love? Let your tongue be the hummingbird and my yoni the Princess. Kiss and trill and suck until my nectar flows.'

'My tongue is weary. Three days and nights spent in your service have left it stiff and dry as an old bone.'

'Which is more than I can say for this!' Honey snapped, waving his floppy member in her fist. 'If you cannot play the man's part, I will try the *farangi*'s mettle!'

'No, Honey,' he protested, but she ignored him, as a girl is wont to do when a lad fails her. He continued, 'The man is still unconscious.'

'If he doesn't waken, I'll take the *farangi* as he sleeps.'

I was the only '*farangi*' in that place, wherever it was, so I had no doubt who she planned to turn to for her satisfaction. Under any other circumstances I'd have been glad to demonstrate my erotic prowess but this was a girl I was sworn to protect from both harm and sin. That she was a fiery little bitch whose every orifice had been plumbed hard and often, I had no doubt. Nevertheless, they hadn't been plumbed by me and I was determined that they wouldn't be. Honour can be a burden but if it were an easy load, it'd have no value.

Her rump swaying from side-to-side, her delicate young breasts outlined by the candlelight, the lustful little harlot crawled towards me like a feline predator. I closed my eyes, feigning sleep, and concentrated on softening the stiff column of my cock. It is a tribute to my self-control that by the time Honey reached me, my flesh lay limp upon my thigh.

She lifted it on her palm and let it flop back down. 'He's as long as a rope's end, and as limp, Bora. Come see what magic I can work, transforming soft hemp into hard oak.' Her flattened hand flipped my shaft from side to side.

Through slitted eyes, I inspected her face. It was oval, with almond eyes that were hooded by creamy lids. Her nose was a small, nondescript button. Her mouth, though full-lipped, was quite tiny, in fact, no wider from corner-to-corner than from the top of her swollen upper lip to the bottom of her pouting lower one. A scribbler of penny verses might have termed it 'a cupid's bow' or a 'rosebud'.

My conscience struggled. I was bound and helpless. If she decided to, there was nothing I could do to prevent the girl from fellating me. Would I then, if she did, be violating my oath to her father? And, at what point would it become fellatio? At first contact or did her lips have to close behind my cock's head for it to count? It was a nice philosophical point, suitable for a Hellfire Club debate.

My conjecture was premature. Her flipping became 'batting'. When that failed to stiffen me she took my shaft in both hands and pumped at it, roughly and crudely. There was no doubt she was a wanton but she certainly lacked the skills of an accomplished harlot. I felt a twinge of sympathy for the lad who'd spent so many hours enduring her clumsy embraces. She began to curse me incoherently, though I caught the words 'mardekeh', 'kir' and 'hashiri', so presumed she was complaining that both I and my cock were worthless and she was horny.

Her fury didn't worry me until she held my shaft to my belly with one hand, made a hard little fist with the other and took deliberate aim at my testes.

I blurted a protest. 'Honey!'

She grinned and pulled her fist further back. I braced myself.

The floor opened up, flooding the attic with light. A great trapdoor crashed. A handsome black head, then a pair of broad but shapely shoulders, followed by two magnificent ebony breasts, emerged. Speaking Persian but with an Ethiopian accent, the sable Amazon announced, 'It's time to go!'

Honey dropped her fist with a snort of disgust.

Three of the most attractive women I've ever met were Ethiopian. This one lacked the delicate beauty of the girl I'd romped with in the clear waters of Lake Tana. She was more handsome than beautiful but she exuded animal sensuality. Her features were Caucasian, with a finely chiselled nose and lips that were full but not everted, as many African women's are. When she climbed up, out of the trapdoor, I judged her to match me in height and perhaps in weight also. Her breasts were massive and tipped by nipples that were as long and thick as the first joints of my thumbs. The indentation of her navel could have held a goose egg. Below that, she was swathed in a white sarong, similar to those worn by the natives of Fiji.

She'd be a formidable bed-partner. Ethiopians count men and women as equals. There are those who'd rather face their men than their women in combat, for the women are the crueller in victory. In matters of lust, I'd found the Ethiopian women I'd known to be both promiscuous and aggressive. But then, it has long been my practice to assume all women are trollops, at heart. I've rarely been proven wrong.

Zema, as I later learned her name to be, stood with her arms akimbo and glared at Honey. Looking like a child beside the giantess, the girl scuttled to the trapdoor and down the steep steps, closely followed by Bora.

Zema turned to me. To my chagrin, she heaved me up and over her shoulder with no more than a grunt. My face dangled close to the cleft of her formidable buttocks. She smelled like fresh-turned earth after a summer rain. My cock lolled against her right breast and there was nothing I could do about it, if she found the contact offensive. Zema bore me down into what appeared to be a warehouse for rugs and hence out into blinding morning sunlight. I was stood on my spread feet, swaying and blinking. A bucket of water took me in the face. Three more followed, sluicing me from head to foot. Being rocked by the water's impact reminded me that my hands and arms were completely numb, though my shoulders ached abominably.

So I wasn't to be murdered, at least, not yet. If they wanted me to be clean it suggested they'd keep me around for a while. My relief was coloured by the thought that the manner of my bondage suited itself very well to torture. Should I be put to the question, I decided, I'd tell all I knew, which was little enough. That both I and Benim suspected the cult to be part of a Russian plot was obvious. I surmised that the coven would act as a fifth-column in the event of a Russian invasion, but that was mere speculation.

Someone put a ladle of fresh water to my lips. I drank and gave thanks, in both Turkish and Persian. When my eyes cleared I saw that we were in an extensive high-walled courtyard. A strange caravan was being loaded by a pack of surly rogues that I took to be Tatars by their scowls, stature, complexions and bow legs. Each was armed with an Enfield rifle, a twenty-foot lance and an assortment of daggers.

The lead vehicle was an oxcart laden with supplies. Behind that were two outlandish carriages, to which teams of eight oxen were being hitched. Each conveyance was shaped much like a railway compartment, but longer and higher and with six wide iron-rimmed wheels that'd have come up to my chin.

There were about a dozen camels and half that number of fine Arabian horses. The former were weighed down with bundles and boxes. The latter were being harnessed.

Zema hoisted me on one broad hip, carried me to the second carriage and tossed me inside. It was immediately obvious that it had been built for transporting slaves but had been modified to provide some degree of comfort. The walls were solid cedar to about five feet, where iron rings were set into them. Above that, there was a carapace of coarse sacking, stretched over a tall wooden frame. It'd admit air and light but prevent those outside from seeing in.

Each wall was lined with a deep wooden bench that was strewn with pillows, animal hides and various cloths, with baggage stowed beneath. I judged the aisle between to be about four and a half feet wide. More iron rings were set into a plank floor that was stained, likely by bodily fluids, but that was now scrubbed as clean as it would come. No doubt this strange vehicle had seen some terrible sights in its time.

Zema followed me into the dim interior. She was joined by a wiry Ethiopian man with a pock-marked face, whom she dwarfed. He held a serpentine dagger to my throat while she cut the thongs that held my left ankle and tied it with cord to an iron ring. My other ankle and my wrists were similarly served, one limb at a time, so that I lay with my arms slightly spread beside me. The change in position was welcome but deucedly unpleasant to achieve. The return of circulation felt as if my arms had been plunged into a furnace. I admit that I writhed a little.

I was left there to contemplate my fate for what I judged to be a little over an hour. I made no attempt to get loose. It had become obvious that the conspiracy wasn't confined to Turkey and Persia. I owed it to my country to uncover its full extent. I owed it to Honey's father and my own honour to follow her until some means of effecting a rescue presented itself.

When there is nothing to be done, a soldier sleeps.

I was awakened by the arrival of two young girls. The first was Spanish, judging by her ivory skin and raven's-wing hair. She had high cheekbones, a Roman nose and a wide, generous mouth. Her black dress covered her from the frothy white lace at her throat to her wrists and to her ankles. It fitted close enough to reveal her lithe, high-breasted figure. There were onyx combs in her hair and a silver cross that had to be a foot and a half long, hanging from a string of what I took to be oversized rosary beads at her willowy waist. She stood, looking down on me with no sign of surprise at the presence of a naked man bound to the floor at her booted feet. After a moment she smiled, stepped over me, and took a seat beside me to my left.

The next girl was a total contrast, dressed as a belly dancer, laden with jewels and tiny silver bells. Her diaphanous emerald skirt was slit to her fleshy hip and rose no higher than six inches below the bejewelled navel of her plump belly. Her abbreviated bolero jacket was unfastened and gaped wide to display the lush inner curves of her sumptuous breasts. She was veiled, but only by a wisp of gauze that accentuated her heavily kohled, slightly slanting eyes.

I greeted both girls in what I presumed were their native tongues – Spanish and Egyptian Arabic – and apologised for my failure to stand. They smiled but said nothing. Zema heaved two trunks, a wicker hamper and a hatbox in after my lovely new companions. The door to our vehicle swung closed. After a few moments, whips cracked and the caravan lurched into ponderous motion.

As if it were a signal, the girls introduced themselves to each other, pointing and saying their names. The fleshy and exotic dancer was Fatima. The patrician Spanish beauty was Maria Theresa followed by a dozen other names that I now forget. Fatima tried Arabic on Maria. Maria tried schoolgirl Latin on Fatima. After a giggling exchange, they discovered French to be a common language. They were soon chatting away like bosom friends – and ignoring the rather large and very naked man who was tethered on the floor between them. Both seemed as refined and educated as girls of their cultures were likely to be. These were no common whores. Whores, perhaps, but of a decidedly uncommon sort.

I had a thousand questions but little information so I turned my mind to how I could make allies of the two young women. A captive can't have too many friends among his captors.

I listened but gave no sign that I understood. Their talk was of girlish things at first: Parisian styles, the latest advances in corsetry and the like. Whalebone was compared to steel in the manufacture of stays. Some time passed before the conversation drifted to the men they were intended for. At first I thought they were comparing the men they were betrothed to but I learned that the girls had never met the men they were talking about – and they weren't cases of arranged marriage. They discussed how to get men to notice them and of how best to effect seductions. That topic led to a chat about erotic techniques that might have surprised the madam of a Bombay brothel.

Maria swore by parsley, as a breath-freshener. Fatima championed the efficacy of vanilla beans. There was nothing for it but for Fatima to step over me to Maria's bench so that they might sniff each other's breath. Inevitably, this led to tentative kisses that gradually became less and less inhibited – until tongues were being noisily sucked.

My cock reacted, much to the amusement of my pretty

companions, who pointed at it and made some quite flattering comments.

Fatima kicked off one curly-toed slipper and stretched a shapely leg out to give my burgeoning erection a gentle nudge with her great toe. Maria giggled and bent to unbutton one of her dainty boots.

I opened my mouth to remind them that I was not an inanimate object. Our strange conveyance creaked to a swaying halt before I could speak.

Twelve

Zema vaulted into our compartment, followed by her countryman. The ebony giantess had covered herself with a voluminous and gaudy ankle-length poncho. Riding bare-breasted through the Persian countryside would, no doubt, have drawn attention. When she saw my priapic state she laughed aloud, stooped and gave my shaft a quick tug, which did nothing to soften it. I was released from my bonds and led down with a noose around my throat and the point of a sword pressed to the back of my neck. The girls stayed behind.

We were stopped on a rutted track that passed between fields of wheat lined with date palms and locust. We'd come to a trilling stream. The oxen were being fed and watered. Tatars gathered round charcoal braziers, brewing tea, just like English working men. I caught a glimpse of Honey and her inadequate beau, Bora, seated on the tailgate of the carriage ahead of us. The bulk of that vehicle looked to be stuffed with baggage.

I was given water and fed boiled mutton with coarse black bread. After, I was allowed to wash and relieve myself, but not in privacy. By the time I was returned to supine bondage in our carriage the ferocious sun was just past high. Sensibly, the oxen and mounts had been left in the shade of a grove of trees. The entire party, I presumed, took a siesta.

Fatima let down a sacking curtain to cover the space above the door at the rear. Our odd compartment was rendered curiously intimate. Maria, giving me speculative looks, unhooked the frogs that secured her dress and pulled it up over her head. All she wore beneath it was a ribbon-tied short chemise in embroidered cotton and her silk hose. She produced a hanger for her dress and suspended it from one of the iron rings.

My eager cock rose in anticipation. Maria pulled the combs from her hair. It cascaded like liquid midnight to well below her waist. My cock twitched. Fatima's toes brushed along my inner thigh. My shaft became fully erect. It'd felt deprived ever since I'd been woken by the sound of Honey berating Bora for his lack of stamina. I assured it that I had no reason to reject either of my new companion's advances, should they choose to make any.

Fatima spread cloths and pillows on her bench and stretched out on them. Maria did the same on her side. Both girls closed their eyes. I cursed to myself and did likewise. As I have said, when there is nothing to be done, a soldier sleeps.

When I woke, a satin pillow had been tucked beneath my head. Maria began soaping my privates with a sea sponge. As she bent over me, tantalising tendrils of her long black hair dragged across my thighs and belly. She still wore her scanty chemise but now it was unlaced and gaping open to her waist. Through the veil of her tresses I was able to catch teasing glimpses of a small but shapely swaying breast.

Fatima had shed her jacket and skirt and was left in nothing but rings and bangles. Although she was kneeling – astride my tethered right arm – the delightful *rondeur* of her body quivered. The muscles beneath her softness were in constant motion, flexing and relaxing in some sort of static *raks sharki*, or 'belly dance'. She was peeling an orange. That simple act sent ripples through her torso. Her shapely hips swayed left, then right, keeping time to silent music. Fatima's head fell back. She lowered a succulent section of her fruit partway into her mouth. Holding it between her lips, she arched over me, lowering her face towards mine. It was a game I'd played before. I jerked up to snap at the orange. She snatched it back. She lowered again. I lunged once more. When I missed, I made an imploring face.

Fatima relented. The orange had just touched my lips when she sucked it back into her mouth but her lips parted and continued to descend. If I wanted the orange, I'd have to follow it. I almost laughed aloud. The first time I'd played that little game had been when I was but fifteen, with a distant cousin who had been a couple of years my senior.

My tongue found the crushed segment of fruit and nudged it aside. I was more interested in Fatima's tongue and the wine of her mouth than in a soggy piece of orange.

I was allowed only the juice of the second segment. Fatima squeezed the slice over her breasts and 'forced' me to suck the juice from her nipples. As my mouth worked, my hand felt heat from the core of her body. She had lowered herself until my up-stretched fingertips could brush across the lips of her sex.

Maria, meanwhile, had washed and rinsed my column, its head, and my scrotum, gently but thoroughly. She dabbed me dry with a soft cloth and anointed my throbbing member with some exotic oil, cooing with delight as she stroked my length.

A throaty voice announced, 'He's ready for me.'

Fatima writhed to her feet and sat back on her bench, her wanton thighs spread wide, with an orange segment held to her cunny. Maria moved aside but still held my cock. Their young bodies had been blocking my view of Zema, ebony, naked and magnificent.

The games women and girls play! There'd been no reason to 'prepare' me for Zema. Short of being dead or close to it, I couldn't imagine not being ready to tup the African Venus. Besides, it behoved me to endear myself to the woman who held me captive. I let my lust show, both on my face and by twitching my member at her. She grinned salaciously. One step took her astride my hips. Her knees bent, lowering her sex towards the bulb that capped my shaft.

I shook my head. Her brows lifted. I signalled with a backwards nod and showed her my tongue.

'You want?' she asked.

'To drink at your sweet fountain,' I told her.

Giggling like a debutante, Zema planted her feet to each side of my shoulders and lowered herself once more. As her thighs spread, so did the lips of her sex. A mass of tight black curls parted to reveal a startlingly pink dewy gash. As her labia spread more, her clitoris was revealed, its shaft as long as my little finger, its head the size and hue of a pale cherry. I made a show of licking my lips. Zema's fingers drew back on her sheath. She fell forward on to her knees and one hand. The tid-bit I wanted and that she was eager to feed me was no more than an inch from my lips. I lifted my head and gripped it between my lips, just behind its delicate helmet.

Zema grunted and tensed. My tongue lapped, slowly at first but accelerating steadily. When her massive thighs clamped my face and she was gurgling, I released my grip. She let out a strangled cry of frustration. Her fist took a handful of my hair to drag my face back to where she wanted it. She was too powerful a woman for me to risk tormenting until she lost control. I tongue-whipped her clit mercilessly and was rewarded by an almighty grunt, a gush of her essence, and her collapse. The softness of her belly completely covered my face. I tried turning my head to snatch a breath but my face had sunk into her as if she were a vast pillow. My feet and hands signalled frantically. I was on the brink of sinking my teeth into Zema's flesh out of my desperate need for air when the two girls finally noticed my plight and rolled her off me.

Zema and I lay side by side, both panting. Maria and Fatima seemed to find this most amusing. Perhaps I would have as well, had I not been the object of their hilarity. Eventually Zema rose up, loomed over me and gave me a sloppy wet kiss, filling my mouth with her thick tongue. I, and my shaft, both hoped this signalled a renewal of our erotic bout, but it didn't. The ebony giantess clambered to her feet, tottered to the rear of the carriage and dropped out over the end. It was not a dangerous feat. Hitched oxen, at their fastest, don't exceed the pace of a light infantry company's quick-march.

I said, 'Maria? Fatima? How may I please you young ladies?'

With a chuckle, Fatima took the place and position that Zema had occupied. A segment of orange dangled from

69

between the lips of her smooth satiny mound. I took it between my teeth, tugged it out and ate it. She replaced it, but this time with a piece of lime. My head lifted. She pushed it back, gently. I was allowed to watch as her fingers worked the slice all the way into her cunny. I expected to be required to retrieve it but she motioned to me to rest my head on my pillow and continue to watch as she stuffed a second, third and fourth segment into her lower mouth.

Holding my face immobile between her hands, Fatima reared up and forward until her sex was immediately above my lips. I looked up over the rolling curves of her tummy and between the jiggling mounds of her breasts. Her face creased in concentration. Her belly rippled. I opened my mouth just in time to catch, first, a few drips of juice, and then a small acidic flood. Fatima strained. A wad of mangled pulp emerged and plopped into her waiting palm.

I told her, 'Brava!'

Grinning mischievously, Fatima duck-walked backwards. Maria held my shaft, aiming it straight up. Fatima lowered herself. My dome nudged her cunny's lips apart. She lowered another inch and I realised why she'd douched with lime juice. Either the acid had neutralised her natural lubrication or it'd shrunk her, internally, as it might purse a mouth, or both, but her cunny resisted my invasion as effectively as an unwilling and virgin bum. Fighting against my bonds, I thrust upwards as well as I could.

'So tight,' she moaned. 'I am your maiden bride, big English. Force me to accept my fate! Sacrifice me! Make me scream. Have no mercy! Pierce me to the quick!'

A hymen resists once and then is sundered. Fatima's sheath fought me inch by inch. Maria held my shaft until half its length disappeared and then she was overtaken by lust. She leaned over me to suck my tongue. She nipped my nipples between her small sharp teeth; and did the same to Fatima. She stood to dance an excited little jig, then sank down, pressing her humid cunny to the instep of my left foot as she slavered and moaned over my testes.

I worked my hips from side to side, wriggling my cock deeper and deeper into the Egyptian. Fatima threw back her head in a delirium of pleasure-pain. Her fists crushed the ripe softness of her own ample breasts, extruding flesh between her fingers.

The compression, the dragging on my cock's head, were an exquisite torment. I was close to becoming desperate to plumb the minx's depths when suddenly the resistance disappeared. Fatima dropped the last two inches, taking my full length. Her pubes ground down on mine. I realised that the lime juice might have contributed to her tightness but most of it was from the contraction of her powerful internal muscles.

I told Fatima, '*Salaam*', acknowledging her erotic prowess.

She responded with a further demonstration, sending ripples of constriction and relaxation the length of my shaft. We grinned at each other, as Freemasons might do after exchanging cryptic signs. She and I recognised each other as past-masters of the venereal arts.

With blatant glee, Fatima bounced and squeezed and rotated her hips in a bravura performance of erotic gymnastics. Her arms extended to each side and undulated as if they were boneless. Her shoulders shook, jiggling the bountiful mounds of her breasts.

Maria's mouth deserted my sac. No doubt Fatima's gyrations had made her position, with her face between Fatima's bottom and my scrotum, difficult. The lovely young Spaniard rose up behind Fatima. Her left shoulder twitched, dislodging her chemise to her elbow. Her right shoulder shrugged. White cotton slithered down her slender young body. Her breasts were shapely, though no larger than would pleasantly fill my hands. She was a little slim for my taste, with the arches of her ribs visible, her belly flat and her hipbones a tad too close to her skin. Her mons was prominent. It was veiled by a mere wisp of silky black hair.

Her body arched. She leaned forward, over Fatima's head. Maria took one of Fatima's lush breasts in each hand and jiggled them. Fatima bent her head back to reach the dangling treat of Maria's left nipple, on which she suckled avidly.

I found the Sapphic display, along with Fatima's incredible internal skills, delightfully arousing. Nevertheless, my bondage irked me. My cock was being well tended to but I'm a man who likes the feel of a woman's body in his hands and the taste of her skin on his tongue. In the lists of lust, I am more of a 'doer' than a 'done-to', by preference.

I did what I could. My bonds allowed me some small movement. I was able to thrust up, at least, if not far.

The girlish lovers separated long enough to allow Maria to circle Fatima and stand astride me, pubes-to-face with the Egyptian girl. Fatima's spread hands clutched the cheeks of Maria's bottom and dragged her close. Maria knotted her fingers in Fatima's hair for the same purpose. I could watch the dimples in Maria's lean little rump dance and the dark eye between her cheeks wink as she flexed her cheeks but I couldn't see what Fatima's mouth was doing. I could hear it, though. The snuffling and slurping were music to my ears. Ere long, the insides of Maria's spread thighs were glistening with her spending or Fatima's spittle, or both.

Fatima's right hand released its grip on Maria's bottom. Two fingers, clamped together, wormed upwards into the Spanish girl's cunny, thrust thrice, withdrew and forced their way into the tight channel of the girl's bottom.

The sudden rude invasion pushed Maria over the edge. She let out a sharp cry and staggered backwards, tripping over me and sprawling by my head.

Fatima, her cheeks wet and shiny, gave me a beatific smile, gyrated her hips hard and fast, grinding down, let out a long sigh and toppled to the side.

My cock flipped out from her warm wet cunny, and was left, standing, feverish and achingly unfulfilled. I contained my impatience for five or ten minutes before craning sideways to Maria and giving her tummy a gentle nibble. She sat up. Her eyes went from mine to my erection and back. She cocked her head in a silent question. I gave her a solemn nod, as if having my cock's needs attended to was of little interest to me, but if she was eager to take care of them, she had my gracious permission.

Maria bobbed her head in thanks and moved closer, to sit cross-legged between my thighs. She arched over me. Her mouth hovered above my rigid shaft. The contrast between the nobility of her features and their lascivious expression delighted me. She contemplated my cock for a moment, as if deciding where to start. It wagged at her. She took a firm grip just below its head and slavered it with the flat of her tongue. Her hair tumbled, veiling what she was doing from my sight. I grunted disapproval.

Understanding, she swept her hair back and lowered her parted lips. They met my purple helmet in a soft kiss. I felt her tongue at my cock's eye. Moving at a damned leisurely pace, her head descended. Her lips spread. They engulfed my glans, paused, then worked lower, taking my shaft into her mouth a fraction of an inch at a time. She'd engulfed no more than three inches when she pulled back, even more slowly, with her wet lips mumbling on my rigid flesh.

Fatima rolled over to rest her face on my belly and watch Maria's work. Perhaps a muscle in my abdomen twitched, for Fatima laid the flat of her hand on my pubes, as if to caution me from thrusting upwards. I had no such intention, of course. Anticipation is all, or close to all, in matters of lust. I had no wish to hurry. Fatima's head was blocking my view of Maria's face. I halfway sat up for a better view.

Maria's lips descended again, just as slowly, but travelling an inch further down my column. She shook her head and swirled her tongue over my dome before retreating. Her next assault took her yet another inch lower. Instead of shaking her head, she bent it to one side, forcing my cock into the pouch of her cheek. The soft wet flesh there buffed my hardness. The dear girl's cheek bulged obscenely. She withdrew, completely, and studied my cock's head once more. When her eyes lifted to meet mine, they were brimming with tears. I wondered for a moment if she regretted what she was doing but she smiled and told me, 'It is *so* beautiful.'

Her hands gripped my thighs. Her body rose up and she turned, tilting forward as her head tilted back on her neck, lining her mouth up with her throat. Maria plunged down.

The full length of my cock disappeared. I felt it butt the back of her throat and then her throat working and, to my joy, I realised she had actually managed to swallow at least the head of my cock and perhaps a third of its shaft. Selin, the Hindu odalisque at Benim's court, had performed a similar but lesser marvel. Fatima gasped, then clapped and exclaimed, '*Magnifique!*'

Maria's tears rained on my pubic mound as she bobbed, fucking her own throat with my cock. Spittle ran from her mouth and drooled on to me. I could not deny her the reward she so obviously craved.

I warned her, 'I'm about to spend!'

She drew back just enough that when my cream flooded, it was into her mouth, not directly down her throat.

The night was cool but I was snug. I slept with Fatima's head on my left shoulder and Maria's on my right, and under a quilted silk coverlet. A shapely thigh was draped across my left leg and a slender one over my right. From time to time, during the night, I was woken by idly caressing fingers or by soft lips nibbling at my neck.

I dreamed of Isabel's loving arms twining around me and of hot buttered crumpets with strawberry jam.

Thirteen

Come morning, I was taken out by Zema and her mate, again held back by a noose and prodded forward by the point of a sword. We'd reached higher and less fertile country. All that grew was scrubby shrubs and little yellow flowers that I didn't recognise.

I was given a bucket of water to carry and was steered towards a clump of bushes. When we came to a patch of something low and thorny, I made to circumnavigate it out of respect for my bare feet.

The little man pulled me back to a straight and prickly path, sneering, 'He has the feet of a pampered sodomite, like all damned English.'

The noose about my throat snatched tight and jerked me backwards. I recovered and turned. The little man was on the ground with a bloody nose. His sword lay in the dirt, as did the end of my tether. Zema's fist was still clenched.

She berated the man for insulting me, calling him 'Melku-with-a-sick-worm-between-his-legs.'

He gave me a look that'd have blistered the hide of a rhino. When I offered him my hand he spat at it, clambered to his feet and circled me to retrieve his weapon. Zema, I hoped, noted that I had stood between Melku and his sword and had not tried to take it or escape.

When we reached the stand of bushes Zema had Melku pay out some twenty feet of line, thus affording me a degree of privacy.

On my return from my ablutions, I found the girls breaking their fast with bowls of hot black tea, Jacob's

Cream Crackers, goat's cheese and fruit. I was returned to supine bondage. Maria held a bowl of tea to my lips. Fatima spread cheese on crackers and fed me. I took pieces of apple and segments of orange from between their lips. It was the most lascivious confinement I could imagine. All of my wants were catered to, except my need to walk free. I was like some exotic wild beast, securely caged but pampered, *en route* to The Zoological Society of London, there to be exhibited for the public's edification.

I reminded myself that I was being carried in relative luxury towards my twin goals of scotching the conspiracy, whatever it was, and of rescuing Honey. I had no idea how either might be accomplished but was sure something would come up.

With our meal done, the girls returned to their favourite pastimes, flirting with each other and teasing me. Fatima flaunted her bountiful breasts by wearing nothing but her gauzy skirt. Maria, more subtly, wore a fresh chemise, this one with a draw-string neckline that she wore off-the-shoulder fashion. The pair busied themselves, as women do, rearranging pillows and cushions; straightening and folding cloths.

Maria said, 'He should have something beneath him.'

I agreed but said nothing. My back was beginning to resent the bare rough wood. I've slept on worse surfaces but not without being free to change my position.

The girls fussed, sorting through bright squares of silk, lengths of white and unbleached cotton and oddments of a dozen varied fabrics. Their 'work' seemed to necessitate them stepping over me frequently and occasionally pausing with their feet astride my head, affording me ample time to gaze up their skirts.

Eventually they decided that I should rest on three layers, the tanned hide of a zebra below a pair of cotton sheets. My opinion, when I'd expressed it, had been ignored.

Maria rolled the zebra skin up and put it by my head.

Fatima knelt astride my hips. 'Sit up, English.'

I sat up, with unnecessary but welcome help from the girls. Maria pushed on my shoulders while Fatima tugged on my neck. My rising put my face on a level with Fatima's. As Maria unrolled the hide down to my rump, Fatima and I sampled each other's tongues. Maria paused for a few moments before saying, 'Down, English.'

I lay as flat as I could with half the rolled skin tucked under my lower spine.

Each worked a hand under me to cup one of my buttocks. 'Lift,' Maria commanded.

I raised my hips as high as I could, forming a bridge that wagged my shaft inches from their noses. They fumbled beneath me, unrolling the skin, with each of the young beauties' cheeks 'accidentally' brushing my member. Inevitably, it reacted by stiffening and moistening.

Maria said, 'Do you smell honey, Fatima?'

'I believe I do, little sister, but whence comes this tempting odour?'

Maria giggled. 'Could it be from the giant stinger of this monstrous English bee?'

'Tasting would be the test,' Fatima mused, fluttering her eyelashes at me. She took a smear of my seeping on her finger and held it to Maria's lips.

Maria sucked Fatima's finger slowly, cocked her head and announced, 'I swear the creature leaks honey-wine. I must sample more, from the very source.' She bent over and took the dome of my cock into her talented mouth.

Fatima scolded, 'Sister, dear, we have a bed to make. Let us complete that chore before we enjoy the fruits of our labours.'

A sheet was rolled. Once more, I was helped to sit up. Somehow, in the wriggling and tugging, Maria's neckline got pulled down to her left elbow, leaving one nubile breast free. Nipples were dragged across my lips. The hands that helped lift my rump brushed my sac. Between times, sinuous tongues invaded my willing mouth. As each sheet was successfully put in place, one girl or the other sampled my 'honey'.

With the job done, Fatima announced, 'Now we may feast.' Two girls' hands wrapped my shaft and pumped in slow unison. Two tongues lapped at my cock's helmet. Two mouths took turns covering it. My scrotum tightened . . .

77

As I anticipated, it was then that Zema made her appearance.

'He's ready for me,' she announced. Her poncho sailed through the air.

I lay back to await her pleasure. Zema knelt astride my hips, parted herself, took my shaft in her hand and sank on to me. Being fucked by Zema was like being masturbated between the palms of two buttery hands. Her cunny was capacious but muscular and mobile. I bucked up at her a few times. She flattened a hand on my chest and commanded me, 'Be still!'

Like a frigid wife, I lay back and allowed Zema to control the performance, even though it was against my nature. Her man-sized hands kneaded the flesh of my chest bruisingly. Her hips ground and rotated. Two breasts, each bigger than my head and black as fresh-poured tar, bobbled and swayed before me. Perhaps Zema noticed the way my eyes followed their gyrations because she grabbed me by the back of my neck and pulled me up to her bosom. My lips clamped on a rubbery nipple that very near filled my mouth. I suckled as hard as I could, drawing an appreciative grunt from the depths of her massive chest.

She became frantic. Her loins rose up and thudded down. She leaned towards me, grinding her pubes on mine. Her skin slithered on me, oiled by her sweat.

I managed to twist my head aside for long enough to blurt, 'Fatima, help her to reach her joy!'

Zema thrust her nipple back into my mouth. I could see nothing, for her great breast was pressed to my face, covering my eyes, but I felt a hand slide between Zema's body and mine, down low, where my shaft entered the black beauty's cunny. The hand seemed to seek, then find, and begin to rub.

Some days later, in one of those gentle moments between erotic bouts, Fatima told me, 'Zema *a une queue pour un clito!*' I couldn't agree that Zema had a cock for a clit because that would have meant that the cunnilingus I'd performed on her had been a kind of fellatio, but I saw her point.

Between impaling herself on my cock and having her clit's sheath worked by Fatima's clever fingers, Zema reached her *petite mort*, scalded my balls with her juice and toppled sideways. The girls waited respectfully for her to recover and depart before returning to the game Zema had interrupted.

Maria took the first long lascivious lick. She paused, frowned, and licked again.

'What is it?' Fatima asked her.

'He has a different flavour now.'

'Silly! Of course he has. He has the essence of Zema's cunny on him. Do you like the taste of a woman?'

'*Oui!*'

'Then you shall have more.' Fatima stood and lifted one foot on to a bench, spreading her thighs above both Maria and me. '*Gamahauche ma p'tite chatte*, Maria.'

Maria licked her lips and looked at me. 'But our poor *poilu* is in great need.' She gripped my shaft and wagged it to demonstrate just how great my – the 'stud's' – need was.

'His need will keep,' Fatima told her. 'Waiting can be a pleasure. He can watch and wait while you pleasure me.' She thrust her mound at Maria. '*Katha ath nan*, Maria – caress my cunny. Make me spend a thousand thousand times, and then a thousand times more.'

Maria grinned at me. 'Is possible?'

I shrugged. 'Try!'

She knelt up to bring her face level with Fatima's pubes. 'You can see?' she asked me.

'Yes, thank you.' I was really warming to the girl. Not only did she dote on performing fellatio, a quality that any man would find endearing, but she had a wicked sense of humour.

The aristocratic young Spanish girl, making sure not to block my view, pressed a thumb on each side of Fatima's cunny, parting its lips. 'A pretty little *almeja*, no?' she asked me.

'A fine little clam, to be sure,' I agreed.

She pressed harder, enough to expose the shaft and head of Fatima's clitoris. 'And there's the *pipote* I was looking for!'

It's only in southern Spain that '*pipote*' – sunflower seed – is used as slang for clitoris. I consigned the implications to my memory. Someday it might be important for me to know where each participant in the plot came from.

Maria had pursed her lips and was blowing gently on the bared head of Fatima's clit. The Egyptian closed her eyes and bit her lower lip. Her hips moved subtly. The tip of Maria's tongue flickered on the straining tid-bit for a second or two.

'More,' Fatima moaned.

'Waiting can be a pleasure,' Maria reminded her. Holding Fatima's lips apart with the fingers of one hand, she extended the middle finger of her other hand and slid it slowly up inside her victim.

'Yes!' Fatima sighed.

'I am going to make you very much wet,' Maria threatened.

I could see by the way her wrist moved that she was rotating the pad of her fingertip on the sensitive spot behind Fatima's pubic bone. She must have been skilled at that caress, for Fatima's knees quivered and moisture seeped down over Maria's hand.

Maria put her face close and inhaled. 'So sweet!' she exclaimed.

Fatima groaned, '*Sharmutta!*'

'Bitch, am I?' Maria teased. '*Te voy hacer la sopa!*'

The threat, to eat Fatima's cunny, didn't seem to intimidate the girl. She knotted a hand into Maria's long black hair and dragged her head in close, into a cunny-to-mouth kiss.

I, awkwardly, raised myself on one elbow.

The feast began. Maria proved to be as enamoured of cunny as she was of cock. Her face burrowed between Fatima's lower lips, spreading them wide and smearing them across her own cheeks. Her head shook, then nodded, then rotated. I could not see what her tongue was doing but I enjoyed using my imagination.

Fatima spread her arms to grab two of the iron rings set in the wall. Her thighs strained wider apart. Her entire body quivered with delight, then tensed. A hard ripple ran down her belly. The tendons in her neck stood out.

She cried, 'I die!' Her knees flexed, as if she were about to topple, but she recovered and straightened. 'More!' she demanded.

Maria peeled her chemise off and returned to her succulent banquet. I managed to wrap my fingers around her slender ankle to give myself the illusion of participating in the amorous games. Fatima lifted her left foot from the floor, up on to the bench, in order to spread herself wider and give Maria easier access to the warm pink fruit between her thighs.

Men can be very lustful. I'm living proof. Some women, however, those who have shed all modesty and have totally freed their inner lasciviousness, can enter states of ecstatic desire, of ferocious sexual hunger, that transforms them into ravening beasts.

That day, I was privileged to watch as two lovely girls goaded themselves and each other along the intricate path that leads step by step from amorous play to mindless frenzy.

Maria doted on love's various liquid manifestations, be they male or female. Fatima was addicted to her own climaxes. Unlike some women, who swoon after a single orgasm and thereafter flinch from being touched, Fatima's first burst of joy made her all the more eager for her second, and then third, and so on, each surpassing the others in intensity.

Maria's face burrowed into Fatima, slurping and lapping, withdrawing from time to time for the girl to suck in great gulps of air before returning to the fray. Fatima ran the gamut in expressing her glee. At one moment she'd be giggling; the next rapt in frowning concentration. She laughed. She cried. Obscenities tumbled from her sweet lips, intermingled with declarations of undying love for Maria. At a climax, she shouted, sobbed or moaned or sometimes screamed as if in agony. Strands of her hair were plastered across her face. Her entire body became coated in a thin sheen of perspiration. The odour of her sweat mingled with the scent of her cunny, deliciously thickening the air I breathed.

Fatima was still writhing when Maria finally sunk back on her heels. 'My tongue,' she managed to fumble out. 'Tired. Ache.'

'Fingers!' Fatima demanded. She looked like a runner three parts through a marathon, exhausted but determined to continue.

'*He* must watch!' Maria declared.

'Yes!' Fatima agreed, vehemently. The Egyptian stepped down from the bench on wobbling legs and set one knee to each side of my head.

Maria knelt astride my chest, her knees tucked into my armpits. I looked up between two lovely bodies, one lean and lithe, the other plump and voluptuous. Their mouths met. Maria's nipples brushed across Fatima's breasts. Each reached down to seek and find the other's cunny. Not four inches above my head, fingers worked into squelching folds of flesh; thumbs discovered clits and attacked them with more vigour than I, a gentle man, would have.

My fingers curled but could reach nothing. I turned my face to the side, to lick the inside of Fatima's thigh. Lifting myself, I was able to trail my tongue higher and reach skin that was seasoned by her seepage.

One of them grunted. A light splattering dampened my face. Their hips jerked, grinding mound on mound, then slithered as they manoeuvred as best they could to press clitoris to clitoris. For twenty breaths, Maria humped upwards while Fatima held still. There was a gurgling cry and then it was Fatima's turn to bump and grind while Maria braced.

Their mounds parted, stretching liquid strands. It was Fatima's hand that snaked down between their bodies. Fumbling, she managed to trap both of their clitorises between her finger and thumb at once. The two buttons of flesh were rolled on each other, inspiring another climax by one of them, though I knew not which.

Their frenzy was not yet done. Without a word but each understanding the other's intent, they halfway rose. Maria's right foot lifted and nudged Fatima's left thigh away from my face. Fatima's right leg bent up as she planted her foot beside my chest. They sank down, Fatima astride Maria's thigh, Maria straddling Fatima's leg.

Their hips moved as if they were riding at a trot that soon became a canter and then a furious gallop that led to them both being thrown with great screams of delight. I thought they were done but I underestimated the minxes. Maria, sprawled across my body, reached down to Fatima's foot, dragged it up between her thighs and humped at its heel. From the confused movements beyond my head, I gathered that Fatima was likewise making vigorous love to some part of Maria's foot. Curious, I twisted my head and craned my neck backwards but the tangle of lovely young limbs defeated me.

Maria, rising to yet another orgasm, bounced her bottom up and down on my chest. I had no objection. She was light enough that I wasn't discomforted. I'd have liked to have been granted better access to either girl's body than occasionally managing to lick the dew from the skin of a thigh, though.

At last, Maria sobbed, 'Enough!'

Fatima, moving with leaden limbs, heaved herself around and crawled wearily over both me and Maria. I think she intended to continue the erotic bout in some way but her fatigue overcame her. She slumped across Maria, who was sprawled supine across me, with my poor neglected cock trapped, stiff as an oak staff, between the small of her back and my belly. The girls slept. Sometime later, so did I.

Fourteen

Fatima said, 'His *arma* looks very uncomfortable. Do you think we should take care of it?'

I opened my eyes. The girls, both still naked, sat opposite each other, the heels of their bare feet digging uncomfortably into my naked belly. My rigid cock, the subject of their discussion, was being toed idly while they debated whether or not to assuage its needs.

'It'd rise again, in time to greet Zema,' I offered.

They trapped my shaft between the sole of Maria's foot and the ball of Fatima's and rolled it while they considered my remark.

'She prefers you to be desperate,' Fatima told me. 'I think she's afraid that her size could intimidate a man's *zib*.'

'My *zib* fears nothing,' I assured her.

'We are instructed to arouse you to the point of madness, every day, but not to let you spend until Zema is done with you.'

'When will she arrive?'

'When it suits her.'

Zema *did* arrive, at that very moment, with Melku. They'd come to take me out for my daily ablutions, not for Zema to roger me. When I returned for a breakfast of tea and Gentleman's Relish on crackers, I found the girls were clothed, after a fashion.

'It will get colder,' Maria explained. 'We will need things to wear, to keep warm.' She'd found a length of jade silk, perhaps a table covering by its fringe, and had fastened it

84

under one armpit with a brooch and at her waist by her beads and cross. The silk was too narrow to overlap. A strip of skin an inch wide showed all the way down her right side. Her right leg was completely bare.

Fatima had devised her garments from two squares of purple satin, each folded into a triangle, one knotted at her plump hip, the other supporting and tied between her ample breasts. I found the effect, something like two risen but unbaked cottage loaves nestling in a gay cloth, quite enchanting.

The girls had strung a cord across the width of our carriage and hung it with sheets. Now they had a place of privacy. The rest of the morning and after our boiled mutton lunch, was spent with them giving me a scandalous fashion show. They posed and promenaded like *filles de joie*, in skirts that were slit at the front, up to their navels, veils that hid nothing, lengths of cloth that tied below their breasts but left those love-toys naked, and as many saucy *modes* as their prurient young minds could concoct.

Fatima was covered in what I took to be a fisherman's net and Maria was naked except for a gauze loincloth when Zema returned. This time she opted to kneel facing my feet, gripping my ankles, providing me with a rare view of her mighty buttocks flexing and quivering. I was pounded lustily for a good twenty minutes before she flooded my balls once more, rose groggily and tottered away without a word of thanks or so much as a backwards glance.

The girls came and stood over me, looking down at my engorged shaft. 'Shall we?' Maria asked Fatima.

'If one of you doesn't do something, soon,' I warned them, 'I shall spend untouched.'

Fatima fisted her hips. 'Well, we can't have that, can we!'

Both dropped to their knees. Fatima took my cock in both hands. Maria positioned her parted lips ready to receive my liquid blessing. It didn't take long, the first time.

And so it was, for the following eight days and nights. The girls played games that aroused me. Zema arrived, mounted my cock or my face, and once my fist, halfway to my elbow, and took her pleasure. After she was sated, the girls and I played.

The sun told me we were heading north by east. As time progressed, we needed more layers of bedclothes to keep the cold out at night. Our portions of mutton grew smaller until on the eighth day the lunch that was delivered was just black bread, olive oil and salt. I counted myself fortunate that both Maria's hamper and Fatima's hatbox were well provisioned. We lacked for little, although the fruit ran out.

Mid-afternoon on the ninth day, our carriage came to a lurching halt. The girls knelt up on a bench to peer through the sacking wall.

'Something's amiss,' Maria told me, 'but I can't see what.'

An ox moaned piteously. Another took up its cry. Harnesses jingled. Men swore.

Zema and Melku appeared at the back. 'We have an entertainment,' she announced. 'You two,' she told the girls, 'will watch from in here.'

I was untied and noosed and prodded at sword point again. I admit that my stomach chilled as four surly Tatars lashed me, spread-eagle, to the spokes of a wheel of our conveyance. People have been tied to wheels to serve as targets for arrow or spear; to be lashed; to be branded; to be broken with hammers or – worst of all, to my mind – to be left there while the wheel turned, carrying the victims round and round, crushing their hands and feet and battering their heads.

But I was left, standing there, helpless. There was a commotion. An ox bellowed. The reason for our halt was revealed. One poor animal, pulled by a halter and the ring through its nose, limped, dragging one foreleg. It seemed the beast had stepped into a hole and had broken its leg. The only thing to be done was to put it out of its misery. I hoped someone would put a bullet through its head, but that was not to be.

Zema strode out, magnificently naked, swinging a gigantic kukri – the crooked blade of choice for Gurkha warriors. This particular weapon was both longer and heavier than any I had seen before.

Two Tatars braced the beast's head. Zema took a wide stance, swung high and brought the blade down on the nape of the ox's neck, severing it cleanly. That was no mean feat, I allowed. Few men could wield a blade with that skill and strength.

The ox knelt and then toppled. Tatars rushed forward with bowls and flashing knives. Steaming blood filled the bowls but also splattered in a wide circle. Within minutes, the ox was a tattered heap of raw bloody meat. Tatars drank deeply, some mixing arrack with the blood before quaffing. Steaks and joints and ragged ropes of giblets were tossed on to braziers, though some of the men couldn't wait and gnawed the meat raw.

A cheerful fellow offered me a bowl of blood, which I politely refused. His mate held a skin of arrack to my lips. That, I didn't turn down.

The Tatars began to sing and dance. I was impressed by the complexity and elegance of their steps. I'd witnessed Azerbaijani dancers perform similar steps before, but only female ones.

It became an orgy, with Tatar mounting Tatar. Zema, still bare and drenched in blood, brought me a piece of the ox's half-burned, half-raw liver. She held it to my mouth with one hand while the other caressed my member idly until I was done. She left me to disappear under a heaving mound of naked Tatars.

My position was becoming uncomfortable. The way I was tied, my scrotum rested on the wheel's iron hub, and the metal was chill. I looked about me, hoping to spot Zema and beg to be returned to the carriage. Instead, I saw Honey, skulking round the edge of the Bacchanalia. It occurred to me that she might hold a grudge. If she meant me harm, there was little I could do to defend myself. The thought softened my member until it lolled limp, partly resting on the wheel's cold hub.

Honey crept closer. A finger at her lips cautioned me to be silent, not that any cries of mine would have been heard above the hubbub. Her purpose became clear. The little harlot wrapped a hand behind my neck and stepped up to stand, legs spread wide, on two of the spokes. Her free hand reached down between us for my cock. I could resist its urge to stiffen but Honey, in that position, squatting in the air as it were, her cunny spread wide, seemed likely to succeed in stuffing my flesh inside her own, soft or not.

Logically, I could not fault myself if my vow were broken that way. Logic is of little use when a man feels guilty.

I tried to writhe and throw her off. My bonds were too secure. The little bitch had the head of my cock in contact with the wet lips of her cunny when Zema rescued me. Honey was plucked away like an infant and carried off facing backwards, tucked under Zema's left arm while the flat of Zema's right hand delivered whacks to Honey's bottom that could be heard even over the din.

Some hours later, Zema returned, bleary-eyed, with a knife in her hand and an empty wineskin over her shoulder. 'Nice English,' she said. She lifted one foot up on to a spoke, in imitation of Honey's attempt to mount me. Her knife hand went down towards my flaccid staff. I flinched. She caught herself, put the blade between her teeth, and reached down again, to caress me. I reacted, although she was rancid with dried blood and arrack dregs.

Her first foot fell off the spoke. She tried again, with the other foot on another spoke, and almost toppled. 'Tomorrow,' she promised me. Her blade sawed through my bonds.

I led her up into the carriage, where soft giggles told me my girls were observing us from behind their curtain. I spread myself on the floor. Zema tied knots that a child could have pulled apart, and left me.

At dawn, Melku arrived without Zema. I surmised that she was still recovering from the previous night's revels. My left wrist and right ankle had come loose in the night. The little man gave me a strange look and tugged the other knots free. When he put his noose over my neck he pulled it tighter than he'd done before. I had to scramble to keep up with him as we left the carriage, or else choke.

Melku was beginning to irritate me.

He made me march at speed, through saw-grass and marshy puddles. When I was slowed by my feet sinking into mud, I felt the tip of his sword bite through the skin at the back of my neck.

Enough is enough.

On our return, Melku, somewhat bruised, led. He wore the noose. I carried the sword.

Zema, back in her poncho, was waiting at the tailgate. When she saw Melku she burst into laughter. I handed her both the sword and the end of Melku's tether, with a flourish and a little bow.

She let him go, to slink off, head down.

I looked straight into Zema's eyes. 'Noble Zema,' I told her, 'I swear, by my honour and in the name of Queen Victoria, my sovereign and liege, that I will not attempt to escape from your custody. I will remain your prisoner until you have delivered me to wherever we are going. I give you my word as an English gentleman.'

She looked at me speculatively, searching my eyes, then dropping her eyes to my cock. Perhaps she was wondering whether, if I enjoyed the liberty of a parolee, she'd be denied free use of my masculine attributes. Eventually, she nodded.

Both to exorcise any fears she might have and to exercise my new licence, I crouched, ran my hands up under her voluminous garment, took hold of her thighs and heaved her up into the carriage. I vaulted after her. Her eyes were wide. I doubted any man had lifted her bodily since the day she'd become a woman.

Daring, I took her garment by its neckline and tore it asunder. Without further ado, I assaulted her on all fronts; my tongue insistent in her mouth, my hands kneading her massive breasts, my cock stabbing into her secret folds. She lay as if numb for a full minute before her thighs wrapped my hips and she thrust up at me, giving as good as she got.

I held myself back until she bellowed a climax, then flipped her over. My hands pulled her hips up and back. I went into her again, as a dog does a bitch. Once more, I pistoned into Zema, driving her to her peak and over it. As she subsided to the cedar floor, I turned her yet again. With my teeth at her throat, I sank four fingers into the hot mushiness of her cunny, found her massive clit with my thumb, and drove her to her third orgasm in less time than it takes to consume a decent breakfast.

Fatima brought a length of printed calico to cover Zema's nakedness. I've never visited Ethiopia so my Amharic is virtually non-existent but Zema looked at me and mumbled words that included, '*barya*' and '*negus*' so I assumed she was calling me an enslaved king, or a king of slaves, or some such. I stroked her cheek and called her 'my Sheba', after the beauty who'd seduced Solomon. Her face turned coyly aside. She giggled. I swear, if she hadn't been black as coal, she'd have been blushing.

Gathering the calico around herself, Zema left us. For the first time, I was alone with Fatima and Maria, unbound. I rose to my feet with a deliberately ominous look on my face. The carriage was, perforce, my abode for the nonce. It was time for me to establish who was master of my mobile house.

Fifteen

Maria had fashioned herself a sort of sari out of a length of scarlet shot-silk. She'd styled it to leave one arm, shoulder and breast, bare. Fatima was wearing a triangle of green velvet, knotted at her left hip. Both had tinted their lips and nipples crimson. Fatima's eyelids had been gilded. The hussies had prepared themselves for yet another morning of rousing my lust and denying me satisfaction until Zema arrived.

But Zema had come and gone and I wasn't bound, helpless, on the floor.

'We . . .' Maria blurted.

'I . . .' Fatima started to say.

Both fell silent before my stare. I let them suffer for a full minute. When they were fidgeting but trying not to, I strode between them, into the depths of our conveyance, and sat on a bench. 'You've enjoyed teasing me while I was helpless,' I said.

Maria mumbled, 'We took care of your need, after a while.'

'Sometimes you did. Sometimes you didn't.'

Fatima toed a knotted silk rug. 'Sorry, English.'

'You will be disciplined, both of you.'

Maria started, 'You can't . . .'

'I can.' I crooked a finger at Fatima.

Looking at her own feet and holding her hands behind herself, Fatima crept towards me. The closer she got, the less fear she exhibited. Most Arab girls have experienced corporal punishment. Many have learned to like it. By the time she reached me her hips were swinging a defiant challenge.

I spread my knees and pointed to my left thigh. Fatima shook her head. I started counting, 'Five, four, three . . .' She was draped across my leg before I reached 'two'. I pulled her hands behind her and gripped her wrists in my left hand. My right snatched her only garment aside.

Maria, her eyes big, asked me, 'What are *you* going to do to her?'

Fatima answered for me. 'Spank me, silly!'

'Can he do that?'

Fatima flexed her buttocks. 'Are you going to stop him, Maria?'

'Watch and learn,' I said. 'You could be next.'

'No!' Maria fled to the back of the carriage.

I ignored her. My right leg hooked over Fatima's, just above her knees. She was immobilised, unable to do more than squirm. As my cock was trapped under her belly, I was quite happy to let her wriggle.

Maria was hovering at the back. She was forbidden to leave our carriage except when escorted by Zema and no doubt feared the Ethiopian more than she did me.

I caressed a smooth hemisphere of Fatima's bottom. She tensed. For the entire time I'd been held captive, up till crushing Zema's breasts, my hands had been denied contact with female skin, apart from briefly brushing a thigh or a hip or a cunny's lip, '*en passant*' as it were, or occasionally holding an ankle.

I stroked, savouring the satin smoothness. I kneaded, delighting in the resilience. I tickled and I cupped. Fatima slowly relaxed. When the muscles under my fingers were limp, I lifted my hand and brought it down, hard.

Fatima yelped.

Maria, drawn by impure inquisitiveness, tiptoed back. She knelt not a foot from the arena of action, eyes bright with perverse curiosity.

I lifted my hand again. Fatima's bottom tensed. I waited. The imprint of my fingers slowly bloomed, livid against pink. I smacked once more, the other cheek, then the first again, quickly.

Maria's eyes grew wider. She hunched over with her fists, knotted together, pressed into her pubes. I reached over her back, to where her improvised sari was tucked in, and tugged the end loose.

Fatima began to pant. Her legs, from her knees down, flailed. I slapped and slapped. Her bottom blushed from the crease of her thighs to an inch below her tailbone. Every five or six blows, I paused to caress her burning skin. I'd reached thirty before Fatima began to moan in a tone that wasn't entirely from pain. I touched her between the backs of her thighs. Her ripe little cunny, squeezed between her legs, was weeping.

With a satisfied grin, I adjusted her legs, parting them further. I compressed her pubes in my palm, lifted my hand, and smacked three fingers down directly on to her pouting slit.

She gasped, jerked, and lifted her bottom even higher.

I *knew* her. Women in general might be hard to understand but Fatima, and her pain-craving sisters, are open books to me. Once you recognise one, all you have to do is gauge the intensity of their perverse needs and they are yours. I beat a rapid tattoo directly on to the cushiony beauty of Fatima's sex. My left hand released her wrists. She was no longer capable of resistance. I took a fistful of her hair and arched her backwards so that I could watch her face. Her cheeks were wet with tears. She was drooling. Her eyes were glazed and her expression blank. For Fatima, all that existed was the urgent rhythm of pain that I was inflicting on her.

She made fists, one clutching air, the other around Maria's wrist. Her hips bucked, rising to meet my every blow. A high-pitched keening, a sound I'd never heard from her before, shrilled from her throat.

Her head turned, despite my grip on her hair. Fatima looked into my eyes and in an incredibly calm voice, almost sighing, said, 'Yes!'

She slumped, spent.

I told Maria, 'Feel how hot her bottom is.'

She stretched out a tentative hand. A fold of her sari came free.

'No – with your mouth.'

Maria knelt close. Her sari unravelled down to her slender waist. She brushed her lips across Fatima's burning skin.

'Tongue! Taste it.'

Her tongue lapped a scarlet cheek.

'Now here.' I took Maria's head by her hair and directed her face, pressing it between the Egyptian's thighs, bringing her mouth to the bruised and swollen flesh of Fatima's cunny.

'Nice?'

She nodded with her tongue fully extended, its tip between Fatima's engorged lips.

'Higher!'

She raised an eyebrow.

'*Beso negro*,' I said. 'You understand?' I'd learned the expression from a Spanish maid in the employ of Lally Madison, one of London's most fashionable courtesans. The practice – the insertion of a tongue into an anus – had been all the rage the year before. Many gentlemen declared it the most intimate and thrilling act that a woman could perform for them. I myself had acquired an extra degree of popularity with the ladies when it was bruited about that I was not averse to returning the compliment. What's good for the goose, after all.

Maria gave me a blank stare. I was surprised, considering how addicted she was to oral service. Perhaps she just hadn't heard the expression before.

Fatima would have stayed contentedly draped over my knee for as long as her nether parts were being toyed with. I extended the middle finger of my left hand to Maria's lips. There was no need to instruct her. It seemed that whatever her mouth was offered, it accepted with gratitude. Her cheeks hollowed. Her tongue lapped. Once my finger was wet, I plucked it away and put its tip to the pucker between the globes of Fatima's bottom.

The Egyptian tensed. For a moment I wondered if I'd misjudged the extent of her experience. Perhaps her bum was a virgin? After all, she was in her early twenties. Many women don't embrace being buggered until their sensuality

94

peaks, in their thirties. My doubts were dispelled when, in response to the gentlest pressure, the tight pin-hole relaxed and softened, inviting my finger to explore. I prodded my way in, savouring the drag and the rubbery resistance. Beneath Fatima's tummy, my shaft twitched, anticipating the pleasures that Fatima's rear passage would afford it, eventually.

Maria's avid eyes followed my finger's progress. With two of my finger's knuckles engulfed, I bent it a fraction and lifted it an inch. Fatima's bottom had no choice but to rise higher. I took Maria by the back of her neck and told her, 'Between her cunny and her bum – lick her there.'

Maria extended her long, narrow and very flexible tongue. It flickered over that small and exceedingly sensitive area, dabbing and dancing and then delivering long lascivious licks. Fatima lay and quivered, luxuriating in the delicious sensations. From time to time, her back passage clenched on my finger.

I pushed and pulled, just a fraction of an inch. My finger pressed to one side and then the other. Fatima didn't resist but those internal muscles are strong. They have to be persuaded to relax. A vigorous buggering would have opened her up nicely but I'd decided to save that game for later.

Fatima sighed, long and deep. The constriction around my finger loosened. I plucked it out and took the cheeks of her shapely bottom in my hands, to tug them gently but firmly wide apart.

Maria's eyes widened when she saw the treat I was offering her. Her chin lifted. As her body rose, her sari slithered down to pool at her knees. Maria's tongue stretched out. Its tip circled the dark rear entrance to Fatima's body, tickling the striations of its pit. The Spanish girl sucked in a deep breath. She pushed. Her face turned from side to side as slowly but surely she worked her sinuous tongue into Fatima's bum-hole.

'Good girl,' I told her. 'Deeper now. Tongue-fuck the little bitch.'

Maria's head drew back and pushed forward, slowly at first but accelerating. Fatima began to moan. Saliva dripped from Maria's lips and pooled in the soft crater of Fatima's anus.

My cock called out to me. Rarely had I seen a bum so ripe for sodomy as Fatima's was at that moment but I am not whimsical in matters of sex. I had a plan and would not be distracted from it by a passing fancy. Self-control is paramount. My object, that day, was to teach these two girls exactly who their lord and master was.

When both seemed rapt, Maria in her tonguing and Fatima in being tongued, I stood up, dragging both with me by their hair. Fatima whimpered. Her bottom wriggled. Her hands fluttered from her nipples to her cunny and back again. She was in a delirium of lust.

Similarly, Maria writhed against my grip, her tongue straining to reach something, anything, sexual.

I lifted my left foot up on to the bench. My left fist bore Fatima down before me. My right hand dragged Maria in close behind me. Maria's hands parted my buttocks. Her face squirmed into their divide. Fatima took my shaft in one hand, my testes in the other, and closed her lips around the crown of my cock.

I fought the urge to fuck Fatima's sweet little face. Holding still, I let her gobble on me, lips mobile, tongue slavering. The tip of Maria's tantalising tongue found my anus and probed. I didn't hold back. My eyes closed. I focused on the obscenely delicious sensations and let the pressure build and build and build until I gushed, flooding Fatima's mouth.

As a rule, I make sure to compliment any sexual partner who has contributed to my climaxes. I didn't, then. The lovely little bitches had taken great glee in tormenting me and using me as their erotic toy. They needed to be taken down a peg or two.

As I released my grips on their hair, the girls moved to embrace. I pulled them apart. The cords that had bound my wrists and ankles served to truss my companions, each seated on the bench opposite the other, both with arms extended and wrists lashed to iron rings. I believe that Fatima expected me to indulge in some erotic cruelty and was looking forward to it. She was right, but not as she imagined. I stretched out on my 'bed' and luxuriated in the pleasure of sleeping on my stomach, at last.

Sixteen

My fellow passengers on that strange journey were all three quite young, very lovely, and what I can only describe as 'erotophiles'. They weren't nymphomaniacs, not even Honey. Nymphomaniacs, unfortunates who suffer from raging unquenchable lust, are sad creatures who are rightly confined to Bedlams, for their own and the public's safety. Fatima, Maria and Honey were all devoted to Eros but not to the point of being crazed. They could be sated. They could delay their orgasms to extend the pleasure of anticipation. They enjoyed sex.

I've read the works of Jacques Bernoulli and Gerolamo Cardana, so I have some small understanding of the mathematical science of 'statistics' and the laws of chance. It couldn't have been by happenstance that three young girls, all lovely, all passionately but not insanely devoted to Eros, were on the same journey. I know that young people are usually lusty. I know that youth imparts beauty. Even so, not one girl in a thousand would have fit the criteria these three did – young, lovely and happy to be depraved. Someone had gone to enormous lengths to find these girls and induce them to join the Wolf's sect.

I could think of a dozen nefarious uses such girls could be put to. I needed more information, but that likely awaited me at journey's end. Questioning the girls overtly might do my cause more harm than good. More intelligence is gathered by listening than by asking questions.

I awoke and rolled over. Above me, four pretty feet were making languorous love to four shapely limbs. My lustful captives, unable to touch in any other way, had stretched out their legs so that they might run the soles of their feet together and, by slumping against their bonds and by balancing their bottoms on the very edges of their benches, bring toes into caressing contact with knees, and even a few inches higher.

How frustrating for them! To have delicate little pink toes, so mobile, offering so many erotic possibilities, within a foot of their cunnies but unable, no matter how they strained, to reach their soft wet goals.

These were the girls who had dripped their spending on me, who had toyed with my cock for endless hours and left it aching with need. Frustration suited them.

I rose and rinsed my face in cold water from a canvas bucket.

Fatima pouted and cajoled, 'Please, English?'

Maria told me, 'My tongue is rested, Milord.'

I undid their bonds and was about to position Fatima kneeling up on a bench when Zema arrived with a great platter of badly-cooked ox meat and a gallon jug of watery ale. My little altercation with Melku was bearing unexpected fruit. Zema ate with us. I pulled Maria's wicker hamper into the middle of the aisle to serve us as a table. A meaningful look from me prompted Fatima to roll down the sacking curtain at the rear, granting us a degree of privacy.

'Zema,' I suggested, 'we three are nude. Won't you join us in that, that we may all be at ease?'

She looked from me to Maria to Fatima and made her decision. Her poncho flew into a far corner. She sat at our 'table', to my left, opposite the girls. I dropped a companionable hand on to the smooth hard flesh of her massive thigh. She edged an inch closer. I selected a choice gobbet of meat and lifted it to her lips. Maria and Fatima, sensitive to the direction I was steering the meal, fed each other.

Inevitably, juices dripped on breasts and had to be wiped away – then licked away. Soon, all pretence was dropped. Maria smeared a juicy slice of liver on Fatima's nipple, which then had to be suckled clean. I pulled Zema's breast down on to the platter, used it to wipe up greasy gravy, then took it to my mouth. Zema, as if not to be outdone, dribbled ale on to my cock but then just looked at it, as if unsure what to do next. It occurred to me that the oversized and dominant lovely might well have been serviced orally, frequently, but might not have performed fellatio before. Perhaps her entire love-life had consisted of her mounting and using helpless men, until that very morning, when I'd thrown her on her back and given her a good hard rogering. Even in the drunken revel that followed the death of the ox, from what I'd seen of Zema, she'd taken the active role. She'd fucked her fellow orgiasts. That is subtly different from her being fucked by them.

I laid the platter aside and lifted my legs up to rest on the hamper. My cock stood at forty-five degrees. 'Maria,' I said, 'show Zema what you do with an ale-soaked cock.'

Maria had been roused but left in need and then bound, still frustrated, for the time my nap had taken. She was not about to miss any chance for an erotic romp. The slender Spaniard climbed up on to the hamper, swept her hair back, gave Zema a 'watch this' look, and commenced by pursing her lips over the eye of my engorged dome and slurping up the minute droplet of ale it held.

Zema knelt up on the bench and leaned forward to watch closer, which pressed her hip against my cheek.

'Fatima,' I said, 'come around the other side of Zema. Frig her clit for her.'

Zema gave me a sharp look. 'But she's a girl, not a man!'

'Have you never been loved by another woman, Zema?' I asked.

She lowered her head and shook it slowly. Perhaps she'd been too deep in lust to be aware of the previous time that Fatima had fingered her. I didn't remind her.

'Then now is your chance.' I stroked her flank. 'Be my pupil and I will teach you many joys, my Sheba. The great queen who bore wise Solomon's son was a famed lover of women as well as of men.' Making the myth up as I went along, I told Zema, 'Solomon had a thousand wives and was pleased to share them all with the beautiful Sheba. Many of them became more enamoured of her touch than of his.'

'In truth?'

'When a woman lays with a woman, it is the purest of joys. Ask Fatima. Do you not find rapture in the arms of Maria, my Egyptian dove?'

Shyly, stroking the inside of Zema's great thigh, Fatima whispered, 'Maria's fingers and tongue have taken me to paradise.'

I took Fatima's hand, guided it to the stalk of Zema's clitoris and encouraged it to stroke gently. Zema bit her lip and turned her attention back to the things Maria was doing to my cock. She was coping with her introduction to Sapphic loving by pretending indifference to the sweet thrills Fatima's fingers were giving her.

I was concerned that Zema might feel overwhelmed. Too many new experiences, too quickly, can panic the timid. Zema, who felled men with one blow and could decapitate an ox effortlessly, wasn't the sort of woman that one thinks of as 'timid', but sexually, in some ways, she was a veritable novice.

I crooned coaxing words into her ear. My fingers stroked the under-curve of one generous breast soothingly, as I might have petted a nervous horse. Maria anointed my cock with ale and sucked it off a dozen times. From time to time she bent my shaft towards Zema and raised an enquiring eyebrow. Each time, Zema shook her head. It seemed that until then she'd lived as a passionate Puritan, eager to fuck but nervous to try new things – like sucking cock or browsing on cunny-flesh. It'd be an act of charity to broaden her horizons.

Although Zema refused Maria's offers, what the Spanish girl was doing obviously fascinated her. She leaned closer and closer. Her broad tongue ran out over her lips. I peered down at her sex, where Fatima was frigging her. Those shapely black thighs were spread wide. They rocked to meet Fatima's caresses.

Maria, clever girl, switched from trying to encourage Zema to fellate me. She took the Ethiopian's hand, curled it around my shaft and urged it up and down. Not only did Zema allow herself this pleasure but she took Maria's long hair in her free hand, wrapped it around her fist and bent the girl's head down. Maria's mouth opened wide. She extended her tongue. Zema, no doubt excited by Maria's submissive display, pumped my cock vigorously. I didn't hold back. Jism jetted from my cock's eye, sluicing over Maria's tongue and splattering her face.

Zema whooped with delight.

I gently but firmly pushed her back on to the bench. Maria and Fatima looked questions at me. I swung aside and nodded. The two young girls swarmed over Zema. A mouth closed over each giant nipple. Two pairs of cheeks hollowed. Delicate hands fluttered here and there, stroking the insides of ebony thighs, caressing the generous curves of a sable belly, patting rounded hips and fondling the powerful column of Zema's neck.

Zema leaned back, submitting to the flurry of erotic attention. I took her right hand and brought it up to cup Maria's pubes. Her left hand I steered to Fatima's breast. Without thinking, she kneaded, compressing soft sweet flesh between her hard strong fingers.

I pushed the hamper aside. On my knees, I put my face to Zema's cleft and stabbed into it with my tongue.

Maria and Fatima squealed with delight. They rained kisses on their willing victim, darting their tongues into her mouth, lapping at her armpits, nibbling and suckling at her teats.

Before Zema had time to fully realise that she was thoroughly enjoying the Sapphic loving of two pretty girls, I knelt up, hooked her knees over my shoulders, presented my cock's head to her cunny's eager lips and sank into her.

As I slowly impaled the dusky beauty, I told her, 'You're a bad girl, Zema. How depraved you've become! I do believe that no perversion is now beyond you.'

Fatima chuckled. 'Yes, she's a naughty girl. She loves it when I finger her like this.'

My hands took Zema's thighs and dragged her bodily to the edge of the bench, so that she sat slumped, with her bottom projecting over the edge. I leaned back until our torsos met in a wide 'V.' Fatima had ample room for her vigorous manipulation of Zema's clit. The lovely Ethiopian made an embarrassed sound and then giggled. She was learning to embrace her inner nymph. *We* had accepted her sensuality, which permitted her to do likewise.

The angle between Zema's body and mine pressed the head of my cock up against the back of her pubic bone. I held that position, moving only enough that the spongy area there was massaged by my hard dome. Zema closed her eyes and bit her lower lip. Some women are sensitive there. Some aren't. Zema obviously was.

I touched each of my young accomplices to get their attention. 'Slowly,' I mouthed.

They nodded. Fatima's frigging of Zema's clit became gentle. Maria suckled softly at one of Zema's nipples and tenderly rolled the other. My Sheba's face grew intent. Her mouth worked. Lines of concentration appeared on her broad forehead. Her head lifted though her eyes remained closed. She started to make little mewing sounds that became an urgent pleading.

Her eyes shot open. 'More!' she demanded.

'Be patient, my lovely,' I told her.

Her hands lifted above her head and found an iron ring to clasp. Her hips rose at me. Zema's head lolled from side to side. She whimpered.

'Now!' I announced.

Maria's teeth sank into one of Zema's nipples as her fingers crushed the other. Fatima's fingers blurred on Zema's clit. I watched Zema's face. At the moment it screwed up as if in agony, I shot to my feet, dragging her up with me. I loomed over her folded body, holding the same ring that she clutched. My thighs cut loose, pounding straight down at her, driving my cock as deeply into her fevered flesh as I could.

The magnificent woman's mouth opened to let out a great strangled cry. Inside her, powerful muscles contracted on my shaft. A sudden gush scalded my cock. I drew back, out of her, took myself in hand and let a great gout of foaming jism flop across her heaving belly.

Zema parted lazy eyelids and gave me a foolish grin. 'The

Child is right,' she drawled. 'You are a master of the bedchamber.'

'The "Child"?' I asked.

A frown clouded her brow. 'I've said too much.'

To change the topic, I rubbed my incipient beard and told her, 'I'd really like to shave.' It'd been a dozen days since my face had felt a razor.

She made no promises but the next morning a Tatar arrived with a bowl of lukewarm water and a straight razor. Zema's trust in my parole wasn't absolute. He held a brace of flintlock pistols aimed at me while Maria made lather from a bar of scented Parisian soap and wielded the blade. The flintlocks were primitive weapons. Still, had I made the wrong move, I had no doubt they'd have discharged. Unlike modern bullets, crude balls of lead flatten, even at close range. They'd have made half-inch holes entering my body and have left four-inch ones as they exited.

Fatima dabbed my face dry and held a soft cloth to my chin. I hardly bled at all. Maria wiped and folded the razor.

'No,' I said before she handed it back to the Tatar.

He watched me warily as I directed the girl in cutting lengths from bolts of cloth and in slitting some to my directions. Before she handed the blade back we had a dozen crude ponchos – just pieces of cloth with slits for our heads, that could be tied with sashes to make toga-like garments. I felt we would need clothing, later, though I'd be loath to cover my companions' lovely bodies.

For me, I also had her cut out a square of cotton from which I could devise a sort of swaddling cloth.

From then on, we always had a rear-guard, a rider who trailed our vehicle by a dozen feet, lance at the ready. Sometimes it was Zema who followed and beamed beneficently at our erotic romping. Once, she bore a pigeon on one finger. I remembered that there had been pigeons at Baghdad.

When I took advantage of my new liberty by jumping off the tailgate and retiring from the track to relieve myself, our rear-guard dropped back to linger but he didn't interfere. My captivity was becoming less and less onerous. I was free to practise my yoga exercises and some limited callisthenics, though I missed my Indian clubs and medicine ball. I had sufficient food and water and three lovelies to make love to, though I didn't futter all three every day. There were days I only played with two, or just one, and I do believe I spent a full twenty-four hours in total celibacy, once.

Seventeen

We entered a city. Zema ordered our sacking drapes closed and enjoined me to remain hidden. I supposed us to be in Bukhara, just by my Sufi instincts. My guess was confirmed when we trundled by the Samanides Mausoleum. I'd never visited the deceptively simple structure but I had seen it depicted in several daguerreotypes and wood-cuts.

The air was laced with the odours of camel dung, saffron and sweet curry. My mouth watered. We'd consumed the last of the boiled and salted ox-meat four days before. The bread had moulded. Apart from the delicacies Maria's hamper provided, we'd subsisted on boiled millet.

My hopes, that we'd reprovision in the city, seemed to have been dashed. We exited Bukhara and wended our way up a verdant hillside. My disappointment was premature. Our procession turned into another giant courtyard. This one was attached to a structure that might once have been a monastery.

We stopped. Zema arrived at our tailgate. 'Bring nothing. All will be provided.'

Fatima made to dismount but Zema stopped her. 'Nothing, please. No clothes.'

Our belly-dancer let her skirt, all that she'd been wearing, fall, and dropped down. I tossed the sarong I'd wrapped around my hips and followed. Maria made no bones about removing her improvised toga but picked up her cross and rosary.

Kneeling as if in prayer, she cocked her head at Zema and mouthed, 'Please?'

The Ethiopian thought for a moment before nodding.

We were ushered by Tatars, who *really* appreciated my companions' nudity, into the baked brick structure. Our assigned quarters were a single, large, windowless but quite comfortable cell. It was lit by candles. A robed figure who might have been a monk showed us where more candles were stored.

The three of us were left to appreciate our luxuries – three real beds, with bedclothes, a low table, a chest of drawers and a rather incongruous heavy leather armchair. I'd enjoyed its like in my Pall Mall club. Unfortunately, there were no waiters standing by to fetch me scotch and soda. Maria hung her rosary and cross over a sconce.

Fatima squealed with delight when she discovered, in an anteroom, both a water-closet and a large copper bathing tub that was already filled with steaming water, with soaps and towels laid close at hand.

'You found it. You shall have first turn,' I told her.

'The bath's big enough for two people, if the two are small,' Maria pointed out.

'Very well,' I allowed. 'Leave me some water, please.'

Giggling, the two lovelies lowered themselves into the tub, one seated at each end. I returned to our boudoir, half hoping I'd find some fabulous treasure, such as a book to read or blank paper to write on. There was none such. I roamed the room idly inspecting the brick walls. There were chinks in some places that might have served as peepholes. No matter. If the residents wanted to spy on my girls and me at our sport, I wished them joy in it. The chest of drawers was empty, except for a single mothball.

I came to Maria's rosary. When I inspected it closely I discovered that each large glossy bead had been cunningly carved into a depiction of a vulva. Christianity comes in many stripes but this was a form of worship more in keeping with Hinduism. If it *had* been of Hindu origin, the string of *yonis* would have been accompanied by at least one *lingam*. I tried the cross's crossbar. It turned. I tugged. Like the handle of my swordstick, it pulled out to reveal, not a blade, but an intricately carved life-sized pink and white jade phallus.

106

I'd never seen a man's penis so intricately gnarled and veined, but this one had been designed to please the sense of touch, not that of sight. In fact, put to its intended use, it'd be invisible.

Spain is a very Catholic country. Devout people often seem to find blasphemy erotic. Half the forbidden French literature I'd read had concerned nuns flagellating novitiates or priests buggering nuns, either in cloisters or bent over altars. I considered taking the toy to the girls, to enhance their watery play, but at that moment three little old men appeared, each bearing a steaming dish of some sort of lumpy pease pudding.

I called to the girls that supper had been served, and quickly ate mine with the horn spoon provided. They joined me, pink-skinned from the hot water and smelling enticingly clean. I resisted their temptation. A real bath, no doubt tepid by then, awaited me.

When I returned, they'd pushed the three beds together. They were lying side by side, face up, legs apart, each idly fingering the other's cunny.

Fatima sat up to greet me. 'Please, English, teach us something new?'

The thirty-four fundamental positions described in the *Kama Sutra* were easy enough to remember and they were variations on congress alone. With two eager pupils at hand and our play by no means limited to ways cocks can join cunnies, I had no doubt I could have rung the changes nightly for a year or more. And yet – the triple bed was a siren. It seemed like forever since I'd slept on a mattress. Call me lazy or impugn my manliness, but at that moment I wanted nothing more than eight hours of uninterrupted sleep. Even so, a gentleman should never leave a girl's lust unslaked, unless it be by way of disciplining her. I thought I had the answer to my dilemma in Maria's cross. I'd let them serve each other while I relaxed.

'No, Fatima,' I said. 'Tonight, sweet little Maria will school you.' I crossed to the sconce and fetched the perverse rosary. Tossing it on the bed, I said, 'Show Fatima how you play with your toy, Maria.'

The girl clasped her mouth, rolled over and buried her face in a pillow. 'Can't.'

The fair gender never fails to amaze me. The girl had sucked me dry on many occasions. I'd gifted her with 'pearl necklaces' half a dozen times. She'd directed my shaft into her friend's bottom and urged me to plumb deeper depths than was possible. Now, no doubt because of the sacrilege involved, she was turning coy on us.

Fatima blinked at me. 'What?'

'The cross and rosary – inspect them.'

She turned the blasphemous toy in her hands. 'Oh! The beads are . . .'

'And the shaft.'

She twisted and tugged and soon found out how to unsheathe the phallus. 'What fun!' she exclaimed, and slid it between her lush lips for a long lascivious suck.

'Show us how you use it, Maria,' I prompted.

She shook her head.

'Then we shall find the way of it by trial and error, won't we, Fatima?'

The voluptuous Egyptian nodded so vigorously that her lovely titties bounced.

Maria's demeanour said that she was deeply ashamed to have been caught in possession of her profane toy. Perhaps she was. There are, however, many people of both sexes who find their own embarrassment exciting. The way her slender form shivered hinted that she was such a person.

I took up her rosary and trailed it down the length of her spine. She shuddered but her bottom dimpled as if she were pressing her pubes down on the bed.

I whispered, 'Sacrilege.'

Her shoulders hunched up to her ears.

'Let me guess how you desecrate your body with this obscene tool,' I said. 'Here, Fatima.' I pressed Maria's buttocks apart. 'Make her wet, first.'

Fatima arched over Maria, worked her mouth and drooled, aiming the string of spittle at Maria's pucker and scoring a perfect bull's eye.

'Well done,' I said. The rosary fastened with a loop

around a bead, so there was nothing rough or sharp at its end. I put a bead to Maria's sphincter and pressed on it. She tensed. I was insistent. The first bead sank out of sight. Her bum's hole closed behind it.

'How holy you must be by now, Maria! How many hours have you spent, telling your beads in this manner?' I pressed another bead into her. 'What do you pray for, may I ask?' The third and fourth bead met little resistance. I followed the fifth with my finger, prodding as deeply as I could. 'Do you ask that you be given into the charge of some salacious priest, one with a cock like a donkey, and sodomised by him as you kneel before the holy altar?'

By then Maria was quivering and her back was hollowed. I pushed a sixth bead into her, and the seventh and eighth.

'Or do you seek damnation?' I asked. 'Is it devils with red-hot iron pizzles that you crave?'

At that, she gasped and shook her head so vehemently that I knew I'd struck home. I'd seen Honey embrace her own degradation. It seemed that Maria had similar inclinations. Fatima, on the other hand, seemed to be more sanely candid about her sensual nature. Perhaps I hadn't probed her murkier depths, yet.

When the tiny mouth of her bottom had swallowed a baker's dozen of the beads, I deemed Maria sufficiently distended. I put my arms beneath her and turned her over. There was still a length of beads loose that sufficed for me to lift the phallus to her mouth.

'This is Satan's insatiable member,' I hissed. 'Suck it!'

Eyes clouded in erotic reverie, Maria took the obscene thing between her lovely young lips and gobbled voraciously on it.

'What a perverse little witch she is!' Fatima exclaimed, admiringly.

'Kneel astride her face,' I commanded. 'Maria, share! Plunge it up into Fatima's cunny, then suck it.'

Maria obeyed, with a will. The phallus went from her mouth and into Fatima for half a dozen strokes, then back to be orally worshipped again. Fatima helped by making a fan of her fingers and frigging it to and fro across the exposed head of her own clit. In no time, the Egyptian was dripping her sweetness on to Maria's welcoming face.

I half-turned Maria from her narrow waist down. Sitting astride her left thigh, I raised her right leg and hooked her ankle behind my neck in a variation on the Pestle position that is described in the *Kama Sutra*. It is a pose in which a man can easily control the depth he penetrates. I moved forward, butting the crown of my staff against Maria's soft portal. With gentle fingers, I parted her delicate petals. My cock eased into her and found her vestibule to be no tighter and no looser than on the dozen or more times I'd fucked her before. When I pushed deeper, however, the bulk of beads, pressing up from below the muscular membrane, halted me.

'Am I hurting you?' I asked.

'Do it!' she barked.

Despite her invitation, I eased into her, working my way firmly but gently. The beads moved under my cock. When the obstruction became less and I felt free to push harder, it was as if they rippled along the underside of my shaft.

With Maria fully impaled, I paused.

She growled, 'Fuck me hard, English. I can take it.' She returned to pistoning jade into Fatima, her mouth stretched wide open so as to catch as much of the Egyptian's splattering liquors as possible.

I rocked. Beads moved beside and beneath my shaft. Once I was sure I'd do Maria no damage, I stroked into her, neither fast nor slow but with that steady rhythm that I can maintain for hours, if need be.

It was Fatima who changed our pace. She leaned towards me, still astride the other girl, so that Maria could continue to dildo-fuck her and lap at her clit. Her tongue laved Maria's heaving belly, down to the little pink button that protruded from between my victim's lower lips. The extra attention moved Maria to writhe beneath me. I could have restrained her but I remembered my first intent – to let the lascivious wenches sate themselves and leave me to get some sleep – so I accelerated.

Maria's face was hidden beneath Fatima and the only sounds she made were wet gobbling noises so I had to judge how imminent her climax might be. When her lower abdomen flushed and knotted, I took hold of the string of beads. A convulsion creased her belly. Something like a muffled sob alerted me. I tugged. The beads emerged, one at a time, plopping from Maria's anus. Her prolonged gurgling confirmed the accuracy of my timing. Her orgasm was not just massive, but prolonged to last for a good dozen heartbeats.

I finished in Fatima's mouth. Sure that Maria would take care of Fatima's need, I let blessed sleep overcome me.

Eighteen

I awoke as the middle of three human 'spoons'. Fatima felt me stir and wriggled her warm little bottom back at me. Maria felt the movement and put an arm over me to take hold of my shaft, no doubt to facilitate its introduction into Fatima's back passage. Before any such progress could be made, the three wizened pease pudding bearers returned. We rose to break our fast.

Somehow, the tub was full again. I let the girls have first turn. I've seen the sun set behind the Taj Mahal. I've watched the white stallions of Lipizza dancing. Of all the beautiful sights I've been privileged to witness, none compares to the living and moving tableau of those two girls at sport in their tub, seen by the rosy flickering light of a dozen tall candles. Yes, it aroused me, but it transcended the merely erotic. I was moved to compose a hymn to Aphrodite. Unfortunately, I've since forgotten most of the words, but it was a fine composition as I recall.

Fatima stood up to rinse off. Maria slapped her neat little bottom for her. Fatima fled, squealing. Maria followed, flicking a wet towel. I took over the tub, thankful that they'd surrendered it before it cooled to tepid.

I didn't linger in the water. I would have but the yelps and giggles from the next chamber piqued my curiosity. With a towel knotted about my hips, I joined my girls.

It seemed that the tables had turned, which was a revelation. Fatima had frequently flaunted her bum at me, wordlessly asking for a spanking. Maria had never done that

112

and yet it was she who was kneeling up on the seat of the armchair, arms embracing its broad back, and it was Fatima who was wielding the wet towel so vigorously. Maria's lean flanks were already scarlet. Her face was flushed and wet with tears.

Fatima grinned at me. 'I was punishing her for her blasphemous toy,' she explained. 'But when she'd accepted the prescribed twenty strokes, the little *sharmutta* begged for more.'

I crossed to Maria and cupped her pubes in my palm. 'Her *yoni* is drooling like a beggar at a banquet, Fatima. She's enjoying her beating. You, of all people, must understand that.'

Fatima simpered. 'Me, English?'

'Yes, you.'

'Then her punishment has been no punishment at all.'

'No, but perhaps we can make it so.'

Her face lit up. 'How?'

'First, she must be made a little less comfortable.' I lifted Maria and set her down kneeling on the arms of the chair with her thighs spread wide.

Fatima flicked her towel upwards, making it snap. 'Shall I beat her on her cunny?' she suggested.

'Later, perhaps. I think that inflicting another sort of distress might be more amusing.' I fetched the jade dildo from the beds. Crouching beside Maria, I worked the phallus up into her cunny at an angle, so that its base pressed against the back of the chair. I'd have to hold it in place but that was no chore.

'Try a good hard slap,' I told Fatima.

The towel cracked across the backs of Maria's thighs. In reflex, she jerked forward, impaling herself.

'There,' I explained, 'the more you punish her, the more she'll sin. How will she resolve this dilemma, I wonder?'

'Tricky,' Fatima agreed. Her arm drew back. She took careful aim. The towel's wet end landed.

Maria's jerk sank three more inches of jade into her cunny. She yelped, '*Peccavi*,' retreating to a Latin confession in her extreme distress – or in her ecstatic bliss. The two are easily confused.

'Yes,' I told her, 'you have sinned. That is your nature.'
Fatima struck again.

'Then I must be punished,' Maria sobbed.

'You are being punished.'

'More! Worse!'

'In what way?' I asked, amused to allow a girl who craved pain to prescribe for herself. I thought it would be most illuminating.

'Like this!' Maria plucked the dildo from my loose grip. She swung round to face Fatima, still kneeling up on the chair's arms. With both hands behind her, she worked half the phallus up into her rear passage and arched herself backwards to rest her neck on the back of the chair. Pushing her belly at Fatima, she demanded, 'Be merciless!'

The Egyptian had her own ideas. First, she went to the bathing room and returned with three fresh towels, each one dripping wet at one end. She took a carefully measured position to one side of her victim, took a deep breath and lashed out. The stinging end cracked precisely on the lean mound of Maria's pubis. The girl yelped and jerked but although in no way restrained, made no move to defend herself. This was what she wanted. This was how she reconciled her salacious nature with her religious guilt.

I was learning more about both of my young companions. Maria craved more pain than I'd have guessed. Fatima, such a sweet and roguish girl, who considered being spanked as jolly good fun, was revealing a streak of cruelty worthy of – no – not worthy of the Inquisition, as I was about to say. Her delight in inflicting pain was limited to subjecting *eager* victims to it. It was akin to the pleasure I take in spanking willing subjects. I'd never lay a hand on a woman who didn't crave it, and nor, I guessed, would Fatima.

Fatima was taking her time, perhaps giving Maria every chance to plead for mercy. The Egyptian paced from side to side, eyeing her victim, selecting her next target. Standing directly in front of Maria, Fatima set her shoulders and swung. On the front-hand swing, the towel slapped the inside of Maria's left thigh, just above her knee. On the return, it hit the same spot on her right thigh. Back and forth the towel swung, each time landing a few inches higher. Between each blow, Maria pumped the dildo up into her own rectum.

The Spanish girl, her hair sodden and her eyes wild, turned her face to me. 'Help me, please?'

I knew she wasn't asking me to come to her rescue. She wanted me to help her endure. I took her hair in my right hand and pulled it down behind the back of the chair, forcing her to arch even further. My left hand held her slender throat in a grip that was gentle enough not to impair her breathing but firm enough that she'd know her life was in my hands.

When the towel struck high, almost at her groin, her mouth gaped wide in a silent scream. I covered it with mine and invaded her lax wet mouth with my thrusting tongue. From the corner of my eye I watched as Fatima drew back her towel again. Both I and Maria anticipated it would fall directly on her sex but Fatima fooled us. It slapped across Maria's delicate young breasts, precisely on her nipples, hard enough to rock her body left and then right.

Maria sobbed around my tongue – and then sucked on it. The pleasure her pain was giving her seemed to have rendered the girl delirious. She strained like a bow, her body *demanding* more torment.

Fatima gave her what she wanted. A dozen blows across her breasts left them streaked with crimson and transformed her nipples into hard brown nuts. Once more, the slaps progressed, moving down Maria's body, each overlapping the one before as if Fatima was painting Maria with pain and taking care not to miss a single spot.

Maria's mouth slobbered under mine. Her face was as flushed as if it had been included in the beating. The wet flicking slaps reached her navel, and lower, but at a slower pace, as if Fatima wanted to prolong Maria's ecstasy of agony for as long as possible.

At last a blow landed directly on Maria's mound. The girl forced her knees even further apart, off the arms of the chair, so that she rested on her shins. She wanted to present her most tender flesh as unprotected as possible.

Fatima stepped back. She tossed the towel she'd been wielding aside and selected a fresh one. Her arm reached out, flicking the end of the towel at its target. She was gauging the distance so that when she swung, only the 'cracking' end of her weapon would strike the parted oozing lips of Maria's cunny.

When she struck, it was hard and fast. The towel blurred, up and down, up and down, beating a rapid tattoo. Maria twisted and shuddered in my hands.

I asked her, 'Enough?'

She shook her head. Despite my hold on her, she convulsed like an acrobat, flinging herself upwards from her kneeling position to get her feet flat on the arms of the chair. Arched backwards in a wrestler's bridge, she *fucked* up at each descending blow.

My cock had become iron. No one had touched it but I was witnessing the most incredible demonstration of un-bridled raging lust I'd ever been privy to. I've seen and performed some rare feats in my life but at that moment I was in awe.

I didn't count but Maria's cunny must have taken a score or more direct slaps before she screamed and collapsed into the chair. I lifted her with great reverence and carried her towards the beds. Halfway there, the dildo fell from her bottom and was ignored.

When I straightened, Fatima eyed my engorged wagging stem. 'Shall I?' she asked, extending a hand.

'Thank you, but no. Do *you* need to ...?' I raised an eyebrow.

'After *that*, no, but thank you.'

It was strange, but we both spoke in hushed tones, as one might in a cathedral. Perhaps we were. Perhaps Maria's bravura performance had transformed our simple cell into a temple of lust.

Nineteen

We spent four nights and three days in that windowless cell, judging by the eleven identical meals of pease pudding we were served – one on our arrival, three a day and one on the morning of our departure. Maria, understandably, slept on her back for the last two days.

When we were taken outside, changes had been made to our caravan.

Half the Tatars had left us, to be replaced by a dozen imposing Cossacks in scarlet felt coats and tall astrakhan hats. They were armed with a sabre and a brace of pistols apiece, plus an assortment of daggers tucked into belts and boot tops. One, I noticed, carried an ancient blunderbuss across his pommel.

The oxen were gone. Teams of extremely large horses of a breed I didn't recognise had taken their place. The smallest of the magnificent beasts was a good twenty hands tall, I swear. They were built like Shire horses but without the feathered fetlocks and they were as shaggy as Shetland ponies about their bodies. The air smelled of burned horn so I guessed that the horses had recently been shod.

There was a water-cart hitched behind the lead carriage. It was nothing more than an enormous barrel mounted on wheels. The tops of both carriages had been covered with lengths of oilcloth.

There were changes inside our carriage, as well. Our clothes, from Maria's modest dress and three immodest chemises; Fatima's skimpy jacket and gauzy skirt, to the last

117

of the items that we'd improvised for play or utility, were all laid out on one of the benches, pristine clean, flat-ironed and folded neatly. The cloths that had served us as bed clothes had also been laundered.

There was a faint smell of carbolic in the air that, with a small damp patch of floor, suggested our travelling home had been scrubbed clean. In addition to our abundance of fabrics and hides, there was now a great heap of precious furs. I recognised sable and ermine and ocelot and lynx but many of them were outside my experience. Isabel, I'm sure, would have recognised every last one – and priced it within a pound.

Three large earthenware pitchers had been lashed to a wall, standing on a bench. A ladle hanging close by told me they were full of water.

A water cart and now three pitchers? I surmised we were heading into dry country, although the oilcloth suggested the opposite.

Maria's hamper had been topped up with dried figs and dates. Someone had added pomegranates and limes to Fatima's hatbox, which had been down to a single jar of crystallised ginger. Most foreigners think that Englishmen are addicted to limes, so I took their inclusion as an act of kindness. I resolved to set a couple of fruits aside, in case Fatima took a fancy to repeating her 'puckered cunny' game. I was also thinking of protecting her from scurvy, of course.

The girls fussed around, storing their clothes and inspecting the furs. As is the way with the fair sex, they could not resist trying the luxuries on.

Two burly Cossacks heaved a huge leather-bound trunk over the tailgate and followed it with a bag in the style made popular by Prime Minister Gladstone. Their third delivery was a girl, who remained stiffly upright as they lifted her bodily and set her down on her feet. The three of us stopped what we'd been doing and turned to face our guest.

She was of middle height, with enormous dark-brown eyes that were tilted and set a little further apart than classicists maintain is the perfect proportion – one eye's width. Their spacing gave her a timid look, like a fawn at bay. As for the rest of her appearance, all was concealed. She wore a stiff brocade cape in green and gold, with arm-slits, that was fastened by frogs and fitted her like a tent. Her head was wrapped in a black scarf, embroidered with gold thread, that covered most of her face, leaving just her eyes exposed.

Those eyes looked from one of us to the others in patent shock. Maria had draped her shoulders with a snow-lynx cape but was otherwise nude. Fatima, bare, was trying out the sensations that a fox-tail tippet afforded when stroked upwards between her thighs. I was simply naked, but I imagine my size was intimidating.

The poor thing scurried to sit on a bench, where she remained motionless, staring at the floor.

I picked up my 'swaddling cloth' and knotted it about my loins. My girls made to embrace our newcomer but she shrank down into her cape like a turtle so they didn't insist. Maria tried Spanish and French and Latin on her, but was ignored. I tried Hindi and Parsee with the same result. Both of my girls performed dumb-show introductions. Fatima took our guest's fingertips only to have them snatched back and disappear inside her cape.

I suggested that we leave her be and give her time to adjust to her new surroundings. The girls concurred but were not content. After about an hour, when our caravan was already rolling, they plied her with fruits and sweet-meats, all of which she ignored.

Maria sauntered casually to where I sat and straddled my knees. 'She can't see, because of my cape,' she told me. She loosened my sparse garment and let it fall to the floor between my feet. Her left hand cupped my testes as her right stroked my shaft, typical of a wise woman who is about to beg a favour. 'She's been summoned by the Child, am I not right?'

'So it would seem.' The more knowledge of this 'Child', whom I'd only heard mentioned once before, I feigned, the more those who knew more were likely to let slip.

'And the Child only calls girls who are of a like nature to Fatima and me, is it not so?'

119

I waited for her to continue.

'So, if she is like us, why is it that she spurns us?'

I shrugged. 'Is it not possible that the Child could have many reasons to summon girls?'

Maria made a moue. 'Perhaps.' The tips of her fingers trailed up the underside of my shaft. 'You should take her, English.'

'You mean by force?'

'If need be.'

'I don't do that.'

'You've forced me.'

'At your request. Playing at rape is very different from the real thing.'

'She'll spoil everything.'

'How so?'

'She'll sit there like a nun. How can we . . .' Her fist wrapped my column and pumped it by way of explanation, 'when she just sits there, face like a prune, and frowns on us?'

I chuckled. 'Face like a prune? But we haven't seen her face, except for her eyes, and they are lovely.'

'A woman can tell. Why else does she hide behind her veil?'

I closed my hand over her fist and stilled it, the better to concentrate. 'Maria, all will be as before. Our sport will continue. If it offends our guest, so be it. Perhaps, in witnessing our joyful games, she will be moved to participate.'

Maria thought about that. 'Well, in that case . . .' She tossed the cape aside, moved to sit astride my hips, steered my shaft into her cunny, and began to ride.

Over her shoulder, I watched the new girl. She didn't stare. She didn't avoid looking at us. Her eyes looked straight ahead, as if we didn't exist.

Perhaps it was childish but from then on, we three entered into a secret and unspoken conspiracy to somehow reach the caped girl and evoke a reaction from her. Maria showed Fatima that no bruises remained on her body, despite the intensity of the wet-towel flogging she'd endured so happily.

The process necessitated displays of her private parts and was performed directly in front of our stranger. A little later, the jade dildo made an appearance and was demonstrated, again, in our guest's line of sight.

Those lovely eyes didn't blink.

Our first meal since our return to our carriage was delivered. I set a steaming bowl of lentil soup down beside the girl. We all watched and waited. Soup challenges a veil. She simply turned to her Gladstone bag, extracted a square yard of cambric and draped it over her head. The bowl of soup disappeared beneath the linen. Listening intently, we heard the sounds of it being drunk.

When we were brought water for washing, she vanished behind the draped curtain. Maria wanted to follow her but I forbade it. Privacy is important when people are confined together. Come nightfall, Fatima, Maria and I snuggled together under a heap of furs. The girl, as far from us as she could get, covered herself with a voluminous ermine blanket. There was movement under it. Her brocade cape appeared and was set aside without more than three slender fingers emerging.

Our diet had improved. We were served three meals a day – lentil soup and tea for breakfast, boiled rice for luncheon and more rice, with a small portion of curried goat, for supper. We had our fruits, both fresh and dried, should we hunger between times.

Several days passed without incident and without our shy turtle emerging from her shell. Zema didn't visit. I missed her. Then, one dawn, it was Melku who delivered our soup. I stood at the tailgate and took two bowls from his hands. When I'd passed those on, I bent for the next two but he only handed me one. I delivered that into Fatima's care and turned back to take my portion. Melku, looking up directly into my eyes, spat into my bowl before handing it to me.

I, of course, upended it over his head.

He drew his pistol so I was forced to jump down and take it from him. Things might have got ugly but Zema arrived and sent the little man off with his head ringing, no doubt, from her backhand blow.

Sooner or later, I decided, I was going to kill Melku.

It was two days after that when Zema visited once more. I greeted her with a hearty wet kiss and a fondle but she wasn't there to be sociable.

'The leader of the Cossacks, Igor Varnokov, knows of your repute as a swordsman,' she told me.

I smiled. I am not a vain man but was gratified that my name was known so far from the capitals of Europe.

'He requests a demonstration of your skills,' she continued.

'A demonstration?' My heart beat faster at the prospect of holding a blade again.

'Will you cross swords with him, just for sport, no more?'

'By all means.'

'Then come.'

I girded my loins and followed her, to be met by the Cossacks' raucous laughter. The sight of a grown man clad in nothing but a cloth a newborn might wear had to be quite amusing. I smiled and nodded with my teeth so tight together I heard them grind.

The field was flat and flinty but my feet had calloused during the journey so my lack of boots was no great handicap. Zema handed me a sabre. It was about three inches longer than I was used to and imperfectly balanced. I gave it some trial swings, letting its hilt grow to know my hand. As we became acquainted, I let my Chi flow down my arm and into the steel. Soon, the blade and I were one, and I was ready.

The circle of Cossacks parted. I am tall but Igor topped me by at least six inches. He'd have weight and reach on me. His head was shaven. He had a prognathous jaw and a beetling brow. His face bore six or eight duelling scars. I did not, however, assume he was a mere brute.

My judgment was confirmed when he addressed me in German with a trace of a Heidelberg accent. 'Richard, you defeated the French army champion.'

I nodded.

'A Cossack is not like a Frenchman.'

I nodded again.

'Tell me,' he said, 'would you like your scar here . . .?' He touched his right cheek. 'Or here?' A massive finger traced a line down his left cheek.

'I already have a scar on my left cheek. If it isn't too much trouble, the right?'

He laughed. 'No trouble, Richard. Shall we?'

He came at me *en flèche*, which, had our duel been in earnest, would have proved fatal for him. I stepped aside, merely deflecting his blade. He recovered from his charge and turned to face me. I saluted him. He approached me more cautiously, striding until close and then stamping into a low lunge, aimed at my thigh. I defended with a bind that disarmed him. Watching me over his shoulder, he darted to his fallen weapon and snatched it up.

I saluted him. He came at me swinging a flurry of blows, intending to confuse me and beat me down by sheer brute force. I effected a *froissement* to take control and disarmed him with a little more force than was strictly necessary. His sabre flew over the heads of his companions.

Igor bellowed. He grasped his right wrist in his left. 'You have destroyed my arm, Richard! Wait!'

He marched off. I knelt on one knee before Zema and returned the sabre to her, as a knight from a more gracious time might have done. Coyly, she accepted.

Igor returned and tossed a leather bottle at me, left-handed. 'A prize,' he announced. 'For being the winner, and for not spoiling my so-pretty face, huh?'

I snatched my gift from the air and gave him a flourishing bow. 'You almost had me,' I lied. His rueful grin told me he didn't believe me.

My prize proved to be about a quart of vodka. Back in the carriage, I offered it to the new girl and was rewarded by an almost undetectable shake of her head. Neither Maria nor Fatima had any such qualms, although Fatima spluttered her first sip. What followed wasn't exactly a Bacchanalia, but approached one.

Strong drink seems to make my yard indefatigable. The girls took this as a challenge. I'd had both, in both bums and cunnies, when they, giggling, challenged each other to a

123

duel. Maria produced a gold half-hunter from her baggage. Each girl was to be allowed five minutes of fellating me, alternating. The one who drew my climax from me was to be the winner, with a prize of having the loser serve her on command for a full day.

Fatima went first. She didn't even try to take me to orgasm, that turn. Looking up at me with saucy eyes she laved my privates with a lascivious tongue in such a manner as to stiffen my cock even further but not give it satisfaction.

Maria, not to be outdone, dangled my testes, one at a time, in the hot soft cup of her mouth and tongued them but without so much as touching my shaft for her allotted time.

From time to time my girls threw sly glances towards the newcomer, who they had taken to calling 'The Maiden'. To them, this was a pejorative epithet. As the girl seemed not to understand a word they spoke, I doubt it bothered her.

Fatima swigged from the bottle and dropped to her knees. This time she seemed in earnest. Her lips closed tightly on me. She took hold of my thighs. Her head bobbed so hard that my balls slapped up under her chin and so fast that her face seemed to blur.

Maria, standing beside me, kissed me deep and long while I fondled her small but delectable breasts.

'Time,' I announced.

Fatima relinquished her oral treat and stood, with a strand of saliva stretched from her mouth to my cock. Maria knelt. I took Fatima into my arms to kiss her but paused.

'Your mouth's bleeding, Fatima,' I said.

She touched her lips and inspected the blood on her fingertip. 'I don't hurt,' she said.

I moistened my thumb and rubbed it across her mouth. When I inspected her lips, they were unmarked. I looked down. There was a dribble of blood on Maria's chin.

'Oh!' Fatima exclaimed. 'One of us must have bitten you.'

She proved right. There were two tooth-shaped indentations in the underside of my helmet that oozed droplets of blood. It was my fault. A fully-aroused cock feels pleasure but is numbed to pain. Fatima was a skilled and careful fellatrice but her background was Muslim so she'd never tasted liquor before, and the vodka was likely one-eighty proof. With her half-drunk but enthusiastic and me rendered insensitive, an accident was almost inevitable.

I told them, 'No matter,' and poured vodka on my wound to cleanse it. That was another mistake. My cock might have been numbed but it wasn't totally dead to feeling. Luckily, Maria's mouth was close at hand to both suck away the stinging liquor and kiss my wound better.

I found this so amusing that I sat down on the bench to enjoy my laughter without the strain of standing upright. Fatima joined me but her joints seemed to have softened. She slithered from bench to floor, tucked her hands under her face and began to snore softly.

Maria looked at me. 'Do I win?' she asked.

'By default,' I replied. This quip struck us both as so hilarious that we ended up beside Fatima, and then we slept.

My small wound was never a bother to me until the day, long after, when my Isabel noticed the tiny twin scars.

Twenty

The Cossacks allowed me freer rein than the Tatars had. Perhaps I'd earned a modicum of their respect. I was allowed to trot behind our conveyance for my daily exercise. I was watched when I sought the privacy of bushes, but from a discreet distance. The one freedom I was definitely denied was that of passing ahead of our carriage. Perhaps there was something or someone in the other vehicle that I wasn't supposed to see – or someone who wasn't supposed to see me.

One dawn, I wandered into an unusually fertile little grove for that part of the world. The sound of rhythmic grunts stopped me. Advancing with caution, I discovered Igor flat on his back with Zema riding him hard. He saw me and winked. I winked back and crept away.

As I answered nature's call, I formulated a theory that she was attracted to the strongest man in any company, but preferred one she could dominate. On the other hand, perhaps Igor had a bigger cock than I. I chose not to dwell on that thought. In any case, I had discovered why Zema had ceased her recreational visits.

Later that same morning, the landscape changed. It had been dry and inhospitable but now it became arid and palpably hostile. The horizon was blurred by sandstorms but I could just make out some crescent dunes that had to be two hundred or more feet high.

We'd entered the Taklaman desert. Little wonder we carried extra water. It's the driest land in all of Asia. It also explained the furs. Although at that time of year it'd be blazing hot most of the day, at night it'd drop well below freezing.

Our caravan slowed and crunched to a halt. I looked out of the back. Our trailing Cossack had shed his felt coat and Astrakhan hat. Now he was clad in a loose white shirt and burnoose. When I dropped off the tailgate and trotted as far forward as I was allowed, I saw woven straw mats being attached to the horses' harnesses, to shade their heads. Our journey was about to become difficult. I just hoped we weren't hit by a tornado. They're as common in the Taklaman desert as showers are during an Irish spring.

Back in our carriage, I warned the girls, 'It's going to get very hot. We'll have to do our best to keep cool.'

Fatima asked me, 'Does that mean we should take our clothes off?'

I grinned. It was a funny question. Her 'clothes' consisted of a single long narrow strip of silk, tied loosely around her hips and trailing almost to the floor.

'Yes,' I said. 'You'll just have to sacrifice your modesty, I'm afraid.'

Maria nodded towards The Maiden. 'How about her? Does she have to undress?'

'That'll be up to her,' I said.

Fatima pressed her strip of silk into the slit of her cunny. She liked the way that looked. 'Then I hope it gets *very* hot.'

'Be careful what you wish for. You might get it.'

Maria, in her chemise that was slit on both sides from hem to waist, took a ladle of water and poured it over her left breast. 'This is how I'll keep cool.'

I admired the way the water rendered the cotton transparent and clinging but had to warn her, 'Water will be precious for a while. Don't waste it.'

'Then *I* shan't,' Fatima declared. She went to Maria, to suck the damp from her flimsy garment. She just happened to purse her lips on the exact spot that Maria's nipple poked at the cloth.

I made my voice stern. 'We're only just entering the desert. It'll likely get warm today, but tomorrow it will be warmer. From now on, we do as little as possible between sunrise and sunset. At night, it'll be very cold. We'll huddle to our hearts' content.'

Maria frowned. 'Does that mean we sleep all day and futter all night, English?'

'Yes, I suppose it does.'

Fatima clapped her hands. 'How delightful! That's exactly how I've always wanted to live.'

The rest of the day was something of an anticlimax. It got about as warm as an English August and cooled off just enough that we were pleased to have covers to wrap our shoulders with. The next morning justified my warnings.

A loud dry hissing woke me. I looked out of the back. A crescent of sand that had to be five hundred feet high was marching diagonally across the way we'd come at about the pace of a leisurely walk.

'Cover all the openings!' I ordered. Our oilcloth roof cover extended down to within about eighteen inches of our wooden walls. I started snatching up cloths and wedging them into that space as best I could. When the girls joined my efforts, I made sure that the sacking blind at our rear was secure and then covered it in cotton sheets. It became dark. We'd blocked out a lot of the light but the sky I peeked at through a crack had turned into the underbelly of a shaggy grey-brown monster. Lightning crackled. Thunder shocked into us less than a second later. Fatima squealed. Maria bit her lip. The Maiden blinked.

There was a howl and we rocked and the howl became a banshee scream. To our left, where we'd missed openings, horizontal streams of fine grit invaded our carriage. I pulled my girls down to the floor and extended my hand to The Maiden. There was fear in her eyes but she still ignored my invitation.

Fatima screamed a question into my ear. I couldn't make the words out. We could do nothing but cuddle close and wait. I gave the girls reassuring grins even though I suspected that we might be in the path of a tornado that could spin us a mile into the air, if it so decided, or else dump a thousand tons of sand on to our heads.

And then it was quiet.

We waited, and waited. I wanted to be sure that the blessed stillness wasn't an illusion brought on by our having been deafened. Rhythmic grating prompted me to look outside. Cossacks with shovels were clearing our wheels. I jumped down to help but Igor waved me back.

'Our work, Richard,' he called. 'Where you are going, they don't want you to arrive with a broken back.'

'Then this is the second time you've protected me from a back-breaking task.'

He laughed. 'The first is my pleasure,' he assured me. 'If you have any similar chores you need help with, Igor is your man.'

'You'll be the first I'll call on,' I promised.

Back inside, the girls had fetched besom brooms I hadn't known we'd had, from their private area, no doubt. I put my feet up on a bench and watched them work. Maria's svelte muscles flexed and rippled. Fatima's bounty jiggled. I'd never considered housework as worthy of watching, before, but I'd never had housemaids who toiled naked before, either.

The Maiden, of course, did nothing except lift her feet when Maria swept under her.

Our carriage moved about fifty feet and then stopped, no doubt on firmer ground. I spread cotton sheets for the girls and me. We lay, naked, with kerchiefs on hand for moping our brows. They weren't needed. The air was so dry that as we perspired, the moisture was sucked away. The girls' health was a concern. I, being English, was more tolerant of extremes of temperature. They, being foreigners, might well be subject to heatstroke.

I tried once more to encourage The Maiden to strip and join us, and was once more ignored. With nothing else to do, I slept.

Supper arrived at dusk – our usual rice and curry, but served cold. By then, the heat was moderate. I left the carriage for a short walk The temperature dropped so quickly that my skin felt it happen – as if I was wading into a cold river. I climbed back inside. Maria and Fatima were making a 'bed' from layers of rich furs. Although the aisle

129

was but four and a half feet wide, they'd made space to either side, under the benches, so there was ample room for three very friendly bodies.

We huddled and cuddled, with a little friendly fondling. The day's heat had drained the lust out of us. At some point I woke to the sound of The Maiden's teeth chattering. I poked my head out and made what I hoped were enticing noises. Cold nipped my nose. I pulled back under the covers. Fatima patted my thigh, perhaps to reassure herself of my presence. My shaft twitched but with no urgency. I slept until my bladder woke me.

An hour after dawn it was hot again. Maria and I spread ourselves on sheets. Fatima decided to test whether a bench would be cooler to lie on. She chose a spot where, when she let her arm dangle down, her fingers brushed my cock. That was pleasant. Even when there's no rogering in the offing, a little friendly caress can keep the juices flowing and the spirit elevated. The backs of her fingers nudged my limp shaft away from her. A little tug flopped it back. I put my hands under my head and let her play. A few more wags had me semi-erect. I considered whether to turn over and take my cock out of her reach or to have her stroke me off. If the latter, I'd need a cloth to wipe myself with and getting one seemed like a lot of bother. On the other hand, I could have had her use her mouth on me, but would that be fair, considering the heat?

I was still considering when a sigh, a rustle and a soft thump distracted me. I turned my head to be confronted by the cleft of Maria's bottom. She was rising to go to The Maiden, who had fallen to the floor.

'She's fainted!' Maria cried.

Fatima, very firmly, said, 'We'll have to take her clothes off.'

The Maiden was lying in a heap. Even through her cape, I could see she was panting like a dog. I scooped her up and stretched her out on the bench. She was much lighter than I'd expected. 'Wet cloths,' I said.

Fatima was already working on the frogs that fastened the girl's cape. I unwrapped her head and face. Fatima gasped.

The Maiden was totally bald. Little wonder, having lost her crowning glory, that she kept her head covered. Her face was red but dry and her lips were cracked.

That aside, she wasn't beautiful or even pretty in the usual sense. Any woman would have envied her enormous lustrous eyes and sweeping lashes but her face was too feral to be conventionally attractive. She had prominent cheekbones, a narrow pointed chin and a thin-lipped mouth that was generous to a fault. Her face was a tad overlong between her eyes and her mouth.

All this was overshadowed by the nakedness of her skull, which was finely sculpted and almost Coptic in its elegant proportions.

'Here!' Maria told me, handing me a wet cloth blindly. Her eyes were big and focused on The Maiden's hairless head. 'Is – is it from some sickness?'

'I see no signs of that,' I reassured her. 'I think she's either bald from choice or that someone has imposed baldness on her.'

'How cruel,' Fatima said.

I squeezed a few drops of water between The Maiden's lips. Her poor swollen tongue touched them. I gave her more moisture. Fatima pulled the girl's cape from under her.

It was little wonder she'd swooned. She wore three layers of embroidered chambray tunics. The top sleeve came just past her elbows. The one under that reached her wrists. The last one just covered the tips of her fingers.

Maria and Fatima busied themselves with The Maiden's bows and buttons while I bathed her face and head. One by one, the garments were tugged away, and finally the matching trousers.

Her bald head had surprised us. Her body was no less striking. Her skin was the colour of what we used to call 'nursery tea' – half tea, half milk. She was long-waisted and sleek as an otter. The girl had virtually no breasts but her aureoles were so puffy they were hemispheres and her nipples were one-inch spikes, jutting from their centres.

But it was her tattoo that drew our attention. It was of a green snake. Her left nipple had been coloured jade, with the

131

narrow line continued to cross and circle her halo before vanishing under her left arm. From there, it circled her body. It crossed her right hip from behind and dangled its head. Her labia formed its parted jaws. The long prominent ridge of her clit's sheath had felt the artist's cruel needles. It had been tinted to serve as the serpent's carmine tongue.

Maria and Fatima stared. 'That must have hurt,' Fatima observed.

Maria licked her lips. 'Unbearably.'

Fatima nudged her. 'Are you going to get yours done, your clit?'

'Of course not! Well, I'd have to think about it. Perhaps. Who'd . . .'

I interrupted. 'Fetch me a ladle of water. Both of you, dampen cloths. Bathe her gently, mark you.' I remembered a medical lecture I'd attended in Calcutta. 'Concentrate on her wrists, her underarms and her groin – where the blood is closest to the skin.'

There was a little friendly spat over who got to sponge the girl's groin. I reminded them, 'She'll be with us for a long time. Now we've seen her naked, she shouldn't feel compelled to cover herself all the time.'

As if to make a liar of me, The Maiden stirred. As she realised she was bare, she wrapped her arms around herself in the manner of Aphrodite Rising, which has always struck me as more coy than modest.

'My clothes,' she croaked, in English.

'Your clothes were killing you.'

'You've – you've *seen* me.'

'We've had that pleasure.'

'Please don't make fun of me. Maria and Fatima are both lovely. I'm – not.'

I used my 'avuncular' voice. 'Maria is a slender nymph. Fatima is as voluptuous as a houri from Paradise. You, you are exotic. Better, I believe you to be unique. There are other nymphs and other houris but I can't imagine there's another girl, anywhere, who is beautiful in the special way in which you are beautiful.'

I noticed that the wet cloth Fatima was cooling the girl's

privates with was being pushed between the snake's jaws.
'Fatima!'

'You said to apply it where her blood is closest to the surface.'

I repeated, 'Fatima!'

Reluctantly, she recovered her cloth.

I let water from the ladle dribble between the girl's lips, restraining her from taking too much too quickly. 'Well, now that you're talking to us, tell us your name.'

'Asp.'

'Your tattoo, is it a religious symbol?'

'No – it was given me for the sake of the exhibition.'

'What's she saying?' Fatima asked.

I translated. Of Asp, I asked, 'Exhibition?'

'There was Jacko, the dog-boy, Ormossa, the fat lady, and we had a mermaid in a jar, and . . .'

'You were tattooed to be put on display?'

'And my hair was removed.'

'You were shaved?'

'A potion was rubbed on me. That's how The Child heard of me, through the witch who made the potion.'

As I translated Asp's words, Fatima and Maria became more and more sympathetic but, as was their nature, also pruriently curious. I was asked to ask Asp if she'd been forced to perform perverted acts for the public's amusement. I refused to translate those queries. Asp wasn't used to us seeing her body, yet, and she was still weak from her heatstroke.

'You must rest,' I told her. 'When the heat abates, we can talk more.'

She reached for her clothes.

'No. If you wish, Maria will find a sheet for you to cover yourself with.'

When the growing coolth woke me, Maria's arm was extended and her hand was beneath Asp's sheet, holding the girl's ankle. I was pleased. We four were forced to be companions. It was better if we were companionable ones. To be honest, I shared the girls' prurient interest. Asp was a true exotic. Curiosities and secrets have always fascinated me, especially living ones.

Asp sat up wrapped in her sheet while we supped. After, I entertained the three by reciting *The Tale of a Bull and an Ass*, from *A Thousand Nights and a Night*. It was slow telling, for I had to recite it in French, for Fatima and Maria, and repeat it in English, for Asp. It transpired that her only other tongue was Uzbekistani, which I did not and still do not, to my shame, speak.

In the tale, fifty fair concubines embrace a like number of lowly white slaves while their mistress takes her pleasure of a gigantic and ugly black man. My story progressed no further. Fatima and Maria insisted that I elaborate on each and every of the fifty-one couplings, providing details of 'where his tongue was' and 'what her fingers were doing'. Before my imagination was exhausted, the cold fell upon us. I arranged our order of lying with a mind to abating any fears Asp might have entertained. She took the extreme left, with Maria beside her, then Fatima and finally me.

No sooner were we all cosy under our pile of furs than Fatima snuggled her head back against my chest and wriggled her bare bottom in my lap. 'You told me that by night, we would futter,' she whispered.

'Asp . . .' I started.

'You promised.'

I surrendered to the lure of her squirming bum. 'Slowly and gently, so as not to disturb the others?'

She agreed, 'Slowly and gently. We have all night.'

I wrapped her curvaceous little body in my arms. My fingers found her nipples. I nuzzled and licked into the crook of her neck, a caress I'd discovered she particularly enjoyed. Fatima was less patient. Her fingers curled around my shaft. Her back hollowed, hitching her bottom higher. She steered my cock up between her thighs to the lush warm wetness of her cunny and rubbed its dome between her nether lips and against the hard little button at their juncture. Her gasps were subdued and breathless but within a few moments she gave a delicate shudder and sighed.

'You said "slowly and gently",' I reminded her.

'That was to give me the patience for "slowly and gently". Now, tease me, please?'

'And what manner of teasing does my little harlot have a taste for tonight?'

'This manner.' Once more she guided my shaft, this time presenting it to the pucker between her bum's cheeks. Her grip was just behind my cock's head. She rubbed my dome against her opening with increasing pressure until the tight portal to her rear passage relaxed and the head of my cock, just the head, entered her.

Holding me there, she twisted her neck to get her tongue to my mouth. As we kissed, I pressed, gently, but her grip tightened, holding me still.

With a last lascivious lick of my lips, she murmured, 'Just that deep, no deeper. That's the best part – when the thickest part of you passes through the narrowest part of me.'

I rocked. My cock's head plopped through the stricture, and plopped out of it. Each stroke was held in check by her clutching fist. I felt Fatima shiver in my arms in time with my entrances and with my exits. The urge to plunge deep came to me but I resisted. From her swallowed moans and tiny quivers, I was sure that she too was fighting her desire to be totally impaled. My lust stretched and sang, like the string of a violin that was being played even as it was tightened. It became more extreme when I felt that although Fatima's left hand was restraining me, her right was busy at her cunny.

There was no sudden rush to climax. One second I was slowly sodomising her and enjoying the incredible tension. The next, I spent. My jism had simply flowed out of me.

I was still trying to decide whether I was disappointed or not when Fatima whispered, 'Now go deep,' and released me.

My erection hadn't softened. I was easily able to slide gradually into her very depths. There I probed, still with slow easy strokes, while Fatima fingered herself through three climaxes and I enjoyed my second.

As I fell asleep I heard a giggle and the subtle susurrus of fur on fur. The giggle was Maria's. Had she and Asp, while I was concentrating on Fatima, also been practising their own 'slowly and gently'?

Twenty-one

The following night, after supper, Fatima asked me for another story. I said, 'We should take turns amusing each other. Maria, what can you do to entertain us?'

She jumped to her feet and went to her baggage, from which she retrieved her neat little boots. With those on, she wrapped one square of fringed satin around her shoulders and knotted another about her hips. '*Cante Jondo*,' she announced.

I translated into French and English for the others, 'A slow song.'

Maria's right foot stamped. Her arms uncurled upwards like a pair of swans extending their necks. Her fingers snapped. Her voice – wasn't very good. I enjoyed her performance more when she sang a *Duende*, which was faster and involved a lot more stamping. It didn't take her long to stamp her shawl right off. By the time she was done, her improvised skirt had also fallen and she was performing in nothing but her boots.

How strange it is, that a man can live in a woman's company and enjoy the sight of her womanly charms several times a day but when she is dressed and then slowly removes her clothing, his eyes are delighted afresh and with more intensity.

Her performance done and applauded, Maria threw herself on to a pile of furs. Fatima leaped atop her, tickling her mercilessly. I watched sheet-wrapped Asp. She made a move as if to join in the romp but drew back before completing it.

'They'd welcome you,' I told her. She shook her head.

Maria and Fatima ground their pubes together and kissed deeply but the cold fell and put an end to their sport.

For our night's snuggling, I allotted Maria the far left position, with Asp between her and Fatima. There were giggles and once a deep chuckle. I could feel furtive movements but couldn't tell who was caressing who, or who was being caressed. Not wishing to interfere with Asp's adjustment to our situation, I turned my back and slept.

The following evening Fatima volunteered to provide our distraction. As soon as the oppressive heat lifted she vanished behind the curtain to prepare. When she emerged, her face was painted, her eyes kohled and her lips vivid. There were jingling bangles of coins at her wrists and ankles and chiming cymbals on her fingers. She'd resumed the costume I'd first seen her in, a minute bolero jacket and a slit gauzy skirt, worn so low that had her mound not been pumiced bare, she'd have displayed at least a hint of pubic curls.

Like Maria, her dance commenced with her arms rising above her head and poised there like the frame of a lyre. The pose lifted and parted her jacket in such a way as to expose the inner and under curves of her full young breasts while intermittently concealing her nipples.

Fatima's cymbals tinkled. Her hips moved, describing a small tight circle, then a wider one, and wider, until the diameter of her sway exceeded that of her hips. Her torso undulated. Her tummy hollowed and swelled. It was as if Fatima's flesh had become liquid. She rippled and flowed.

Her left breast quivered deliciously. Her right joined in. She spread her feet and thrust her pubes sharply forward. The muscles in her tapered thighs flexed and trembled. It seemed as if not a single one of her muscles was still. Her body as a whole swayed to a slow rhythm while her softer parts obeyed another, more urgent, beat.

Very slowly, she leaned backwards. Her knees bent towards us, for balance. She tilted and tilted until her long hair brushed her bottom and her breasts were pointing straight upwards. Holding that position, she shivered all over for three long beats before she convulsed, tossing herself into the air, and landed with her legs spread wide, one foot pointing to her left and the other to her right.

We applauded until our hands stung.

'The way you bent your back, Fatima!' Maria exclaimed. 'Your spine must be made of India rubber.'

I noticed a gleam in Asp's eyes and remarked, '*Snakes* have flexible backbones.'

Maria and Fatima turned to Asp. Maria asked, 'Is that why you are named for a snake, apart from your lovely tattoo?'

Asp looked at the floor.

'Show us!' Fatima demanded. 'Show us your back-bend.'

'One entertainment for each night,' I said. 'Tomorrow will be Asp's turn.'

She shook her head.

'I told you a story. Maria sung for us. Fatima danced. It's only fair, tomorrow, you perform.'

When we settled for the night, I gave them freedom to choose their positions. I ended up with Maria's back to me, and Asp between her and Fatima. I didn't detect much movement. Perhaps my little minxes were saving themselves.

At breakfast, both Maria and Fatima made dumb-shows, teasing Asp about her coming performance. She took it in good part and seemed, to me, to be hugging a delicious secret to herself. When she settled for the day's heat, she still draped herself with a sheet, but carelessly, with one slender leg and svelte hip left partly uncovered. I wondered if it was truly a lack of care, or was it perhaps by artifice? Women have that instinct – to tease and flirt – even though many of them would deny it.

It was with some anticipation that I looked forward to the evening's period of moderate temperature. Once our supper was done, Maria and Fatima started coaxing Asp. Asp, coy as a novitiate nun making her confession to a handsome young priest, at first declined.

Maria sat hip to hip with Asp and put an arm around her. 'We're really looking forward to watching you, sweet serpent.'

138

I translated, as I did everything they said. It was a chore but we weren't pressed for time.

'I have no costume,' Asp hedged.

Fatima asked, 'Did you always perform in a costume?'

'No.'

'Sometimes you performed bare, as bare as we three are now?'

'Yes.'

'You've seen me and Fatima and English, all of us, stark naked. Please don't be shy, little Asp,' Maria wheedled, caressing Asp's neck.

'It is more than "bare",' Asp murmured.

'More than bare?' Fatima asked. 'You shed your skin, like a true snake?'

Asp tittered. 'Of course not.'

'Then?'

'When I perform, I . . . It's difficult to explain.'

I said, 'Then show us.'

Fatima sat to Asp's other side and insinuated a crafty hand under her sheet. 'I *do* like your snake, Asp. Can you make it wriggle?'

Asp grinned. 'Perhaps.'

Maria added, 'If your snake dances prettily for us, I'd be happy to feed it.'

'The Englishman is better equipped for that,' Fatima observed dryly. Her hand, under Asp's sheet, bunched over the girl's diminutive left breast. 'If someone pinches your snake's tail, does she poke her tongue out?'

'You're teasing me!'

'And they'll continue to tease you until you satisfy their curiosity,' I warned.

'Very well!' Asp took a deep breath and stood up. Her sheet fell to her feet. Now that the shock of her being so 'different' had passed, I saw her for what she was, a sleek and lovely young woman, erotically sensuous, but in a way I'd never seen before. Her lack of bosom or shapely hips didn't detract from her appearance. Rather, instead of being a woman whose sexuality was more evident in her feminine parts, she was sexual in her entire body.

139

Fatima reached out and ran a finger down Asp's spine. Asp shivered but stepped further away, isolating herself the way a solo performer has to.

'*This* is what I do,' she announced, not without pride. '*This* is what I am.'

She took a stance, feet planted firmly and spread wide apart. I silently cursed the dim illumination. Her tattooed cunny was shaded. I was curious to see if those jaws would move.

Asp began to bend. Her knees went forward, as Fatima's had. Her head tilted back, as Fatima's had. The muscles in her thighs tensed, just like Fatima's. Asp had no tresses to brush across her bottom but her head dropped low enough that had she had hair, it would have.

And she kept bending. The bones in her hips formed sharp angles. The cage of her ribs spread like fans and beneath them, her abdomen hollowed. Her knees bent further. Her body arched more dramatically. Asp's naked skull appeared, between the spread of her thighs – and still she bent.

Asp grinned at us, with the back of her neck pressed up against her cunny, her head shielding her mound.

'What say you, English?' Fatima joked. 'Everything you want, *bouche*, *con* and *cul*, all lined up ready for you.'

I ought to have reprimanded her for her crudeness, but I confess, she was only giving voice to my own thoughts.

Maria stamped her bare feet and cried, '*Bis!*' I think she was asking Asp for some further contortion rather than a repeat of the one we were witnessing.

Asp writhed to the upright position and gave us a quizzical look, as if to question whether we were ready for an even more extreme display of her talent.

I called, 'Please continue, Asp. You have us enchanted with your skill.'

'Yes, go on,' Fatima encouraged.

Asp nodded acquiescence. Her left leg bent at the knee, sliding her foot up her right calf. When it passed her right knee, she pointed it straight out to her left but kept lifting it. Her weight shifted a little, for balance, but otherwise her body was still. Up and up rose her foot, to the height of her shoulders, her chin, the top of her head and beyond, until it pointed straight up at the ceiling. Her two legs, split wide apart, formed a single vertical line, with her left knee tucked behind her shoulder.

As one, Fatima and Maria crouched and went closer. I too was inquisitive about the inevitable distortion of Asp's cunny but I deemed it more gentlemanly not to give way to my base curiosity. Fatima tested Asp's slit with a finger but I couldn't see clearly because her body blocked my view. I did see a reaction on Asp's face, though.

Fatima turned to me. 'She'd be impossible for you to futter, in this position. Her passage is bent, inside. You'd get no deeper than *this* much.' She held her finger and thumb three inches apart.

Maria chuckled. 'I wager English would enjoy the attempt, no?'

I grinned but made no remark.

Asp, with a remarkable show of acrobatic ability, hopped to sit on a bench. There she perched with her left leg still vertical until she folded it neatly behind her own neck.

We three spectators 'oohed' and 'aahed'.

She took hold of an iron ring. Once more she lifted a leg, her right one, and elevated it until it too crossed behind her neck.

Maria crouched and stared. '*¡Ay por dios, que almeta!*' As if compelled, she sank her face between Asp's thighs.

I was concerned that Asp, who we had been slowly coaxing from her timid shell, would recoil. How little I know of the fair sex! Her eyes closed. Her mouth softened. Somehow, she hitched herself closer to the edge of the bench. Even above the creaking of our trundling wheels, I could hear the wet sounds of Maria's feasting.

Fatima said, 'And now we are as one, no, English? *Trois maîtresses et un maître*! What games we will play!' She sat beside Asp and pulled her own legs up, to cuddle her dimpled knees. '*Joue avec moi, Anglais! Lèche moi le clito!*'

I don't believe I've ever refused a request to lick her clit from a lady. I certainly didn't then. Side by side, Maria and

I knelt and lapped. It wasn't a contest, but she brought Asp to climax three times while I only drew two from Fatima. I put it down to Asp having been celibate for some time.

The cold put an end to that little game. We retired to our pile of furs but I was in no mood to delay my own pleasure until the morrow. I was in something of a dilemma. Asp's special talents had whetted my appetite for something erotically gymnastic. It would be a shame to futter her, the first time, in any mundane configuration. Four friendly bodies in one bed is fine for the more commonplace manoeuvres, but I had something more exotic in mind. And yet, my staff was nagging me.

I was still debating how to resolve my problem when Maria and Fatima, the last two into bed, entered head first, as it were, squirming down between Asp and me, so that we were paired head to tail. Maria's mouth served me well. I trust she was equally pleased by mine and that Fatima and Asp reached their mutual satisfactions.

Eventually, I slept, and dreamed of Asp's contorted body and how it might best please me to use it.

Twenty-two

It seemed it hadn't been just *my* imagination that Asp had inspired. Even at breakfast, a time we'd tacitly agreed was for teasing and flirtation but not for more intimate caresses, Fatima and Maria couldn't keep their hands off Asp. If she'd had any lingering doubts about her own attractiveness, they were certainly being dispelled.

They made a game of it. Maria, pretending that Asp's seated legs were in her path, casually lifted one by its ankle until it was higher than her head. While it was so elevated, Fatima 'accidentally' dropped her spoon and in retrieving it just happened to press a kiss on the distorted lips of Asp's cunny. Asp herself was not innocent. Bending to straighten our bed of furs, she held her legs stiff and spread. Before rising, she showed her skills off by tucking her head between her thighs and lifting it to kiss her own bottom.

I was not excluded. As was my practice, once I'd finished my rice, I made my way to the rear of our carriage, ready to trot behind it for a while. On that day, as I passed between the girls, who were sitting two to one side and one to the other, Fatima just happened to lean forward, so that my wagging column dragged across her face. For perhaps half a second, my dome was caught between her lips. Tempted though I was to pause and thrust, I went on by. To everything there is a time, and dusk was the time I'd appointed for coupling.

While I was trotting behind our carriage, we passed a family of wild Bactrian camels, a pair and a suckling calf, not three hundred yards away. Melku let off a shot at them. They ignored him, as he deserved.

When we settled for our afternoon siesta, one of the girls was inspired to dampen a sheet for all three of them to lie beneath. I'm sure it provided coolth. As there was no room for a fourth, I settled on a bench, uncovered. Perhaps I should have reprimanded them for wasting water but I was loath to sound a discordant note. I was determined that my cock and Asp's cunny were soon to become intimately acquainted. A friendly atmosphere would be more conducive to that end than a hostile one.

The sun was red behind the horizon's haze as we supped.

When we were done eating, saucy Fatima giggled and asked me, 'It is your turn to be the entertainer again, English. Do you have another tale for us, or ...?' She looked from Asp to me and back again.

Maria was more direct. 'English is going to futter our little Asp in positions we, Fatima, can only dream of. We will watch. That will be a fine entertainment, to my mind.'

'*Bien sur*,' Fatima agreed. 'I am content to watch and learn, if you and I, my little *salope* ...' She turned to me, 'How you say in English, English, "diddle each other", while we watch?'

I smiled. 'I thought you didn't speak English, Fatima?'

'A little, perhaps. Just a few naughty words.'

Asp stood up and looked at each of us in turn. Out of discretion, I'd not been translating this exchange for her. She'd caught Fatima's brief foray into English, though.

'What are they talking about?' she asked me. 'Who will "diddle" who?'

'They suggest you and me, each other, and have asked if they might watch us,' I replied, utilising an alternative meaning of 'diddle'.

'Oh.' She turned her head aside, blushing. Her hand shielded her mound protectively.

I rose and took her satiny head between my palms. My hands tilted her face to look up into my eyes and held her there for a long moment. It has been my experience that if you allow a woman to gaze into your eyes for any period of time, she will see in them whatever she wants to see.

She blinked. I told her, 'I've wanted you from the moment we uncovered your lovely face and exciting body, but while I am master here, no one does anything that they don't want to do. If you can tell me, honestly, that you feel lust for me, then let us enjoy Eros' blessings. If you do not care for me in that way, tell me now, and I will never approach you again.' My words were coloured by our proximity. We were both naked and standing close enough that my erection bridged the gap, to nudge her just above her navel.

She glanced down between us with a little smile. 'Your sincerity is self-evident, Richard. Although mine is less obvious, I tell you in all candour, yes, I lust after you.'

'You have no reservations?'

'None.'

Fatima started slow-clapping. Maria joined in and added, 'English, that's enough persuasion. In the name of all that's holy, *do* her!'

Women! There's no romance in them.

Asp went up on tiptoes with her lips pursed for a kiss. I'm somewhat tall. There was still a foot between our mouths. I put my hands around her hips and lifted her. Asp's lips were thin and her mouth was wide but her tongue welcomed my invasion. She was sweet as the dew from honeysuckle. Her hands gripped my head as if she feared I'd pull away from her mouth. We nibbled at each other's lips and suckled on each other's tongues. Our kisses were as pure but passionate as a virgin bride and groom's on their wedding night, except that Asp's elevation enabled her to trap my shaft between her thighs and rub them on it.

I raised her higher, trailing kisses and licks down her throat and across the slight swell of her breast until my mouth found the tail of her serpent, the resilient spike that was her left nipple. Again I suckled, drawing as much of her flesh into my mouth as I could.

Asp moaned. She swayed between my hands. Her legs were parting, wider and wider, until her toes pointed horizontally in opposite directions. 'Fuck me,' she begged.

Fatima and Maria cheered, so I presumed that 'fuck' was

145

one English word that both were familiar with. They began to chant, 'Fuck, fuck, fuck.'

Not to be contrary, but because it is my habit to deny a lady until she seems rabid with lust, I heaved Asp yet higher. At that elevation, she was able to grasp a cross-bar in our roof, which made holding her there less onerous. Also at that height, the sweetness of her cunny was inches from my mouth. The spread of her thighs had teased its lips apart. I extended my tongue and insinuated it between her swollen petals.

At the first contact, Asp, the dear, tucked her tail in, lifting her cunny's lips up to greet my mouth. I kissed her, little sucking kisses then deeper, probing ones, exploring the inside of her cunny as I had her mouth. She was sweet and lemony on my tongue but when I inhaled, I was reminded of a surfeit of orange blossom.

Asp's legs, still rigidly held out to each side, began to tremble. 'Please, Richard, do not make me spend just yet. I might swoon, and I have yet to enjoy that special delight I have anticipated since the day we met – of being stabbed to the quick by your . . .' Her words became a delighted squeal as the tip of my tongue gave the head of her clit two quick flicks. 'Not yet, not yet,' she gasped. 'Hold me tight.'

Her back began to curve away from me. Once more, her spine bent, folding her in half, backwards. I braced back and gripped her hips harder. Her legs bent at her knees so that although her thighs were still wide-spread, the soles of her feet gripped my head.

She arched. Upside-down and as bent as a Persian bow, Asp set her hands on my thighs and closed her lips over the head of my cock.

Fatima and Maria applauded.

'Fuck her face!' Maria urged me.

I resisted my cock's demands that I comply. Asp knew what she wanted from each of us. I am no mean cocks-man, but we were exploring exotic realms that she was more familiar with than I. It seemed wise to let her lead.

She tongued and sucked and bobbed, familiarising herself with my dimensions, contours and flavours, but taking care

146

not to stimulate me too far. Her hips tensed under my hands. Asp, effortlessly it seemed, writhed back up. Looking down on me, she asked, 'Lower my cunny to your cock, Richard, and I will fuck you as no other woman has ever fucked you, or likely ever will.'

I let her down slowly. She hooked her right foot behind my neck and let her left dangle. By the time my dome nudged into her wet heat, her limbs were extended in opposite directions once more, distorting her soft portal. I probed into her vestibule without meeting much resistance but beyond that, the passage I sought was warped to one side. I paused.

'Force your way!' she demanded.

And so I did. My hands pressed down on her as my hips surged up. Where her sheath was bent, I straightened it.

Asp gasped, 'Yes!' She looked into my eyes fiercely. 'Now let me go and hold fast!'

I have felt power surge through my veins. I felt it when I entered the Holy of Holies, in Mecca, disguised as a Muslim. Strength roared through me when I, on my own, repelled two score ferocious African warriors and put them to rout at the point of my sabre.

Those feelings were as nothing compared to the puissance I felt when I did nothing but brace myself, standing still as a statue, and was fucked by Asp. The Hindus have the right of it. A man is never closer to divinity than when he is consumed by acts of lust.

Her right foot held my neck. Her left braced upon my thigh. That part of her that was most *woman* gripped my shaft.

Asp's lips brushed my left nipple. She bent back, and down until her body and mine were at right-angles and then beyond, until she kissed my foot's instep. The pressure her sheath inflicted on my down-bent shaft was an exquisite torment. Those subtle muscles convulsed and she was rising, up and up, until her mouth touched my chest again, paused for a heartbeat, and once more descended.

She was incredibly strong in her legs and abdomen. Without use of her hands or arms, she went from head-down to head-up two dozen or more times. Asp's skin became slick with sweat, both hers and mine.

Maria and Fatima, although unable to take their eyes from Asp's incredible exhibition, made free of each other's bodies with their fingers. Their frantic mutual frigging seemed likely to take them to their climaxes long before Asp was done with her acrobatic contortions.

Asp, at the peak of one swing, gave me a saucy grin, as if to tell me that she had even more in her repertoire. I set my feet more firmly and further apart. On her next descent, Asp twisted so that she faced me all the way. Each time she went down, she half-turned at her waist. With her gyrations adding to the delightful torture she was inflicting on my cock, my need became urgent.

I put my hand, palm out, against my lower belly. My thumb's ball found the hard button of her clitoris. Now, not only was my shaft churning her sheath, but every movement she made frigged her clit.

Asp's face tensed. Her writhing became frenzied. Her abdomen rippled, within as well as without. Her eyes rolled upwards.

She screeched, convulsed and went limp. I was ready. My hands took her hips and flipped her entire body upwards so that she smacked against my chest. Holding her thus, I jerked up into her thrice, and let loose the floodgates of my desire.

When I'd done, I set her down on a pile of furs, tenderly, feeling a confusion of benevolent emotions towards her. Surely there is no greater compliment a woman can pay a man than by swooning from the climax he gives her.

Twenty-three

It was an hour or a little more past dawn as best I could judge. It had warmed enough that I was comfortable sitting naked on our tailgate, eating a pomegranate and spitting the pips in the general direction of Zema, who was riding rear-guard. Sometime in the night we'd entered a valley that sloped upwards between two steep hills. The air was redolent with crushed thyme. Had I not been thirsty as dust and somewhat odorous myself, and had I not been engaged in a perilous mission, life would have been quite pleasant.

Our water ewers had run dry three days before. We'd been served scant rations for drinking and none for washing. There'd been no rice. Asp's Gladstone had yielded several coils of kielbasa but we'd made no great inroads into the spicy sausage because of our thirst. Our only other provision remaining was a small pot of pale grey Beluga caviar from Maria's hamper. It was safe until we had ample water to wash it down with, and ideally some points of toast to spread it on.

It'd been two and a half days since our last romp.

Someone hailed Zema from further up our caravan. She spurred past us. I spat a seed after her.

A great drop of water splashed on to my left instep. I looked up. There were clouds gathering and they weren't the unnatural grey-brown sand-laden monsters I'd seen in the desert. Another fat drop fell on my knee. There was a flash that lit up the horizon but the rumbling thunder took several seconds to reach me. I called out, 'Girls! Come quickly. I think it's going to rain.'

Asp shed her skimpy improvised toga and plumped down beside me. Maria and Fatima soon joined us but by the time the Egyptian's shapely rump hit the cedar planks, the rain had become a torrent that blew a full yard into our carriage. It was like sitting under a glorious waterfall. We leaned back on stiff arms, gazing skyward, mouths agape. Raindrop pellets pounded our bodies and filled our dry mouths. We all three gulped until our bellies were replete. We sat up to sluice off our skins with our cupped hands. I could feel the pores of my skin unclog and rinse clean.

The caravan came to a halt, no doubt so that precious water could be collected.

Asp, companionably, reached over to help me cleanse my privates. Inspired by my instant erection, no doubt, she leaned across to suck fresh rainwater from my cock's dome. I lay back, content to let her.

Maria, also inspired, fell back beside me and raised one foot to rest against our carriage's wall, leaving her other leg dangling towards the ground. With her thighs so spread, the rain beat an insistent tattoo on her cunny. Her bottom shifted, adjusting her angle. She parted herself with her fingers. 'Girls,' she exclaimed, 'try this. The rain on my clit – divine!'

I translated for Asp, to my own loss. She deserted my cock and lay back, legs Veed towards the sky. All three of my lovely companions wriggled and squealed but despite the force of the flood, none seemed able to reach a climax. I thought about their cunnies, now rain-rinsed to pristine cleanliness and doubtless aching with need. What man would be so churlish as to ignore the plight of such as these?

I dropped off the tailgate into ankle-deep flowing water. How to choose which soft pink fountain to drink from? Before I could resolve my pleasant dilemma, my *embarras de richesses*, Asp joined me, making my decision unnecessary. She stooped to lap at Maria's cunny, leaving me Fatima's labyrinthine treasure. The downpour had become so intense that I was deafened and blinded to everything except the treat that was in the shelter of my bowed head. Rivulets of rainwater ran down the creases between her belly and her thighs, and a third coursed between the lips of her glistening quim. I sucked from where those three streamlets met, then followed the central trickle upwards. Dom Pérignon never produced so fine a vintage as I imbibed that day.

Asp reached across to stroke my shaft. My fingers found her cunny and then her clit. My girls had become naiads, free and innocent in their depravity. I fancied myself as Neptune, Lord of the Waters, Master of all water nymphs.

Maria and Fatima achieved their climaxes almost simultaneously. Asp and I vaulted back on board, she to squat over Maria's face, I to mount Fatima. Rain pounding on my behind spurred me to ride her hard and fast. After all, she had already spent so I had no obligation to wait on her. As is often the case, however, my efforts reawakened her lust, so that when I was done, she was eager for more. With a grin, she reached for Asp, who had just toppled off Maria.

And so our relay continued. One of us might fall, exhausted, but not before passing Eros' baton on to the next. It was not until darkness, and the temperature fell, that the final lap of our race was done. We dried off, covered ourselves in furs, and slept the sleep of the thoroughly sated.

I woke to shouts and curses. Our carriage swayed forward and fell back with a jolt. I rose, donned my scrap of cotton, and dropped from the rear. The blessed rain had stopped, leaving us with its curse. The ground beneath us had softened. Our wheels were a foot deep in oozing mud. The cries I'd heard were the sounds of Cossacks straining to push us free. Their tempers were foul. A Cossack will ride for a month and then fight for a week, all without food or rest, without a word of complaint. Give him common labour to perform and within the hour he's ready to murder his own mother.

Melku was plodding back and forth, brandishing a long club, achieving nothing. Igor, muddied from toe to head, strained at one of our wheels. We had six. Five of them were manned, leaving the middle one on the left vacant. A whip cracked over the heads of our horses. I squatted behind the neglected wheel, got my fingers around a half-buried spoke and braced myself to heave.

Zema called the cadence. On her three, we all strained. My back was creaking when I felt movement.

'Keep it up,' Zema called. 'It's moving. Don't lose it!'

I hunkered lower. My muscles tensed. We began to roll. A movement caught my eye. Melku's club hit my left shoulder and the back of my skull at once. His second blow was swinging towards my face. I snatched for his wrist and threw myself sideways, under the carriage, out of the path of the following five-foot-tall iron-clad wheel. Melku, dragged after me, was less fortunate than I. His shins crunched under the rim. I looked upwards to watch the floor I'd slept and futtered on pass above me. When the carriage halted, I was sprawled behind it, in its ruts. Melku was close by me, screaming.

Zema strode back to us, shoulders bunched, fists tight.

'He tried to kill Richard,' Igor shouted. 'He did it to himself. Richard did nothing.'

That wasn't exactly true. It'd been no accident that I'd tugged Melku after me. It seemed diplomatic not to correct the Cossack.

Zema went to Melku and looked down on him. He sobbed, 'Help me!'

She nodded and marched off, to return with the Cossack's blunderbuss. When he saw her intent, Melku shielded his face with his arms and begged for mercy, but to no avail. His face and half his head were obliterated.

I had no qualms about his dying or the way of it but it would have been better had it been at my hands, rather than at Zema's. She might be plagued by regrets. I wouldn't.

Twenty-four

The slope was gradual, but always climbing. At times, our path was constricted by a vertical cliff on one side and a drop of hundreds of feet, equally vertical, on the other. From time to time we passed solitary turf-roofed log huts and sometimes herds of scrawny goats. When we saw people, mostly they fled but there were those who welcomed us and fetched provisions. Half of our remaining Tatars left us. They were replaced by half a dozen squat toughs that might have been Gurkhas, though they ignored me when I addressed them in my broken Nepalese.

We ascended high enough that we could peer down on to clouds that looked like watered milk, pooled in the bowls of valleys. It snowed, but lightly. Great forests of fir trees shrank below us until they mimicked fields of grass.

We crested the saddle that connected two mountains and came to a village that was built of square-cut stone blocks. Zema warned us to cover ourselves. I donned my loincloth and one of my crude togas. Fatima did similarly, but her garment was ankle-length. Maria had her severe black dress and Asp her trousers and tunics. Almost as soon as we were modestly clad, we were politely swarmed by a dozen round-faced children. We had no sweetmeats to offer them so I broke a piece of kielbasa off a coil for each one and was rewarded by beams and chatter I didn't understand.

The horses were led away to stables. Three busy little fat women invaded our carriage with straw brooms, leather buckets and chamois cloths. They smiled and fussed and shooed us outside.

Zema greeted us with, 'There is to be a feast in your honour, English.' To my girls, she said, 'There are men here. You will not touch them. If one of them touches you, I will disembowel him very slowly, using a blunt knife, understood?'

A fire was lit in the middle of a great circle of flat stones. We were given leather flasks of fermented *Goji* juice. One *tahr*, a short-legged wild mountain goat, was turning over the fire. Another animal was being butchered ready for the spit. Strings of onions and stacks of *papadams* were set close enough to the flames to scorch, that being the style of the local *haute cuisine*. Youths, both male and female, stamped a circular dance to the discordant music of horns and drums.

I found myself quite affected. It had been a long time since I'd attended a celebratory social event. Although I hadn't realised it, I'd missed mingling with a throng of revellers. The core of it is much the same at a Mayfair ball, a Makah potlatch or a Himalayan *Tiji* Festival. It's all booze and dancing, with the young men sizing up the girls, trying to guess which ones will spread their legs if plied with a sufficiency of strong drink.

Remembering the night of our vodka party, I kept a close eye on Fatima. She, like the other two, was a model of decorum. All three of my girls were scrutinised by youths but with more worship in their eyes than lust.

When we were replete and the fire had died down enough for foolhardy boys to leap through the flames, we returned to our carriage. Zema had posted a pair of Cossack guards that I felt we had no need of. After a little persuasion, they left to seek whatever *Goji* juice wine was left over.

Come dawn, the horses, clean and groomed, were harnessed and hitched. I saw Zema emerge from the largest hut, leading two diminutive cloaked figures. A pair of Cossacks helped the newcomers into our carriage. Zema made the introductions. Jia Li was Chinese, pig-tailed, lovely and elegant in black satin *pyjamas* and wooden-soled shoes. Asuka was Japanese, in full geisha regalia of chrysanthemum-embroidered white silk kimono, obi, white face with painted-on features, with elaborately coiffed black hair pinned by thick wooden needles. Both girls spoke fluent

French. No doubt that was a qualification for whatever duties they all were intended for. Asp didn't speak the language but perhaps her special physical abilities outweighed that disadvantage. I was offended that French had been chosen over English for our *lingua Franca*, but that is the rule rather than an exception. One day, I am sure, English will take French's place as the tongue of diplomacy and international scholarship, as French has usurped Latin's.

I bowed to our new guests and pulled Zema aside. 'Are these young ladies of the same erotic nature as Maria, Fatima and Asp?' I asked, *sotto voce*.

'Each in her own way, yes.'

'I am to cope with *five* such greedy creatures?'

Zema laughed, deep and guttural. 'Surely five pretty little harlots won't intimidate you, English. You have a reputation that, until now, you have lived up to.'

'But *five*?'

'I've been assured that you are man enough for five, and many more. There are great expectations of you. Don't fail the one who has set such store by your masculine prowess, English. She doesn't take disappointment well.'

That was interesting. So, whoever was behind the plot, 'The Child' was female, was she?

It was flattering that I was considered 'man enough' to satisfy five young ladies who were all possessed of incontinent animal passions. What worried me was Zema's 'and many more'. We were not yet arrived at our destination. Our carriage was large enough to accommodate a dozen or so nubile young beauties, at a pinch. What if we collected more *en route*? My question was, had I the stamina and the will to service such an exotic and demanding stable of frisky fillies?

My analogy led me to wonder what 'use' I was supposed to be put to? Was I to be put to stud, like some prize stallion? In prospect, many men would delight in such duties. In practice, they might find them onerous in the extreme. I spent the rest of the morning trotting behind our carriage. Its interior had lost some of its appeal.

My concerns proved premature. We were brought a great wooden platter of hot spiced strips of goat wrapped in warm *chapattis*. I helped a Cossack slide it into the back of our carriage and followed it, salivating in anticipation.

'Where are the new girls?' I asked Maria.

She nodded towards the draped curtain. 'They've been in there all day.'

'Doing what?'

'Primping, as far as I can tell – or rather, the Chinese is primping the Japanese.'

I shrugged. 'She looked fully primped when she arrived, to me.' Towards the curtain wall, I called, 'Our lunch has arrived. It'll be best eaten while warm.'

Jia Li put her head around the curtain. 'Please to wait for Miss Asuka.'

I nodded. Five or six minutes later, Asuka appeared, looking no different than when she'd arrived as far as I could tell. I reached for a *chapatti*.

'Please no,' Jia Li asked.

I drew back my hand, puzzled. Asuka bobbed a curtsey. Jia Li produced a pile of linen doilies. Both knelt beside the platter. Asuka took a *chapatti* between finger and thumb and set it diagonally across the doily that Jia Li held ready. They bowed their heads to each other. Asuka writhed elegantly to her feet, shuffled to me, knelt, and offered me my lunch on her extended palms. I thanked her. She returned to the platter to kneel once more. I lifted my *chapatti* to my lips, only to be stopped by Jia Li's frown and shaking head. Perhaps our manners *had* become lax during our confinement. I set my food down and was rewarded by Jia Li's smile and nod.

The process was repeated for Maria, Fatima, Asp, then Asuka served Jia Li and finally the geisha served herself. Our newcomers smiled, nodded and lifted their portions to their mouths, extending their little fingers like old maids at a tea party. Looking at me, they waited. I took a bite from mine. By then it was cold, but not as cold as the rest of the food would be before I was allowed to get to it.

I forced a smile. 'Asuka, yours is a pretty name. Would you tell us what it means?'

She tittered and looked down. If she blushed, the white on her face hid it. 'It means "Tomorrow's Fragrance",' she whispered.

'But you are as fragrant as cherry blossom today,' I remarked. 'How much sweeter could you be?' The simple compliment seemed to throw her into utter confusion.

I turned to Jia Li. 'And what does your lovely name mean?'

Red-faced, she mumbled, 'Very beautiful.'

'Then your name was well-chosen.' I got up and reached for the platter.

Jia Li wagged a finger at me. She and Asuka selected a fresh doily, taking a deuced long time about it, it seemed to me. A *chapatti* was chosen and bowed over before it was passed to me.

Fatima brushed her fingers together and eyed the platter. I asked, 'Another, Fatima?'

She nodded. Before Jia Li or Asuka could move, I snatched a *chapatti* up and handed it to Fatima, without benefit of either doily or ceremony. She sank her teeth into it, grinning straight at Asuka. Our two new girls stood, bowed, and shuffled backwards to retreat behind their curtain, leaving their *chapattis* half-eaten.

'I think you hurt their feelings, Richard,' Asp said, wryly.

'That's unfortunate,' I said.

Fatima giggled around her mouthful and almost choked.

I took another *chapatti* and considered the situation. As a geisha, Asuka had no doubt been trained to turn every meal where a man was present into an elaborate and flirtatious ceremony. From what I knew, a geisha might entertain at one meal a day, no more. If serving tea was a three-hour ritual, that might be a fine entertainment to a Japanese man but in our current circumstances, sharing three meals a day, and every one with a masculine presence – me – such rigmarole would become intolerable.

Jia Li wasn't a geisha but it seemed that, perhaps during the course of their journey, she'd fallen under Asuka's domination. If we could break through Asuka's rigid reserve, Jia Li would follow.

157

I had to assume that both were erotophiles. Under Asuka's stiff formality and Jia Li's timidity, they had to be seething with lust. If we could introduce the newcomers to some seemingly innocent fun and games, less innocent ones were bound to follow.

I was the problem. If a man was present, Asuka couldn't help but 'perform'. If I 'removed' myself . . .?

Thinking of 'games' reminded me of being forced to amuse visiting girl cousins, when I was a boy and had not yet attained puberty. After my voice broke, entertaining girls stopped being a chore.

But before my beard had sprouted, we'd played parlour games, Cribbage, I Spy, Hunt the Thimble and one game that amused me both pre- and post-adolescence – Truth, Dare and Consequences. I revised the rules in my head and adapted them to our circumstances – and to the end I intended. My version was simpler than the original – just Dare and Consequence.

I signalled my girls to huddle with me and explained my idea in whispered French, then in English, for Asp's sake. They suppressed giggles. I took myself to the rear, lowered the sacking blind and lay down. The girls heaped furs on me until I was invisible. I called, 'You won't see me again until after dark,' and covered myself again, leaving a peep-hole.

My girls resumed their seats. Fatima raised her voice. 'Asuka, Jia Li! There are no men in sight now. We three are going to play a game, just girls having girl-fun. Will you join us?'

Two pretty heads showed. 'Where did he go? When will he return?' Asuka asked.

'English doesn't tell us where he goes, but we know he has made a close friend of Zema,' Maria replied, winking. 'As for how long, he said we wouldn't see him again until after dark.'

'Ah so!' Asuka sighed. Something about her changed. It was nothing obvious, but it seemed that she became more of a real woman. 'I like games. Which one is it to be?' she asked.

'Come sit with us,' Fatima invited.

Maria said, 'The game is called Dare or Consequence. I will be the first Mistress. I will dare each of you, in turn, to perform some deed. If you refuse, you will pay a consequence after the game is done.'

'Consequence?' Asuka asked.

'Six spanks on the bottom,' Maria told her.

Jia Li giggled. 'Please, who will do the spanking?'

'We vote for that.'

'And when you have dared all four of us?' Asuka wanted to know.

'Then another will be Mistress, and so on, till all five of us have had a turn. That way, none of us will be too demanding of any other, for the tables will be turned soon enough.'

Asuka thought. 'So when each has had a turn as Mistress, those who owe consequences take their spankings?' She narrowed her eyes at Jia Li. 'There are those who might refuse dares, in happy anticipation of those smacks.'

'True,' Maria said, 'but accepting the dares can be fun as well, as you will see when we get into the spirit of the game.'

Fatima reached to put a hand on Asuka's kimono-covered knee. 'Try it, Asuka. You'll like it, and we are eager to play with you.'

Asuka nodded. 'Very well. Who will you dare first, Maria?'

'In order as we are seated. Fatima, I dare you to bare a breast for us all to see.'

Fatima put three fingers to her lips in mock shock. After a moment's contemplation, she shrugged her left shoulder out of her toga and pulled the fabric down until her breast lolled free. Jia Li giggled. Asuka pulled a fan from her obi, spread it and covered her mouth, but eyed Fatima's breast over it with some interest.

Maria touched Asp, who spoke no French, to get her attention. She made sucking noises with her lips and then pointed at Fatima's breast. Asp nodded happily and bent to her allotted task. Her cheeks hollowed. She bared her teeth to show that they were sinking into the breast's softness. When she released the delicate flesh, it was wet with saliva and indented with tooth marks.

159

Fatima was flushed with pleasure.

'Asuka, I dare you to – to let down your hair.'

Without hesitation, the geisha began plucking the needles from her top-knot. 'Are you making it easy for me, because I am new?'

'Perhaps.'

'Please don't.'

'You have already performed my dare, Asuka, but I'm sure that Fatima will remember your brave words when she is Mistress.'

Asuka's hair tumbled to her waist.

Maria continued, 'Jia Li, I am sure that you have lovely legs. I dare you to bare them for us.'

The Chinese threw a glance at Asuka, as if asking permission, stood up, reached up under her *pyjamas'* top, and let her trousers fall. Unfortunately, I couldn't see her lower limbs but my girls paid them pretty compliments. Her top reached her hips and just below, so none of her intimate parts were exposed, so far.

Maria said, 'And now Fatima will be Mistress.'

Fatima said, 'As your new Mistress, I reverse the order. Maria, you shall be first. I dare you to unsheathe your special little toy and perform for us as a sword-swallower might.'

Maria had come a long way since the days when the nature of her toy shamed her. She drew the dildo from its sheath with a flourish. Jia Li gasped. Asuka's eyes widened. Maria dangled the jade phallus from her fingers, bent her head back, opened wide, and lowered. Inch by inch, the obscene object descended. When the hilt kissed her lips and it was obvious that several inches had to be down her throat, she released her hold and worked the muscles in her neck, making the dildo bob up and down.

Asuka had the grace to applaud. 'One day, I'd like to try that feat,' she said.

'By all means. Jia Li, you are next,' Fatima said. 'I dare you to come to me, kneel before me, and allow me to do whatever I wish to you for the length of time Maria takes to count to one hundred.'

160

Jia Li licked her lips. 'Anything you wish?'

'Yes.'

'I – I . . .' The lovely little Chinese made up her mind and went to kneel before Fatima, trembling, but not entirely from fear.

Fatima pulled her close, knotted a fist in her hair and bent her head back. Jia Li didn't need to be told to part her lips. Her tongue was already extended when Fatima's mouth descended.

Maria, belatedly, started counting. She didn't hurry to catch up.

As Fatima savoured Jia Li's mouth, her free hand fumbled for the loops that fastened her jacket and released them, one by one. By the time Maria reached thirty, the jacket was hanging from Jia Li's shoulders and Fatima was cupping a delicate breast, with her thumb and finger working on the dark brown cone of its nipple.

Jia Li hadn't objected. Nor had her friend, Asuka. Fatima's hand smoothed down the girl's sleek torso, caressed the delicate curve of her belly and dipped to cup and compress her pubic mound.

'This game,' Asuka asked, 'by the time we come to the last one, what will be the manner of the dares, I wonder?'

'You may withdraw from the game if you lack the courage to continue,' Maria interrupted her counting to offer.

Asuka chuckled behind her fan. 'And leave my curiosity unsatisfied? No, I will see it through to the very end.'

Maria finished, 'Ninety-nine, one hundred.'

As Jia Li returned, shakily, to her seat, Fatima looked at Asuka. 'I have long wondered what a geisha wears beneath her kimono, Asuka. I dare you to show us.'

The Japanese stood, shrugged, snapped her fan closed and laid it aside. Her obi unravelled. With a cocked head and a smile, Asuka slipped her kimono from her shoulders. It might not have been so for all geishas, but this one wore – not exactly nothing beneath her kimono. Her naked body was criss-crossed by tight scarlet silk cords. They ran above and below her pert little breasts, tilting and extruding them. They encircled her hips and descended in a V that framed

161

her puffy little mound while neither concealing it nor impeding free access to it.

Maria gasped, 'Jesus!'

Asp drawled a dry, 'Delicious!'

Fatima asked, 'Do you go about like that all the time?'

'No,' Asuka answered. 'This is special for your Richard. Had he shown more patience and better manners, *I* am the reward he'd have been given.'

'Your loss,' Fatima told her.

'He is a good lover?'

'The best I've ever had,' Maria said.

'Me too,' Fatima agreed.

I was flattered, but my girls knew I was listening. It'd be nice to think that they'd still have praised me had I not been present, but I am not a vain man, as any who know me will affirm.

Fatima took a breath and turned to Asp. 'I dare you . . .' She paused, remembering that Asp had no French. She pointed to Asp's mouth and extended her own wagging tongue.

Asp nodded. 'I get it. You want me to lick someone's cunny. I'm game. Whose?'

Fatima understood the nod, at least. She jabbed her forefinger in the direction of Asp's own private parts.

'Myself? You want me to show off? The Japanese girl thought she had some surprises for us, didn't she. *I'll* show her.' She dropped her trousers and pulled her tunic off. Without visible effort, Asp lifted her knees high enough that she could plant the soles of her feet flat on the bench, one to each side of her slender bottom. Hugging her own shins, she bent herself, lowering her face all the way down to her own privates. Asp's distorted position had parted her cunny's lips. She lapped into herself with rapid little licks, like a thirsty kitten at a bowl of milk.

Asuka let out a torrent of Japanese, reverting to her own language in her excitement. Recovering, she added, 'When *I* am Mistress, my dare will put you to the test, Snake Girl!'

'She speaks no French,' Fatima reminded her, 'but don't be so sure you'll test her. Our Asp is capable of incredible feats.' She made a two-handed flourish towards Asp,

162

indicating that she was passing the role of Mistress on. I wondered how she'd manage to challenge the others when she knew no French. Her mime-shows proved sufficient.

She pointed at Fatima. Fatima nodded, ready to be dared. Asp stood, lifted one foot up on to the bench, and made a show of folding the fingers of her right hand into a 'dagger' and mimed stabbing into her own cunny. Fatima nodded once more and followed directions, one hand holding her improvised garment up to her waist, the other thrusting into herself, deeply enough that all her knuckles disappeared, vigorously enough that her one bared breast bounced.

The air became redolent with the fragrant aroma of female arousal, and it wasn't all from Fatima's copious lubrication. Jia Li was squirming on her bare bottom. Asuka's thighs were clamped together and moving subtly.

Asp monitored Fatima's depraved performance until the Egyptian's face flushed and she bit her lower lip. Then, a hand on Fatima's arm halted her before she reached completion.

Clever Asp! She knew that I wanted all five women to be well aroused before I made my dramatic entrance. Perhaps her cunning came from her knowledge of the English tongue. I firmly believe that the languages we speak influence our abilities. The Arabic ones enhance skills in mathematics and science. Many Far Eastern ones, Hindi and Urdu in particular, increase spirituality. English encourages craftiness. Ask any Frenchman.

It became Maria's turn. Before Asp had the chance to mime her dare, the Spaniard slipped out of her chemise and set it aside. The little minx had become quite the exhibitionist. In exaggerated dumb-show, Asp indicated that Maria was to use her dildo once again, but in the more customary manner. Obediently, Maria stood with one foot on the bench and turned so that all the women could see what she was doing. Unfortunately, that hid the details from me, but I'd seen this performance several times before. I *was* able to enjoy a rear view, the dildo in Maria's fist, thrusting upwards, and the way her tight little bottom clenched and relaxed in response to each stroke. I could hear Maria's

163

pants coming faster and was just beginning to wonder whether Asp intended to let Maria reach her climax, when my lithesome one reached out to still Maria's arm.

Asp turned to Jia Li, who wore that strange look only a deeply submissive woman can wear – apprehension blended with anticipation. The Chinese put a hand to her own cunny and raised an eyebrow. Asp shook her head. She pointed at Jia Li, turned her back to her, bent to lay her hands on the bench and spread her stiff legs wide. Jia Li understood. By the time Asp turned back, she was already in the same vulnerable position she'd seen demonstrated, and swaying her rump as if challenging Asp to do her worst.

Asp started by giving each of Jia Li's cheeks a hard open-handed smack. The girl reacted by hollowing her back and elevating her bottom, inviting, almost begging for more of the same. Depraved Jia Li! Clever Asp!

She made the girl wait but it wasn't a spanking that she had in mind. Asp sucked on a finger and then put her hands on Jia Li's cheeks, to spread them. She spat into the crease, with what accuracy I couldn't tell, and worked her finger into the Chinese girl's bottom, quite quickly and without hesitation. No doubt Asp had discerned that Jia Li's back passage wasn't unused to such invasions.

After no more than six thrusts, Asp put two fingers together for half a dozen more, then three at once for a final six. By then Jia Li was writhing and pushing back. My cock reacted. Eager sodomites, when female and pretty, have that effect on me. Most young women fornicate whenever given the chance. A goodly proportion of the gender will readily perform fellatio. Only the most concupiscent enjoy being buggered. It's a woman's lust that engenders mine most surely. I'd sooner bed a plain woman who seethes with desire than a lovely one who lacks passion.

None of my present companions lacked it, of course. Nor were any of them plain.

My loincloth was making me uncomfortable, so I shed it.

Asp allowed that Jia Li had fulfilled her dare – too soon for the Chinese's liking. Jia Li turned to sit, but Asp restrained her, signalling that she should maintain the pose.

It was Asuka's turn. Asp pointed to her. She nodded. Asp's tongue extended, wriggling in serpentine fashion. Asuka signed that she understood, she was to lick someone, somewhere. Asp pointed to Jia Li's bottom-hole, which I imagined was quite dilated by then, the result of Asp's vigorous triple-finger-fucking.

Asuka looked blank. Asp repeated her mime. Asuka shook her head. Asp had struck on the one thing that Asuka would not do – perform analingus on a girl who she had dominated into submission. I'm sure it was a matter of pride of rank, not of distaste for the act itself.

Asp gave Maria a questioning look.

Maria asked Asuka, 'You accept the consequences of refusal?'

'Six slaps? I accept, provided Jia Li isn't appointed to carry out the punishment.'

'Oh no,' Maria agreed. 'Jia Li would be much too lenient. We're sure to elect someone much stronger and much more vicious.' She turned to the little Chinese. 'I'm sure Asp will allow you to sit, now that your bum isn't required. Now it's your turn to be Mistress.'

Jia Li covered her face with her hands and shook her head. Maria waited patiently. Eventually, the Chinese whispered, 'I couldn't.'

Maria looked around at the others. 'If you can't, you can't, Jia Li. English has a rule that no one shall be forced to perform any act they find repugnant.' She grinned. 'Even so, I think that you should accept consequences in lieu of doing your duty. I propose – six slaps.' She paused. 'From each of us.'

Jia Li looked from between her fingers and nodded. 'I accept.'

'Including from English.'

Jia Li dropped her hands, beamed and nodded enthusiastically.

Asuka declared, 'And now *I* am Mistress, am I not?'

'You are. We await your dares.'

'Then I dare Fatima to perform the act I have just refused.'

Fatima smiled. 'Lick that lovely little Chinese bum-hole? By all means!' She reached Jia Li before the girl had time to assume the required pose. Fatima's hands spun her to face the bench and pressed her head down. Her knee between the girl's thighs parted them.

There was something about Jia Li that inspired others to manhandle and command her. It's a quality only the deeply submissive possess.

Fatima spread the Chinese's cheeks and squirmed her face into the narrow valley. With a great smacking of lips, she slobbered and snuffled, letting everyone hear what it would have been difficult to watch. Jia Li's moans of pleasure reached a higher pitch when Fatima reached between her thighs to frig her clit.

Leaving the pair of girls to their devices, Asuka strode to Asp. She touched one of the girl's ankles, then the right hand bench, and the other ankle, followed by the opposite bench.

Asp nodded. She dropped to all fours between the aisles and lowered her elbows until her forearms were flat on the floor. Her shoulders went forward, beyond her hands. Her balance shifted until she was able to raise her legs and rock like a seesaw on the fulcrum of her elbows. Asp's long slender legs lifted and straightened out in opposite directions until her feet rested on the two benches.

She swayed, once, twice, three times, and heaved herself upwards. When her torso formed a perfect upright right-angle with her legs, she flung her arms out for balance, and stayed there, poised in that precarious pose.

All, except Fatima and Jia Li applauded. Even *I* whispered, 'Well done!'

It transpired that there was more to Asuka's dare than that Asp perform a lissom miracle. 'May I borrow your toy?' she asked Maria.

Maria handed the dildo over. Asuka stretched out on her back with her face directly beneath Asp's cunny. She reached up and wriggled the jade phallus into Asp with a deft twisting motion. Unbid, Asp gave a little bounce, encouraging further penetration.

166

Without pausing in her play, Asuka told Maria, 'Your dare is to serve me, with your mouth and tongue. Do you understand?' She spread her thighs and lifted her bottom by way of explanation.

'Is *this* what you want?' Maria asked. She knelt between Asuka's legs and set her lips and tongue to play between the scarlet cords that bracketed her cunny.

With all five distracted, none looking in my direction, I decided that it was time to make my appearance. I set the pile of furs that covered me aside, stood up, and flexed my legs to make our carriage rock.

Maria looked up from her happy task. 'Oh, *there* you are, English. We'll be right with you, if you don't mind waiting a few moments.'

Twenty-five

I had to wait for more than a few moments. Asuka made Asp spend and was taken to climax in turn, by Maria. Jia Li whimpered and collapsed. With three of the five limp from orgasms and the other two 'in heat' I anticipated a merry romp. My cock was at 'present arms'. I had taken but a single stride in the direction of the carnal treats when a noise behind me halted my progress. I held a fur before my naked loins and raised the sacking at the rear. Time had flown. It was our supper being delivered. A Cossack handed up a great steaming tureen of *Kinema* curry and a fistful of horn spoons but no dishes. We ate from the communal tureen. I am not fond of fermented soybeans but there were *chapattis* left over from lunch, so I didn't go hungry.

Asuka made no attempt to impose artificial formality on our meal. It seemed that her reserve had melted. She and Jia Li exchanged meaningful glances and eyed my shaft, which they were seeing for the first time.

Fatima told me, 'While you were gone, Maria organised a game that calls for forfeits. There are spankings due to two of us. Asuka is owed six smacks and Jia Li thirty. We agreed to select the one to deliver the smacks by vote. I propose that you be that one, English.'

'Indeed! Perhaps we could have a show of hands from you ladies. Who would like me to administer the slaps?'

Four hands shot up, Asuka's being the only one that didn't.

'I accept the honour. I shall also pick the time. We are all replete from our supper. I have found it unwise to bend a girl across my knee when her tummy is full. For now, we shall find less strenuous amusement.' I looked from girl to girl, as if pondering, but I had already decided. 'Asuka,' I said. 'You have been trained in many methods of pleasing men, have you not? Tell us about them.'

'I sing like a nightingale. I dance like a dervish or a flamingo, as required. I play the Sheng moderately well. I tell wonderful stories, and no one performs the tea ceremony as elegantly as I,' she boasted.

'Those are all wonderful accomplishments,' I allowed, 'but what of the carnal arts?'

'Oh! You wish me to describe my pillow skills?'

Fatima interrupted with, 'We all do. Perhaps we can learn something new from you.'

'I – I cannot face Richard and talk of such things.'

'But you'll face him when you do them,' Maria put in.

'That's different.'

'You may turn your back,' I offered.

And so she did. She had a pretty back, shaped somewhat like a cello, with dimples to each side of the base of her spine and a delightfully curved bottom. The cords that bound her transformed mere beauty into a much more appealing erotic obscenity.

'I am practised in eleven positions in which the man need not move to reach his happiness. I know my paces from walk to gallop and when each is appropriate. I am skilled in massage, both with my hands and my feet.'

'Massaging their cocks, do you mean?' Maria asked.

'I am an adept at that, but I meant for relaxation and redistribution of Chi.'

'Is that like "jism"?'

I interrupted before we got too far off topic. 'Chi is a spiritual thing, Maria. Let Asuka continue, please.'

'I can satisfy a man using my yoni, my mouth, my hands or my feet.'

'Not your bottom?' Fatima asked.

'If that is what he requires, but there is little skill involved in that.'

'I disagree. Perhaps we could debate that later, if English agrees.'

'Asuka is listing her erotic skills,' I reminded them.

Maria's expression might have been a sneer on a less attractive woman. 'We all of us here know a dozen ways to get a man's jism out of him. I can't imagine that Asuka knows one that we don't.'

Almost whispering, Asuka said, 'I have studied Lady Takara's Pillow Book. It is possible that there are skills described in that ancient collection of erotic wisdom that you of the West do not know.'

For a moment, my antiquarian interests superseded my erotic ones. 'Lady Takara's Pillow Book?' I asked. 'I don't know that one. Do you have a copy?'

'Alas, no, but if you wish, Richard, I could demonstrate the *Chipatama* Kiss.'

'*Chipatama* means?'

'The head of the male organ.'

That roused my interest. I find that I always respond when a woman offers oral service. I said, 'I'm sure that we would all enjoy a demonstration.'

Fatima coughed in a very pointed way but she said nothing.

I asked, 'Do you need to make special preparations?'

'All I need are these . . .' She fluttered her long delicate fingers. 'And this.' She touched the tip of her tongue.

Maria asked, 'What about your lips and mouth? What about your throat?'

Before Asuka could say anything that might cause friction, I said, 'Let Asuka show us her way, Maria. Later, you can show her yours.'

Maria shrugged.

'Shall we start?' I asked Asuka.

Bowing, with her hands pressed together as if praying, Asuka shuffled towards me. 'Please,' she said, 'to sit on the edge of the bench? I need to reach your parts.'

I shifted to sit on my tailbone, with my cock wagging and my balls dangling.

'Thank you. And feet further apart?'

I spread. Maria brought a cushion. I hitched up for long enough that she could get it under me.

'Thank you,' Asuka said. 'Comfort is important.' Her hands disappeared from my view, below me. At first I wasn't sure that she was touching me but when I concentrated, I could just discern a delicate prickling immediately behind my scrotum.

She smiled and held one hand up for me to inspect. Her almond nails had been filed to sharp points. Asuka laid both palms on my thighs, high up and just inside, where there is a line between where hair grows and where it doesn't. She dragged her nails down my legs, softly and gently, but leaving four thin white lines down each thigh. Holding my knees, she leaned forward and to my left. The tip of her tongue, just the very tip, traced one line, then the next, and so on, before moving to my right thigh. The sensations were no more intense than if a spider had walked down my leg, but they raised the hairs on the back of my neck.

Fatima asked, 'Does that feel good, English?'

I nodded. Speaking might have broken the spell.

Asuka cupped my balls, one in each palm. Those needle nails tickled behind them. The ball of one finger palpitated the spot where I had been scratched, between my balls and my anus. The pressure was slight and yet I felt it penetrate deeply. My sphincter tightened and my shaft lifted. Asuka's pink little tongue protruded from between her lips. I thought she was going to lick me, but it just moved from side to side. I was reminded of snakes I'd seen, tasting the air.

She had my balls separated. I think it was the ball of her thumb that she used to stroke the skin of my scrotum, between my globes. I became aware of my pulse, beating hard in the vein that runs up the underside of my shaft.

She caressed me with one finger and one thumb, the finger pressing rhythmically on my perineum, the thumb stroking between my balls. Her other hand took a grip on my shaft, at last. She held it between her thumb and two fingertips, as she might a flute. I held my breath, forgetting that she'd said she wouldn't use her lips or mouth.

With the utmost delicacy, Asuka turned my cock this way and that, inspecting its swollen purple head. A small bead of clear fluid appeared from its eye. She ignored that. Her tongue flickered. Her head bent closer. Asuka's eyes narrowed, as if she were taking aim. When the tip of her tongue touched me, it was on the rim – the collar of my cock's head. Moving like a hummingbird's wing, delicate as a butterfly's kiss, that teasing tongue-tip travelled the circumference of my dome, pausing to pay extra attention to its knot.

And that finger and that thumb were still pumping beneath me, but with a little more pressure. My cock felt like a balloon, blown up until ready to burst. Were I not a patient man, blessed with preternatural self-control, I'd have been demanding that Asuka suck me. I had that feeling that all men know – that I just *had* to do something to tip myself over that glorious edge.

I resisted it.

Her tongue traced a spiral, getting closer and closer to the weeping eye of my straining cock. Her lips were drawn back in a sort of erotic snarl, as if she were denying them what they craved, my cock.

Another finger began to work beneath me. Without penetrating, it pressed and relaxed on the sensitive rim of my sphincter. I was in an agony of anticipation. *Something* had to happen to relieve my tension.

Asuka's eyes, black as sin, gazed up into mine. Her tongue reached the eye of my cock at last. It dabbed, once. My balls tightened. It dabbed again. I felt the base of my cock thicken. It dabbed for the third time, withdrew an inch, and hollowed into a spoon of flesh.

I wondered why she had stopped just when I'd been so close.

And then I climaxed.

And I discovered why she'd shaped her tongue into a spoon.

Twenty-six

A wolf howled in the distance.

I was grateful for the straw on the ground, for I was barefoot and it was freezing. We'd been hustled from our carriage, only allowed to wear the clothes we owned, and I owned none. Zema had distributed furs. My cloak was sable and quite warm, except it only came down to my knees.

The village consisted of a score of sagging sod huts, a very large stable and a larger warehouse. The latter two had been built from whole pine trees, trimmed, shaped and chinked with moss. Despite the meanness of the hovels, there were signs of prosperity. I'd heard but not seen cattle and chickens and had been fed a bowl of scrambled eggs.

Scabs of dirty snow crusted the lean flanks of the hills. We'd passed a good-sized flock of real sheep, not sheep and goat crosses, which are more common in those parts. A trio of pigeons that hadn't the sense to go in out of the cold circled overhead.

Bustling little people – I couldn't tell male from female even when I saw their creased and greasy faces – were unloading our caravan and loading vehicles much like English dog-carts; a seat for two and a low-walled flat back, with only two wheels. No English dog-cart was ever drawn by a mule, though. These were – all thirty-six of them, by my count. Another peculiarity was that all the mules wore felt over their hooves and the wheels' rims were also padded.

The first cart was filled. It, with Honey perched atop its load, was driven away towards a narrow ravine. I couldn't see far into the slot, for it curved not a hundred feet in. Maria's hamper and trunk were added to the pile of goods in the back of another cart. Zema came to us and led Maria away, to be loaded into it.

One by one, each of my companions was put aboard a cart. Soon, I was left alone. Finally, Zema came for me. 'I am sorry, English,' she said. 'Here I release you from your parole. Where you are going, you may not enter unbound.'

Some three-score armed men were watching us, so I extended my wrists and suffered her to wrap them with a leather thong. To my chagrin, Zema helped me into the back of the last cart. I was somewhat mollified when she, who had never allowed my cock near her mouth during the course of our many couplings, lifted my fur cape aside, bent, and gave me a quick hard suck. Perhaps she was repaying me for something or another, although the touch of her lips had more symbolic value than erotic, it being unanticipated and brief. Perhaps it was simply her way of saying good-bye.

Bora, Honey's Turkish paramour, shared the driving seat with Igor, who took the reins. We rolled with unnatural silence into the ravine. It twisted and turned and became even narrower. My erstwhile home would never have fitted through.

After no more than half a mile, the way sloped downwards slightly and opened on to a geographical feature the like of which I had only seen twice before, and both of those on coasts. Nature had carved a rugged tower of stone with perpendicular sides. It was perhaps a hundred yards across and stood alone, rearing a full fifty feet above us and dropping into a chasm below us for at least four hundred feet. It was crowned by a squat, massive fortress, featureless apart from arrow slits.

The ravine path debouched on to a stone bridge that looked natural in origin but had been enhanced by tools. That bridge was no more than a foot wider than our cart's axle.

We rolled on to the hazardous span. Ahead, a roughly triangular cave, twenty-five feet to a side, waited like a monster's mouth to devour us. There was something bulky lurking just inside the cave's shadow but I couldn't make out what.

Igor reined his mule to a halt in the middle of the bridge. As I glanced at him to ascertain why, he gave Bora a straight-armed shove, toppling him, screaming, into the abyss. Bora's usefulness, whatever it had been, had obviously come to an end. It was fortunate that Honey had already disappeared into the cave, though perhaps she wouldn't have cared. Sympathy for others wasn't one of her virtues.

I was reminded that although I had become mildly fond of both Igor and Zema, they weren't pleasant people.

When we entered the cave I found that the bulky object I'd glimpsed was a gigantic bronze cannon. Its bore looked to be between twenty and twenty-four inches. There was a canvas strapped over its muzzle so I couldn't be sure. Iron bands bound its barrel but I wouldn't have wanted to be near the monster, not before, beside or behind it, if it were ever fired. A bronze cannon with that massive a bore is as likely to explode as discharge.

The body of the weapon had been formed into the likeness of a fantastical snarling wolf, with the barrel projecting from its great maw. All the paraphernalia a cannon requires was lined up in soldierly fashion: two racks, one of sponges on long poles, the other of equally long ramrods and wadhooks, five half-barrels of water, a pile of pre-shaped wads, a titanic brass monkey, complete with its pyramid of iron balls, two neat coils of slow-match, and an orderly stack of packaged charges.

I was taking a mental inventory in case I somehow escaped with the intelligence. If I managed to report to either the Indian Army or John Company, I might have to brief the commander of an armed force, prior to his launching an attack on this place. I prayed that day would never come. The cannon might prove useless after its first discharge but a schoolboy with a catapult could have defended that narrow bridge. If I had been ordered to take this fortress, I'd have opted for a siege, though my supply lines would have been perilously long.

We arrived at an opening to a downward-sloping tunnel,

off to my left, just in time to see Honey, hysterical, carried into it over a Cossack's shoulder.

It was very dim where we were. Twenty or so feet farther in, I discovered why. To my right there was a secondary cave that served as a magazine for the storage and measuring of black powder. There had to be five hundred or more hogshead casks piled against one wall. Before them were copper scales, scoops and funnels and cotton bags, where the powder was weighed and packaged in single charges. Inevitably, there had been spillage. No wonder the mules' feet and the wheels' rims had been padded; no wonder there were no lamps or candles. The shelf of felt slippers, waiting for the powder monkeys to wear, was a wise precaution.

I'd never heard of several thousand pounds of black powder going up all at once. If ever such an explosion were to occur, I'd sooner be far from it than near.

Not far beyond, the tunnel widened and there was light, some from lamps and some from ingenious slots cut through the rock. There, mules were being fed hay from mangers or drinking at troughs. Carts were being unloaded.

Igor jumped down from his seat and came to lift me from the back. I thanked him, though it galled me to need his assistance.

He grinned, nodded, and hit me with a club.

Twenty-seven

I awoke chained to a heavy wooden St Andrew's Cross in the strangest room I've ever been unfortunate enough to occupy. My manacles looked to be made of gold, thick bracelets with 'D' rings attached. My ankles were similarly clasped. The oddest restraint, though, was the band about my waist, which had a strap of the same metal, vertical down my belly, with an offset crossbar of gold at its end. That thin flat strip was at the exact level that my shaft sprouted from my pubic hair. I found that menacing.

The half of the room that I was in was built of unadorned stone blocks. It was lit by both a dozen spluttering flambeaux and the menacing glow of a brazier that had some sort of instruments heating in its coals. I didn't feel like speculating on the uses the instruments might be put to.

The room was divided by a wall-to-wall, floor-to-ceiling wrought iron screen. The other side could have been an illustration from my translation of *The Arabian Nights*, become real, though I didn't think that at the time. My modest opus was both written and published much later.

The luxurious area was made bright by a fine pair of crystal chandeliers such as might have graced a Duke's ballroom. All the walls were concealed behind tapestries, draperies, hanging rugs and swathes of sumptuous fabrics. The floor was covered by carpets and rugs and rugs-on-rugs, and animal hides and furs in a zoological garden of patterns and colours. Not a stone showed.

There was a long table, or perhaps a workbench, for it was equipped with alembics, retorts, bottles, flasks and phials – all of the paraphernalia an alchemist might need. My father, an ardent amateur chemist and renowned creator of bad smells, would have died of envy.

Behind the bench was a set of shelves, bearing earthenware pots. The containers were labelled in a variety of languages and scripts so that I couldn't read them all. Among those names that I could translate were: Aconite, Essence of Nettle, Willow Bark, Ambergris, Ginger, Fugu Liver, Poppy Juice and Black Cohosh. It was a strange selection, ranging from medicinal through intoxicating to deadly.

The room was occupied. I puzzled over the figure who was grinding something in a mortar with her back to me. By size, she was a young girl. By shape, as far as I could see, she was a woman. Her garb argued that she was a child – a white smock over a bell-skirted dress in pink with blue polka dots. It was mid-calf length, with a froth of matching pink crinolines showing beneath. Her hair was the glistening white of fresh-fallen snow and cascaded to the ankles of her naked feet. That made her age – I knew not what.

She turned to look at me. I was no wiser. She had the face of a painted porcelain doll, but with startling yellow eyes.

'You're awake, Richard,' she said in French with some sort of Slavic accent.

I nodded and gave her a polite, 'Madam.'

'I should introduce myself. I am she who they call "The Child". I am not so named for my years, but for my parentage.'

'Indeed?'

'Yes, indeed. My Father was Chingis Khan. He begat me upon a giant she-wolf.'

I was moved to make some amusing comment, such as, 'You carry your six hundred odd years very well,' or, 'And which side of your family do you favour?' I held my tongue. It isn't wise to make fun of a megalomaniac who has you in her power.

The Child continued, 'Do you know why you have been brought here?'

I hazarded, 'So that I might have the pleasure of making your acquaintance?'

178

Her brilliant eyes clouded. 'Are you a frivolous man, Richard?' She snapped her fingers. What I'd taken for a great mound of furs rose up and divided. Two massive wolves, the male as tall as The Child's shoulder, the bitch just a few inches less, padded to her and nuzzled her hands, but with their baleful eyes on me.

The threat was obvious. I said, 'If I have offended you, Madam, please accept my apologies.'

'Accepted. You are here, Richard, to tutor my girls.'

'You have daughters?'

'In spirit. You have travelled with a handful of them, en route to this place.'

That gave me pause. If she considered Fatima, Maria and the rest of my playmates as her 'daughters', how did she feel about my having diddled them all on an almost daily basis? I've faced irate mamas on occasion, but never while naked and fettered.

Perhaps my consternation showed on my face, for she continued, 'You are known to have studied the *Kama Sutra* and various similar works. You have a reputation as an expert in the erotic arts. Your skills have been tested. I'm told that they are practical as well as theoretical. I require that you coach my girls to become supreme seductresses and bedmates. I want them to be houris, Richard, such women as men dream of but rarely meet.'

'May I ask to what end?'

'You aren't stupid. You know of the Hashisheen, I'm sure.'

'The Old Man of the Mountain – he drugged young warriors – they woke surrounded by pliant girls and in the utmost luxury. After a period of debauchery, they were drugged again and when they woke, told they'd been granted a visit to Paradise. If they died in The Old Man's service, they were guaranteed to return. They were assassins who knew no fear, for they welcomed death.' I paused to rub my itchy nose against my arm. 'Is that your intent, Child, to emulate The Old Man?'

'In part. *My* houris will be put to diverse tasks. Some will entertain covens of my werewolves. Some will become close to men of power or wealth. Each will be a seductress, an

179

agent provocateur and a betrayer, all in one. They will not kill by their own hands but they will open the doors that let my deadly werewolf covens in.

'Men are easily swayed by the women who please them in bed. The wisest sage is a fool when his passions are aroused. My soft sweet army of a mere five hundred girls will sway the entire world, once they are set in place. Those they cannot control, they will cause to be slain, whenever it suits my purposes. The Czar has entrusted me with . . .'

'How proud you must be,' I interrupted, 'to be trusted by your monarch, and to trust him, but even Czars are not immortal. What of his eventual successor? Might not he decide to take the weapon that you have wrought out of your hands?'

'I am no fool, to put my trust in kings, Richard. No one but I will know which girls are where, or which code words will command them. I alone . . .'

She raved on about 'fomenting war' and 'securing a warm water port for Mother Russia' but an earlier phrase, 'a mere five hundred girls', echoed in my mind. I repeated it, I thought under my breath. She must have had remarkably sensitive hearing.

The Child giggled. 'Fear not. Your enrolment will not be so great. I will give you but ten girls at a time, for ten days. In that time, you will teach them everything they need to know to lure and then enslave both men and women. There must be no carnal act in which they are not adept.'

'What if I fail to teach them? What if one fails to learn?'

'You will find them eager pupils but in that unlikely event, I am of an economical nature. The Czar is sending me a garrison of Cossacks, a force of one hundred large and lusty men. They will require entertainment. If a girl misses your passing mark, I will give her to them, to use as they see fit. I already have one such girl waiting.'

'Who? Not one of my erstwhile companions, I trust?'

'The Persian girl. The one called Honey.'

'But surely she would make a fine seductress.'

'She might, but she is spoiled. *You* spoiled her. She witnessed your victory over my first coven. She knows that my werewolves are not invincible. That poisonous truth must not spread.'

'She might tell the Cossacks.'

'They have no language in common and I doubt there would be much conversation between her and them even if they did. Cossacks have other uses for pretty girls than to talk to them.'

'*I* know that same "poisonous truth". What if *I* confide it to my pupils?'

She counted on her small slender fingers. 'Then the entire class will fail. They'll all be given to my Cossacks. You will be given to my wolves. I'll find another tutor. Volunteers won't be hard to find.'

'And Igor threw Bora into the abyss to hide the truth about your "werewolves",' I guessed. 'But why bring him so far to die? And what of the other members of his coven?'

'Honey's young lover? Zema made use of his strong back. He helped keep Honey amused. As for the other cowards that you routed so easily, all are long dead.'

'But . . .'

'Enough!' she commanded. 'All will be as I say. You will now meet your keepers and your enslavement will be completed.'

I admit that I bristled. Britons are *never* slaves, and the least enslavable Briton I knew was me. No doubt my muscles flexed in reflex, but it did me no good. Gold is a soft metal but not so weak that I could break bands of it that were three inches wide and half an inch thick.

The thought brought a smile to my lips. At that moment, I was clad in more riches than I'd ever dreamed of possessing but I couldn't so much as purchase a five-penny cigar, nor a Lucifer to light it with.

And so I met my gaolers. Kashk was a tall stringy fellow with a hatchet face and restless hands. His skin was as creased as old leather although he couldn't have been more than forty. By his looks, he might have been Cree, though that seemed unlikely.

The other, Lom, outweighed me by a hundred or more pounds. He was well larded, but with hard fat that would easily absorb blows and would protect his organs from all but the deepest wounds. I thought he might be a Mongol. Both men wore gaudy silk pantaloons and shirts and long sleeveless embroidered jackets.

I took them to be eunuchs – Kashk likely mutilated when fully grown – Lom emasculated before reaching puberty. A young boy who loses his stones rarely misses them. An adult man who is robbed of his manhood is likely to be vicious and resentful of men who are whole.

Lom reached towards my privates. I cringed, inside. I have an abhorrence of having my parts touched by my own gender. His fingers, however, closed on the gold crossbar. I cringed once again. Misery loves company. If I was right and neither of these were fully men, the better to suit them to guarding what amounted to a harem, it could be that I was destined to join their sorry state.

It was something of a relief, then, when Lom only bent the metal into a circle that girded my member.

Before the ring fully closed, Kashk set a half-cylinder of stiff dark fabric between it and the underside of my column. The band of gold was tight but not unbearable. Kashk went to the brazier. I set my teeth. Whatever torture they intended to inflict on me, I *would not* cry out.

He returned with a metal rod that was tipped by a white hot diamond of glowing steel. I tried to think of a quip that would demonstrate my *sang froid*. None came to mind. Lom lifted my shaft out of the way. He used the backs of his fingers, thank goodness. Burning metal came closer and closer to my shrinking scrotum. I tensed. There was heat on the underside of my shaft. I became distinctly uncomfortable but was spared the agony I'd anticipated.

Kashk returned his rod to the coals. My sphincter unclenched. Lom tugged the half-cylinder from between my cock and the gold ring. I breathed a sigh of relief. No doubt the fabric had protected my skin while the heat melted the gold band closed. It seemed likely that the other bands I wore had been united in the same manner but I hadn't been conscious then.

They'd saved the most frightening welding for when I was awake to enjoy it. That was an error. I can forgive a man who inflicts pain on me. I will *never* forgive one who inspires my fear.

The Child said, 'Bring him here.'

Lom was impressively strong. He wrapped his arms around the cross I was chained to and carried it, with me on it, to the grill that divided us from their Mistress. He set me down so close that my chest was pressed hard against the ornate bars. Did she intend us to futter through the grill? This suspicion was reinforced when she brought a pot of salve and began to smooth it over my member. It occurred to me that a six-hundred-year-old woman might have need of a lubricant.

'This lotion is similar to the one my "werewolves" anoint themselves with,' she told me. 'It's a little more potent. You might even find the effect pleasant. There are irritants and stimulants in it that will engorge your member to an extent that few men have ever experienced. At the same time, it contains alkaloid compounds that will deaden your nerves. The combined result is a priapism beyond any that occurs naturally. In other words, Richard, I am blessing you with an oversized and very demanding cock.' She smirked, looking up at me and then back down to my engorged member.

'The constriction about the base of your shaft will add to and maintain the effect.' Her two small hands wrapped my column and pumped it. 'I want you to give my girls practical lessons. My lotion won't make you insatiable, but close to it. If you are diligent, you might be able to achieve orgasm. If not, unslaked lust can make a man quite uncomfortable, or so I have been told.'

My cock grew between her hands. I couldn't see it but it felt as if transformed into some gigantic heavy-headed club. The animal in me ignored my detestation for the nasty little witch. It *demanded* that I break free and ravish her. My self-control, and my chains, restrained me.

'What a fine big member you possess,' she said. Her fingers ran from its base to its aching head. 'Such heat! Such a strong pulse!' She applied downward pressure, which my shaft resisted. 'So strong! It will serve my purposes admirably.'

The Child stepped back. She went to her table and washed her hands in something that smelled like alcohol. I made a mental note that strong spirits might be an antidote to the lotion. Lom dragged me away from the grill. Both of my guards disappeared for a moment and returned armed. My heart lifted. A heavy revolver was thrust into the sash around Lom's mighty girth. It had to be my Dragoon. Kashk wore the sabre my Isabel had given me, to his left. Tucked through his sash, behind him, was my Smith & Smith patent spring-loaded swordstick. I wondered about my Bowie knife and my Derringer. Could they be close by?

So, it amused them to threaten me with my own weapons, did it? That could backfire on them, particularly if they hadn't uncovered my stick's secrets. I tried to concoct a plan but my cock demanded my full attention. From memory, I'd rogered a dozen girls and women since my current mission had begun. That made thirty-six orifices, approximately. No – thirty-five, for Zema's mouth hadn't been available, except for the briefest moment.

Right then, I'd have sacrificed my left testicle for five minutes with any one of them.

I now know that the first application of The Child's lotion made me delirious. I recall being taken down from the cross and stumbling through various chambers and passages at the point of my own sabre. Later, I realised that my cock hadn't grown so long that I shouldered it, like a rifle. Nor had my testes dragged on the ground. The floor under my feet hadn't really been as warm and soft as woman-flesh.

After minutes, or hours, in my fever I couldn't tell, we arrived at my personal cell. It was plain stone but comfortably furnished, with a chair, a table and a narrow bed. Lom produced a ring of keys from a pocket in his voluminous pantaloons and gave them to Kashk.

In the distance, a gong sounded. It had to signal something urgent because Kashk fumbled his keys in his haste.

It seemed that my gaolers didn't plan to allow me any rest on my first night in their charge. No doubt they thought to teach me a salutary lesson. My left wrist was linked to a ring set in the wall about three feet up. My right was chained to a ring immediately below the first but set in the floor. I couldn't stand, sit or lie down. Very soon, my back began to ache. My cock was a constant torment. Even so, at some point, I lost consciousness.

Twenty-eight

A pail of icy water woke me. Another, a little warmer, sluiced me to full awareness. My left arm felt as though laced through by hot wires. My head ached. My cock was still engorged but throbbed less urgently than before.

While I was still chained, Lom shaved me and sponged me down. He wasn't rough. He took care not to spoil my moustaches. Perhaps he thought he could assuage the enmity he'd inspired the day before. If so, he was wrong, but I'd let him think he had. I told him, 'Thank you. You're a fine fellow who is just following The Child's orders. I don't hold it against you.' I don't know if he understood my lying words but my tone was friendly.

My manacles were rearranged so that my wrists were chained to my waist. Again, I was prodded along to a new location, but one that was close by. I was pushed through a wide door made of iron bars. It clanged behind me with my guards on the other side.

'Back up,' Kashk ordered in harsh Marseilles French.

I set my back to the bars. He reached through and unlocked my fetters. They were being very cautious, but this was the first day. Familiarity, I hoped, would breed contempt.

It seemed that The Child's fortress was divided between areas that were forbidding and those that were sybaritic. This chamber was opulent. Like the half-room I thought of as The Child's Alchemical Laboratory, no stone showed. It was lit by bronze lamps and silver candelabra. The furniture was eclectic. The Child had shown foresight. There were tables and chairs and sofas and divans and ottomans and stools, cushions and pillows – anything and everything that a woman might be sat upon, perched on, bent over or spread across to facilitate erotic activities.

There was statuary, some Hindu but much of it looked Italian to me. Figurines with larger-than-life sexual parts coupled in some positions I was familiar with and others that even Asp would have found beyond her. Two of the figures were life-sized, a male and a female. I was to use them as teaching aides, no doubt. His bronze cock was as large and as erect as my own. Her cunny was intricately detailed, but impenetrable, of course. I dubbed them Adam and Eve and then changed my mind. Adam was fine for him but the exaggerated contours of the female statue made Lilith a more apt name for her.

Shelves were laden with dildos, from miniature to gigantic, from featureless to grotesque.

Although my shaft still projected like a yacht's prow, my immediate need was for food, and that there was in plentiful supply. A buffet was set out on a long marble-topped sideboard, with thick slices of ham, chafing dishes of scrambled eggs, steamers full of porridge and a stack of bread rolls, similar to Scottish baps, with a butter dish at hand and, incongruously, a haggis. There was a row of glass jars, each containing either pickles or preserves. A huge pot of coffee was warmed by candles. There were pewter pitchers of fresh milk. How strange, to think that a milkman delivered to that place!

There was far more food than my class and I could eat at one meal. Perhaps it was intended as a full day's supply.

There was also cutlery, of a kind. It seemed I wasn't to be trusted with metal implements so there were knives and spoons that had been carved out of hard wood. You can kill with a wooden knife but it's less menacing than cold steel and menace can be important. I can slay a man with a straw but I doubt anyone would find one threatening.

I looked back. Kashk and Lom were eyeing me through the bars. I gave them my most pleasant smile, which I'm

afraid has sometimes been compared to a puma's snarl. My
fingers tore three baps apart. I smeared them lavishly with
butter and closed them over slabs of ham. Two of them, I
took to the entrance and handed through. The eunuchs
looked shocked at my generosity but recovered enough to
snatch the sandwiches and nod their thanks.

I sat down to enjoy my own sandwich and put my
thoughts in order. The Child was obviously a lunatic. That
made her no less dangerous. Throughout history, lunatics
have become emperors and generals. I cite Alexander of
Macedon and Napoleon Bonaparte. Both of them were
short. The Child was short. Could there be a connection?

Part of her mental disease seemed to be focused on her
own safety. The Child lived in barred quarters, in a strong
fortress, in the remote Himalayas. She was triply protected.
I deduced that she most feared the very thing she was
creating with her covens, assassins. If we can control
something, we need not fear it. She wanted to control an
army of assassins. It all made a queer sort of sense.

Then there was her theatricality and her addiction to
barbaric opulence. How deep do layers of rugs have to be
for comfort? She dressed her eunuchs in silk. She'd fettered
me with gold. There was no practicality to any of those. I
have not studied the sciences of the mind, apart from
attending a few lectures at the London branch of The
English Philosophical Society, but her sybaritic excesses
seemed to me to be external manifestations of her internal
delusions. Did she see herself as a modern-day Catherine the
Great or Cleopatra? There was a connection between those
two mad queens. The story goes that Catherine kept an
Imperial Guard of men seven or more feet tall. She was
reputed to suck ten of them dry each day. Cleopatra's
soubriquet was 'The Gobbler'. If The Child felt a connection
with those royal sluts, perhaps I could turn her mad
fantasies to my advantage. Could I seduce her? She'd
admired my cock, so perhaps . . .?

A gong sounded. Giggles and chattering came from
beyond an archway at the far end of the room. In twos and
threes, cuddling and holding hands, the girls who would

form my first class appeared, led by my five lovely companions. All were naked. All were desirable. For any reasonable man, they would comprise a surfeit of feminine beauty.

The residual effect of The Child's salve rendered me unreasonable. One look at that delightful array of breasts and bellies and thighs jerked my cock to its fullest attention. I wanted them *all*.

Fatima ran to me, jiggling deliciously with every step. 'English!' she cried. 'You are safe! Is it *you* who is to be our tutor?'

Before I could answer she was in my lap with her arms around my neck and her tongue in my mouth. Maria was close behind and hugged my head, managing to flip a nipple across my ear. Asp snaked an arm into the press of our bodies. Her hand found my shaft.

Reluctantly, I struggled free. I had a class of ten girls to consider. It wouldn't be good for discipline if I was perceived as having favourites. I had never been a good pupil, when young. I'd preferred to follow private studies, at my own pace. Now, however, I determined to be a good teacher, even if my role made no sense. A mere man, even one of my considerable experience, was expected to teach the erotic arts to ten lubricious little harlots? In combination, they likely knew more about futtering than I could even guess at. Even so, I had to make a good performance, for all our sakes. There was no doubt in my mind that The Child wouldn't hesitate to throw anyone who thwarted her to her wolves – or to her Cossacks.

Fatima gave me a sheepish look. 'I'm sorry, English,' she said. There was a glass pot in her hand. 'But I have to . . .' She pointed at my shaft. 'If I don't, The Child has other potions, terrible ones.'

I said, 'I understand. Go ahead.' It'd passed through my mind to take the pot from her and apply its contents myself but the thought of her fingers' touch overcame my kindly impulse.

I stood and let her slather. My lust burgeoned. Fatima quickly coated my length in its entirety but then she looked up into my eyes and continued stroking. I tried to think myself into a climax, to no avail. The rest of my class began exchanging glances and whispers. Fatima changed hands. Had I let it go on so long as to tire her arm? With a wrench, I stepped back, plucking my shaft from her hands.

'We will start with introductions,' I croaked.

'And then you fuck me?' a shapely green-eyed redhead suggested.

Ignoring her, I asked, 'Does everyone apart from Asp speak French?'

All, except Asp, nodded.

'Who speaks English?' I asked in my native tongue.

Asp and a tall lean blonde raised their hands.

I looked at the blonde. 'Your name?'

'Hanna.'

'From Sweden?' I guessed.

She nodded.

'Hanna, I'd like you to translate for Asp. Will you do that for me?'

She and Asp looked each other up and down. By their expressions, both liked what they saw. Hanna nodded. 'I will be pleased to look after her, Master Richard.'

'Thank you. From now on, everyone must address me as just "Richard". The nature of your lessons will make formality ridiculous.' Also, I was sick of being called 'English'. I'm proud of my nationality but that isn't my name.

Hanna mouthed, 'Dick' at me, with a grin. Her eyes dropped to my groin. She winked.

'Richard,' I repeated, sternly. I was going to have to keep a tight rein. These lovelies were used to manipulating the men around them. 'Introductions,' I reminded them. 'You will each tell us your name and where you come from, and . . .'

The sound of my sabre being clanged on the bars of the door interrupted me. I turned. Kashk told me, 'Names, yes. Where they come from, no.'

I shrugged. My little ploy at gathering intelligence had been worth a try. I'd likely be able to locate each girl's country of origin from her accent but I'd hoped to pinpoint their towns.

'Very well, give just your names. If you have a bedroom

190

skill that you are particularly proud of, tell us what it is. Name your favourite thing to do with a man, or with a woman, if that is your preference. If there is something you haven't tried yet, tell us what it is.' I paused for thought. There's nothing that can be done that someone hasn't done or tried to do. I explained, 'I don't mean any sexual act that does real harm, nor anything to do with ...' I ran through a list of all the unethical, disgusting or dangerous practices I'd heard of, without accepting requests for more specifics when a girl feigned not to understand. My conclusion was, 'If any of those acts appeal to you, I can't teach them to you. I'd have to fail you.' The expressions on their faces told me that they understood the consequences of failure.

'Very well, Asp, you begin.'

Hanna translated for her. 'I am proud to be very flexible. My favourite is to be put into positions no one else can achieve and then fuck or be fucked, hard. I have done everything I have ever heard of, with both men and women. So far, I've enjoyed them all.'

Hanna went next. 'I have no special skills except that when I climax, my cunny squirts.' She chuckled. 'I could drown the unwary.' Hanna offered a grin all round. She seemed totally uninhibited, which is a quality I admire. She continued, 'My favourite thing is sauna sex. I like men but maybe like women better. I've done everything, I think. Perhaps I will learn new things from Richard, I hope.'

'Sauna sex?' I asked.

'Get hot and sweaty. Slip and slide all over. Lick and be licked. That's the best – lots of girls, all licking me – me licking them.' Her head cocked as she thought. 'Birch beating is nice also.'

I took my hand off my cock, where it had wandered all by itself when I'd pictured half a dozen Swedish blondes, entwined and slithering. 'Fatima?'

'I am Fatima. I am a dancer. I have great control of my muscles, outside and inside. My favourite is to take it up my bum. I like men better, depending on the man. I too hope to learn new things.'

Maria said, 'My special skill is in my throat, right,

Richard? I like big cocks, the bigger the better.' She eyed my rampant member and licked her lips. 'I do everything and like everything, I think.' She paused and looked at Fatima. 'Oh yes, I like women too.'

The next girl was the shapely green-eyed redhead, who had a Greek accent, from the north, I thought. Her name was Iola. She confessed that she didn't know if she had any special skills. She'd only had three lovers and all of them had been virgins when she'd met them. Iola had no way to know how she compared to other women.

'What do you like to think about doing?' I asked.

'Being watched.'

'We can promise you that, can't we, girls?'

That brought an enthusiastic response.

'How about making love to women?' I asked.

'I never have.'

'Why not?'

'I didn't know women did that.' She put a hand on one lush hip and looked around the chamber. In a very coy voice, she asked, 'Would someone show me how women make love to women?'

The response was fervent. Perhaps Iola had only had three lovers but she had the instincts of a siren.

I asked her about rear entry.

'You mean "on hands and knees"?'

Fatima interrupted with, 'A man fucking you up your bum-hole.' That was crude, but explicit.

'No one has ever asked me.' Iola's face grew thoughtful. 'Does it hurt?'

I waited for one of the girls to answer but none did, so I told her, 'Some, at first, but it doesn't have to be too bad.'

'Then it gets to be very good,' Fatima added. 'Just like losing your maidenhead.'

I said, 'Jia Li, your turn.'

She looked at the floor and twisted her fingers together.

'You have to tell us, Jia Li.'

She whispered, 'I like to do as I am told and to be told I am a good girl and sometimes I like to be spanked. Men or women, all the same to me.'

'I still owe you a spanking, don't I, Jia Li?'

She brightened at that, bobbed me a curtsey and asked, 'Now?'

'Later, but I won't forget. You will show the class how a good girl takes a spanking.'

She blushed and sighed, 'Oh, thank you, Sir Richard.'

I didn't correct her for having granted me a title. She so enjoyed using honorifics.

Asuka said, 'I like cords. I like to be bound in helpless positions and then used hard. My skills are in ceremony.' Her eyes twinkled at me. 'And in ritual, including ritual ways to please men.' She looked from my golden collar to the band about my waist. 'Chains might be nice.'

I told my class, 'Asuka has some remarkable skills in her tongue and fingers. She will give you all a demonstration, in due course. How about women, Asuka?'

'If they are good girls and do as they are told.' She gave Jia Li a meaningful look.

'What happened to your beautiful scarlet cords?' I asked.

'Everything we had was taken from us.'

'I'll see what I can do to get them back, or some new ones. We'll need them for the lessons.'

Maria jumped up. 'They took my cross as well, Eng – Richard.'

'I'll look into it. Next!' I pointed to a chestnut-haired girl who was almost as voluptuous as Fatima. Her big hazel eyes, freckles, button nose, deep lips and wide playful grin told me she was Irish even before she spoke.

'I'm Tara. I can make men hard by talking dirty. My favourite is to take two or three big fellows at once. I can hold my breath pretty good.'

'Women?' I asked.

'Never tried.'

'Why not?'

'Never met one who wanted to. I'm willing to try but women don't have cocks, do they? I like cocks. I can't see the fun unless something goes up inside me.'

Maria showed Tara her fist and pumped it up and down.

Tara's eyes widened. 'Oh. Oh! I never thought of that.'

Elsa, from Bavaria, I thought, was shapely but her curves were firm and sturdy rather than softly voluptuous. Her legs were a little short but they tapered nicely, from muscular thighs down to sculptured ankles. She had large solid breasts with tiny pink nipples. 'I like to spank naughty girls and boys. I like to make them lick me until I spend on their faces. I like to fuck them.'

'Your bum?' Maria asked.

She shrugged. 'It is not a big pleasure for me, but I can take it and fake it.'

She wouldn't be my sort of woman, under normal circumstance. Under the current ones, she could be very useful.

Last of all came Chiku. I made a guess that she was from the Cape Colony in the Orange Free Valley. It's a part of Africa that abounds in mullatos, quadroons and octoroons. European men have been taking black mistresses and casually bedding black slaves there since the seventeenth century. Before that, it was Arabs. There has been plenty of time for the bloodlines to mix, often resulting in strikingly handsome men and extraordinarily lovely women.

Chiku's complexion reminded me of old gold. Her hair was close to her skull and tightly curled but her features were mainly European, with the exception of her lips. Those were slightly everted, making her mouth look remarkably sensuous. I wanted her mouth, right then, right there, but I told myself to be patient.

When it was her turn to speak, she strode to the front, padding on long narrow feet with her hips swaying and her belly undulating. Chiku was obviously proud to show off her body's sinuous beauty. 'In the beginning, I did everything a woman can do, just to survive. I found there was no sexual act that I didn't enjoy. Chiku has never said "No". She never will. Try me. Put me to the test.'

I raised my voice for Kashk and Lom's benefit. No doubt they'd be reporting my progress, or lack of it, to The Child. 'Thank you, ladies. I am going to teach you many things, including the positions described in the *Kama Sutra*. Those of you with special skills will teach them to the others. First,

194

so that we may move forward smoothly, we must take care of the deficiencies.'

'Deficiencies?' Maria asked.

'Iola's bottom is a virgin. Also, she's never made love to a woman. Nor has Tara. We'll take care of those three things now.'

Hanna said, 'I volunteer to initiate them.'

'I will make them lick me,' Elsa offered.

'Thank you,' I said, 'but Iola's lovely bum comes first and only I am qualified to perform that little chore. Are you ready for that, Iola?'

'I'll try to be brave,' she promised. Her face brightened. 'Will everyone be watching?'

Twenty-nine

I made my selection from the array of dildos. The one I chose was very modern. If The Great Exhibition had included a display of sexual devices, this one would have earned a special place. It was a simple steel rod, about half an inch in diameter and some five inches long, with a one-inch sphere mounted on one end.

I'd posed Iola, on her hands and knees, on four low benches that were arranged in a square. She liked to be watched. Her position showed her off to her best advantage. Her breasts hung, ripe and full. Her back hollowed slightly, emphasising the lush promise of her hips. With her arms and legs spread wide, every succulent part of her was available.

Hanna sat on a chair facing Iola, ready to brace her. I'd decided to combine Iola's introductions to Sapphic and anal sex. The blonde's and the redhead's mouths were already mashed together and making wet noises. Iola was taking to girl-love with some enthusiasm. I hoped that her bottom would take to buggery equally well.

I asked Fatima, 'May I have some of The Child's salve?'

She eyed my stiff member. 'You want *more*, Richard?'

'Not for myself. To make it easier for Iola.'

'Oh, I see.' She fetched the pot for me.

I dipped the dildo's ball into the ointment. 'Part her cheeks for me, Fatima.'

She set the pot aside but close to hand and told Iola, 'I envy you. I still remember my first time, taking it up my bum. It's special. Don't be scared. Richard is a nice man, which is good, and he has a big cock, which is better. Just relax and take it.'

I set the ointment-coated ball to the pucker between Iola's cheeks. Rotating it, I applied gentle pressure. There was some resistance. I pushed a little harder. Iola moaned into Hanna's mouth.

Looking at Maria, I said, 'Pinch her nipples, but not too hard.'

She obeyed, tugging as she pinched, almost milking. I put some force behind the dildo. Iona's sphincter indented and then gave, allowing the ball to disappear into her rectum.

Iola said, 'Oh!'

Our audience applauded.

'Did I hurt you?' I asked.

'Not hurt, exactly.'

Encouraged, I fed her back passage the full length of the rod, then drew it slowly back, twisting it between my fingers.

'Again?' I asked.

She nodded before returning her mouth to Hanna's. I pumped, at a snail's pace, making sure to thoroughly coat her rectum with the potion.

'Tingles,' she said. 'More?'

I pulled the dildo out, dipped it in the pot again and returned it. There was no resistance. Her anus relaxed at the first touch. I judged that she was ready.

'Brace her,' I told Hanna.

Fatima, anticipating my wishes, pulled Iola's cheeks as far apart as she could. I removed the dildo and set the head of my cock against the tiny opening.

I was trembling. The tension between my potion-induced lust and my self-control had reached a crisis. How much longer could I have kept my passions in rein? I'll never know. All I know is that the beast in me rose up, infusing my muscles with preternatural strength. I took hold of Iola's thighs, taking great pains to ensure that my hands didn't crush her flesh. With a fierceness raging through me, I slowly and deliberately drew Iona back, impaling her inexorably. When I had reached the greatest depth and she had not cried out for mercy, between gritted teeth I asked her, 'Are you ready?'

Through a red haze, I saw her nod. I unleashed my beast.

I remember some of it. I know my rocking dislodged Iola's knees from two of the benches but I didn't pause in my pounding. I held her up with my hands and my cock while Maria pushed the benches back into place. It seems to me that Asp managed to get under us and work on Iola's cunny with her fingers. There was sweat, mainly mine, running and splattering. My hair whipped my face.

I heard Iola gasp, 'More. Don't stop!'

My cock was a truncheon, battering into her. I could have sobbed from my need to spend but relief evaded me no matter how I thrust and skewered and attacked Iola's bottom from every angle. My legs and back ached. I ignored their demand for rest. I blinked with sweat-blind eyes. Hanna had been joined by Asuka and Chiku in bracing Iola, and I was rocking all three.

Eventually, Asp tugged at my left arm. Fatima pulled at my right.

'Enough,' Fatima told me. 'She is done. You must stop now, Richard.'

'Please, Richard?' Asp asked.

I ground my teeth and shuddered. Like a bull elephant shaking off his 'must', I became myself again. With a great effort of will, I plucked my cock from Iola's bottom.

'Did you spend?' Fatima asked me, concern in her voice.

I shook my weary head.

'Come,' she said.

With four or five girls supporting me, I was guided to a sumptuous divan and helped to lie down.

Someone said, 'Poor man.'

I wanted to protest the sympathy but had neither the will nor the strength. The only part of me that was still able to stand was my monstrous stiff cock. All ten lovelies clustered around me, even Iola. Fatima lifted my head, sat, and lowered it into her lap. Asp threw a leg across me to set her foot beside my hip. With her other foot still planted on the floor, she lowered herself. Her serpent took my cock into its mouth and swallowed it. Asp sank down on to my shaft until the lips of her cunny overlapped the golden ring that encircled its base. She swayed as she raised and lowered herself, working her clit on my cock's smooth metal cuff at the nadir of each stroke.

With both of Fatima's breasts being dangled over me and one of Tara's being offered to my lips from the side, my vision was limited. I didn't see who it was that steered my fingers to, and into the yielding humidity of her cunny. My scrotum was caressed. Lips and tongues worked on my toes. It was likely Hanna who lapped the sweat that trickled down my side.

How sweetly solicitous my girls were! As agents of Russia, they were my country's sworn enemies, but I felt no enmity towards them. They were not to blame. Every one of them, no matter whence she came, had been a pariah in her own land, denigrated and persecuted for no greater crime than being overtly sensual. The Child had offered them acceptance and even appreciation. Those are supremely seductive. It was little wonder they were in her thrall. They had no more choice in following her than goslings do in trailing after their mothers.

Asp climaxed, sagged and climbed off me. Hanna took her place with a grin.

Tara exclaimed, 'By all the Saints, we have us a man with a cock that faileth never. If we only had two more like him, we could all be made content.'

I remembered her boast of enjoying three men at a time. 'You mean that *you* could be made content, my greedy little colleen. What about the rest of the girls?'

Their laughter broke the tension that my inability to climax had engendered. I'd recovered enough to hump up and meet Hanna's vigorous downward thrusts. Whoever I was finger-fucking – I believe it was Chiku – spent on my hand. Hanna grunted and dismounted. I took the opportunity to extract myself from the press of flesh with my cock no closer to discharging than it had been when I'd broken my fast that morning.

We paused to eat our lunch – left-over food from breakfast. The eggs had congealed but the ham was fine. Once more, I fed the eunuchs, sending Fatima to make the delivery. Lom wouldn't care but Kashk had enough man left in him to enjoy the sight of her lush body.

We brushed our fingers off and wiped our mouths.

'The *Kama Sutra* devotes many pages to the art of kissing,' I announced loudly, for my guards' sake. 'We have a great deal to cover in ten days and I'm sure you have all been kissed, often. For that reason, I will teach you each kiss once and once only. You must concentrate.'

Maria asked, 'Are you going to show each of us every kiss, Richard?'

'No. I want you to form a line. I will name the kiss and then demonstrate it with the girl at the front. She will pass it on to the next girl, and so on down the line. The first girl will go to the back of the line after she has passed the kiss on, so that each of you will get a chance to be . . .'

'Kissed by you,' Fatima interrupted.

I didn't argue. The girls lined up, with Asp first and Hanna second, ready to translate for her.

'I think we can practise the three "Maiden's Kisses" all at once.' I took hold of Asp's shoulders. 'First, there is a simple lip-to-lip.' I brushed my mouth against Asp's. The little tease ran the sole of her foot up the back of my calf. 'Next, the maiden grows bolder with the "throbbing kiss".' I projected my lower lip and slid it between Asp's. 'With the third maidenly buss, the little minx teases her lover with a delicate touch of her tongue, but no more than a touch.' I demonstrated. Asp's lips parted. She swayed forward to rub her cunny on my thigh. Somehow, I resisted her invitations.

My plan – to make this lesson less of a strain on my self-control, was being severely tested, and we hadn't got past the 'innocent' kisses yet. I sent Asp to the rear of the line with a smart whack on her rump to speed her.

Hanna took her place with a look on her face that warned me of temptation to come.

'The *Kama Sutra* differentiates between kisses with different pressures,' I almost gabbled. 'You need no instruction in "soft, medium, hard", I'm sure. We'll move ahead to the lip kisses. These do not involve tongues,' I added quickly. My lips closed on Hanna's lower one, then her upper one, then nibbled on them both together. That's a caress that strikes me as extremely dull, but it's in the book.

Somehow my hand was on Hanna's hip and she was undulating against me as we kissed. In my naked priapic state, her writhing was much more effective than had I been clothed and not yet erect. I sent her to the back, without a pat on her bottom, even though she twitched it at me.

I covered 'Battle of the Tongues' with Elsa, wishing she were Chiku, and then realised that although the *Kama Sutra* lists many more kisses, they only differ from each other by the time of day and the state of relationship rather than being true physical variations. I wasn't going to be cheated out of Chiku's mouth, though.

I announced, 'I'd like to get to at least the first two positions for lovemaking today. To save time, I'll simply demonstrate the rest of the kisses, without describing them.'

Fatima's mouth and mine met like old friends, not that familiarity lessened my pleasure. Maria seemed intent on swallowing my tongue, as usual. Jia Li surrendered her mouth, letting my tongue and lips play as they wished but initiating nothing. Asuka simulated passion but was too predictable. The flick of her tongue's tip on mine was always followed by it lifting to offer the nectar pooled beneath it. She had a trick with curling her tongue and trilling that invariably preceded a strong rhythmic suck.

Tara told me, 'Until today, I'd never kissed a girl. Now I'm kissing nine of them.'

'How are you enjoying it?'

'Very much. Now kiss me!'

She had very mobile lips, which I enjoyed. She was a little more aggressive than I liked but my mouth soon tamed hers. I'm happy to say that I left her panting and starry-eyed.

Iola was pliant in my arms but tentative with her kisses. Perhaps she was still recovering from her first experience of being buggered.

And then it was Chiku's turn. Lips that are slightly everted remind me of a cunny's lips, not in appearance but in vulnerability. With such a mouth, even one of the 'maiden kisses' is an intimate act. I took Chiku's elegant face between

201

my hands and bent to brush my lips on hers. She was tall. I didn't have to hunch right over, as I'd had to with Jia Li and Fatima. I recapitulated the entire repertoire, from the purest to the most prurient. She squirmed against me, rubbing her breasts across my chest and thrusting her hips up and forward to press and part the petals of her sex about the base of my column. I felt her go up on to the tips of her toes and when that didn't raise her high enough, she made a little jump. Her legs wrapped around mine. The wetness of her slid down the length of my shaft. She paused and did a little shimmy. It was then that I realised she was frigging her clit on my golden ring.

'You need it, don't you?' I said.

'Mmmm.' Her tone spoke more eloquently of her desire than any words could have.

I broke from her arms, set her down and announced. 'The first position is called "*Indrani*". I don't need to tell you that a man should never enter a woman before she is aroused and her cunny seeps its dew. To save time, I'm going to assume that Chiku here is already wet and eager.'

A couple of the girls giggled. Hanna drawled, 'When is she not?'

'Better make sure you're in the same condition, Hanna. You could be next.'

'Promises.' To Iola she said, 'You can give me a hand.' She guided the Greek's fingers to her cunny. 'You need the girl-girl practice.'

I took Chiku's arm and led her to the divan. 'In this position,' I said, posing her as I spoke, 'you are on your back with your knees pulled up to touch your breasts.' I climbed up. 'Your feet are tucked into my armpits, to take some of my weight.' With my body straight as a lance, my weight on my toes and on the soles of her feet, I smiled down on her. 'Am I too heavy for you?'

'Please hurry up!'

'I enter her, thus.'

The girls huddled close to watch as my cock's engorged head parted Chiku's tight black curls and slid up inside her.

'She can control the depth of penetration by pushing up with her feet.'

'But I don't want to,' Chiku said. 'Fuck me hard, Richard.'

And so I did, and with my cock's ring flicking across the startlingly pink head of her clit, she climaxed before more than ten minutes passed. As gently as my raging lust allowed, I rolled her aside and pulled Hanna down under me.

'Indira can easily lead into the position called "The Flower in Bloom". Get your feet up close to your hips, Hanna. Lift your bum on your palms. Tilt up towards me.'

Hanna had likely tried that position a hundred times before, but rarely with a man of my dimensions and never with one whose cock was banded with gold. I went into her smoothly but with gusto. She rewarded me with a deep grunt. For a while, I limited the depth of my thrusts. My concern was that gold ring. Cunnies are less delicate than many men give them credit for but I didn't want to bruise my girls there if I could help it.

Hanna, however, thrust up at me with such vigour that I was buried to the hilt. She lubricated copiously. My thrusts squelched. Her fingers clawed at my arms. Her face twisted into a lustful grimace. Our audience urged her on, 'Let it go, Hanna!' 'Show us how much you can squirt, Hanna!'

Hands reached between us to tweak her nipples. Someone, I believe it was Maria, got a finger to Hanna's clit, so I leaned back a little to give her room.

Hanna half-sat up beneath me. Her belly creased and contracted. Aromatic juices, so hot they felt they were scalding me, squirted out from between my shaft and her cunny's lips. I withdrew, still rampant – still aching. Almost croaking, I announced, 'Next, "The Churn".'

Thirty

Kashk said, 'Turn right.'

I memorised, *Fifteen paces, turn right.* 'Where are we going?' I asked.

'She wants to see you.'

'What for?'

'She says you're a player of chess.'

I was and am, but not an accomplished one. Once I had the honour of playing a friendly game against the French champion, Pierre Saint-Amant. He trounced me.

So The Child wanted to play chess with me, did she? Scotching her fiendish plans had to take priority over saving Honey. Sitting across a board from her, even with a sword at my back, I'd have an excellent opportunity to crush her larynx and possibly rip her throat clean out. I knew that Kashk would run me through but unless he was lucky and pierced my heart, I had some chance of surviving, unless Lom shot me dead, which he most certainly would.

Very well. So be it.

I consigned, *A hundred and four paces, turn left,* to memory. We entered the stark chamber that was divided by The Child's ornate grill. Damn it, the chess table was set up abutting the bars. She'd be reaching through them to play. Even so . . . If she reached through and I grabbed her wrist and snatched her forward against the wrought iron, my other hand *still* had a fair chance of finding her throat.

Lom held my cocked Dragoon on me while Kashk freed my right wrist from my golden belt. I flexed my fingers, already feeling the wet crunch as they crushed The Child's larynx. Kashk reconnected my manacle to a foot-long chain that was attached to my metal collar. I sat. Yet another chain came into play, running taut from my waist down to a ring set in the floor. I wasn't going to be lunging at anyone. It'd be all I could manage to do to play a piece of mine that had reached the far side of the board.

The Child appeared in a little girl's dark-blue velvet party dress. Perhaps I was being honoured. More likely, she had dressed up to intimidate me by pointing up my nakedness. If so, her effort was wasted. I'd gone bare for so long it seemed natural and my unfailing erection, although a problem, was certainly nothing to be ashamed of.

'There are things I need, for my teaching,' I told her.

'Such as?'

I recited my list. She allowed that I could have them. 'Shall we play?' she invited.

I had white. My opening gambit was for 'Fool's Mate'. She avoided the juvenile ambush and routed me in eight moves. My next ploy, in our second game, was to offer my queen's knight as bait to trap her queen. She took the bait but avoided the trap.

'How ironic!' she exclaimed.

'What is?'

'You have not been dubbed but you are, figuratively speaking, a knight in the service of your Queen, Victoria. Symbolically, you just sacrificed yourself, but to no avail.'

I gave her a puzzled look.

'You – the chess piece – it represents you and you just . . . Never mind.' From then she played quickly and spitefully, decimating my pieces. She announced, 'Check and mate,' and swept off, no doubt to find more intelligent company, such as her wolves.

My gaolers led me back to my cell by a different route, adding to the mental plan I was compiling. Kashk danced ahead, wielding my sabre, practising lunges and making a poor showing of it.

'Stamp harder with your leading foot,' I told him. 'Keep the trailing leg straighter and lower. Be a jabbing lance.'

He tried again, performing no better.

'Bravo! You have a natural talent for fencing.'

The fool positively glowed.

A door to the right opened. A thin man, all in black, including his turban, emerged, wearing a bulky satchel and carrying two unlit lamps. When he saw us he darted back and snatched the door shut. I'd had almost two seconds to glimpse beyond it. There was an arrow slit through which I'd seen the night sky, tinged with pink at the horizon. A narrow and steep stone stairway spiralled downwards but not up.

Now I knew which direction West was. My assumptions, that we were in the upper structure and that there was a 'below the stairs' where the chores were taken care of and where menials resided, were confirmed.

I wondered how well a gigantic wolf could negotiate a precipitous spiral staircase.

That night I was allowed the use of my bed, with both wrists chained to the wall above my head. I reviewed my mental architectural sketch. It had too many gaps to be of much use but I'd keep working on it. Perhaps the girls could be induced to divulge some information about their quarters.

The gong sounded once, and perhaps a quarter-hour later, again.

I felt somewhat smug about our little chess tournament. Megalomaniacs are quick to accept that other people are stupid. My first encounter with The Child's salve had rendered me both delirious and horny. The second, applied by Fatima that very morning, had stiffened my yard and dulled it but it hadn't affected my intelligence as much as before. Even my lust, though still made intoxicatingly strong, hadn't been so overpowering as it had. There was no doubt in my mind that I was developing a resistance. That was an asset. It was imperative, however, that I conceal my small advantage. I'd started my deception by playing chess so badly that The Child had been convinced my brain's functions were still blunted. I would continue it by acting the satyr with my pupils.

I could do that.

That night I dreamed that I heard wolves howling and when I woke, they were.

Thirty-one

The freshly-catered buffet was as generous, and as odd, as the previous ones. I sent a platter of overcooked bacon to the eunuchs, via Iola's delicate hand. The devilled goat's kidneys were half raw and stringy. I made do with quince preserves spread on *chapattis*. There was too much chicory in the coffee.

While I ate, Fatima anointed my cock.

'The success of a spanking,' I announced, 'depends as much on the one who is spanked as on the one performing the act.'

Both Elsa and Jia Li perked up.

Tara wanted to know, 'But a man puts a girl over his knee and whacks her bum. What does she have to do with how it turns out?'

'You'll see.' Turning to the rest, I said, 'If you've ever been spanked, put your hand up.'

Fatima, Maria, Jia Li and Chiku each raised an arm.

'If you enjoyed it, put the other hand up.'

The same four responded.

'So – everyone here who has tried it has enjoyed it. Most of the rest of you will as well, *provided* it is performed correctly by *both* parties.'

Tara said, 'I still don't understand . . .'

'You will. An awkward spanking gives no pleasure to anyone. One that is elegantly performed can be exciting. People become addicted to being spanked but one that is clumsily executed can be a disaster. You see, a spanking is like a duet, a dance for two. In a waltz, a man leads and a woman follows. If the man misleads or the woman fails to follow, they could stumble and fall.'

Jia Li, Asuka and Fatima looked puzzled by my reference to a 'waltz'. I reminded myself that my pupils came from many cultures. To clarify, I continued, 'When tumblers or acrobats perform, throwing and catching each other, they must both be skilled.'

Tara, still unclear, asked, 'But the man *forces* . . .'

'And the woman willingly bends to that force, even though she pretends to resist it. She has her moves to make, her grace to contribute. I will demonstrate with the aid of . . .' I looked from girl to girl, deliberately teasing. '. . . Jia Li.'

She squealed with delight before recovering her usual demure expression.

'Often, a girl who has merited a spanking will be fully clothed. We will pretend that Jia Li is wearing a dress and a pair of drawers. Are you ready, Jia Li?'

She nodded eagerly.

I strode to her, took her by the nape and marched her to an upright chair. I sat with my left knee pointing straight ahead and my right turned down and aside. 'Note the positions of my legs.' I pulled Jia Li down over my left thigh. 'Now, I can trap her thighs.' My right leg crossed over both of hers, just above her knees. 'You see how she is contributing? If she had started kicking before I had her pinned, she could have fallen or have been harmed. Now, now that I have her safe, she can present a pretty picture of a maiden in distress by flailing her legs from her knees down. Be careful, though. Never kick harder than the man can cope with.'

'In your case, that means as hard as she can,' Chiku guessed.

'Not all men who spank are as large as I am.'

Jia Li kicked, but not vigorously.

'To pretend to protest "with feeling" a girl might reach behind herself, trying to cover her bottom with her hands. This gives the man a chance to grab her wrists and pin them

209

to the small of her back.' I demonstrated, with Jia Li's assistance. 'If, however, the girl is more in the mood to "surrender," she will keep her arms down but hollow her back, raising her head. That is a signal to the man to take hold of her hair.' I released Jia Li's wrists and wrapped her long black hair around my fist. A pull on it bent her backwards.

With doubt in her voice, Tara said, 'So *she* is signalling to *him*, telling him what she'd like him to do.'

'Exactly. That's what seductive women do – give hints to men about what they'd like – even about things they want to be *forced* to do against their protests. A siren can be so subtle that she makes her men think that they are doing what *they* want to do, when it's really *her* initiatives.'

Iola frowned, as if finding the concept hard to grasp.

I continued, 'Now I lift Jia Li's skirts . . .' I mimed doing so. '. . . and pull her undergarment down to her knees. Now her legs are tangled. I am free to admire her bottom at my leisure.' I stroked and squeezed Jia Li's smooth firm haunches. 'I am not only enjoying caressing her, as she is happy to be caressed, but I am teasing her. It is a paradox of spanking that even girls who adore having their bottoms tanned are nervous about it at this stage. Jia Li, are you scared?'

She nodded as best she could with my hand in her hair.

'Are you also thrilled?'

'Please?' she whimpered.

'Please start or please don't start?'

'Yes. Both. I want it. I'm frightened of it.'

I smiled at my class. 'Strange, isn't it?' My fingers squeezed Jia Li's flesh. 'She craves what she fears. Right now, there's a knot in her tummy.' I lifted my hand. Jia Li tensed. Her sleek little bum clenched. I stroked it some more. She slowly relaxed. I gave her right cheek its first swift whack, not hard but not gentle, either.

'As you saw, I waited for her to become calm and for her muscles to soften. If you are over a man's knee, as she is, and want him to get on with it, that's what he is waiting for.'

I asked Jia Li, 'Do you like to count?'

She shook her head. 'Can't.'

'Some girls like to count each slap out loud. Some can't keep track after the first few blows. I'm going to give Jia Li thirty, unless she stops me by calling out "enough". No girl should accept a spanking without having a way to ask for it to stop.'

Jia Li's cheeks twitched.

'She's impatient. We won't keep her waiting.' I slapped again, clipping alternate cheeks, keeping up a steady rhythm. 'This is painful for her,' I said. 'It always is at first. She's enduring it and wondering why she was so silly as to volunteer but there comes a time, about – now – when the hot glow penetrates and spreads and becomes intense pleasure.'

Jia Li was writhing and sobbing. Her breath came in short gasps.

'She's really enjoying that?' Tara asked.

Still slapping, I asked Jia Li, 'Shall I stop?'

'No, no, no, no, no!'

'You see?' I vocalised the end of my mental count, 'Twenty-eight, twenty-nine, thirty!'

Jia Li wailed and humped her blushing bottom up at me.

'She's desperate for more, poor girl. She could likely climax from it if I went on long enough.' I flipped Jia Li over, releasing and trapping her legs once more, and bent her backwards over my knee until her head brushed the floor. My hand forced her knees apart, exposing a swollen clit and an engorged and saturated cunny.

'Maria, she needs your tongue.'

The Spanish girl knelt at our feet, parted Jia Li's nether lips and set her mouth to work.

'Now I want you all to pair off. Decide between you who gets the first spanking. You'd better agree on how many slaps before you start. Any questions?'

Elsa said, 'There's nine of us now. Who gets left out?'

'I think that you do. You know how to spank, don't you?'

'Of course.'

'And you'd find it very difficult to let yourself be spanked. If you were, you'd get no more pleasure from it than I would, right?'

'Thank you, Richard.'

At that moment Jia Li's little shiver told us that she'd climaxed. I picked her up and carried her to the divan. 'Come here, Elsa. Jia Li needs more than one climax. I imagine that watching me spank her has made you horny?'

'Yes.'

'Then you two can comfort each other for the rest of this lesson. Don't forget to be masterful and demanding, Elsa. She needs that.'

Fatima looked at my cock and asked me, 'What about you, Richard? Don't you need . . .?'

'I can wait,' I said, hoping it was true.

They paired off quite quickly, no one objecting to anyone else. Of course, there were natural pairs. Asp and Hanna seemed to have taken quite a fancy to each other, perhaps because of Hanna's services as a translator, perhaps because they could converse without the others understanding. Fatima and Maria were old friends. Chiku was having fun teaching Tara the Sapphic arts so that left Asuka and Iola as the last pair by default.

I wandered around my 'classroom' adjusting a knee here and directing a hand there, alert for any real cries of pain. There were none, but the sights, sounds and aromas stimulated my senses so intensely that my lust became unbearable. If the statue of Lilith had been made of anything softer than bronze, I'd have ravaged her then and there.

Tara, she who boasted of accommodating three men at a time, rolled off Chiku's knee with both hands clutching at her own groin. 'Holy fuck!' she groaned. 'Me sainted Mother would never believe it. Who'd have thought a bum-beating could make a girl so horny? Do me, someone. In the name of all that's unholy, somebody do me.'

Nothing fuels my passion like the knowledge that a girl is consumed by lust. Tara's pleas fanned my fires. I strode to her and gathered her up in my arms, facing away from me, warm soft bum pressed against my belly, and carried her to where Adam stood with his bronze shaft stiff and ready.

Tara soon understood my intent. 'You're as twisted as me Da's shillelagh, Richard,' she told me.

'Lucky for you that I am.' I heaved her up at Adam. She spread her thighs wide to greet his metal cock. Her arms wrapped around his bronze neck. With a little manoeuvring, we lined up her cunny with his prong. She sank down, impaling herself. Her hips began to pump. I stilled them. 'You like more than one man at a time, don't you?'

She nodded. I mounted Adam's plinth, guided my staff up between her plump rosy buttocks, and thrust. The metal member that filled her cunny rendered her back passage doubly tight. I surged up for half my length and paused, in case I was hurting her.

'Do it, fuck you,' she shrieked.

I gave her the rest of my shaft. It felt strange, fucking against the thick metal column's resistance, but lust overcomes all. I pounded into her. She was unable to move much, being doubly impaled, but Tara was very vocal. There was no mistaking her joyous cries when she climaxed, nor her continued desire when she called out, 'Don't fucking stop, you fucking English fucking bastard! Don't you *dare* stop!'

It was my thrusts that were sliding her up and down Adam's member, so, in effect, I was rogering her from the front and from the back at the same time.

Reverting to her native Gaelic, Tara screamed, '*Taim ag teacht!*'

I'm not conversant with the language but I recognised 'I'm coming!' One happy holiday that I'd spent in County Cork, when I was but a lad, there'd been a parlour maid . . . But that's another story.

Now that Tara had warned me of her climax, I forced my thrusts to judder to a stop and caught her before she collapsed. I admit that although I lifted Tara off Adam's unyielding pole with great tenderness, I couldn't resist a few more grinds into her bottom as I did so.

We paused in our studies for lunch. Halfway through our meal, a pretty bare-chested lad with gilded curls made a delivery to the eunuchs. I sent Tara to collect it. The girls gathered round as excited as though it were Christmas. The Child had kept her word. Everything I'd asked for, she'd provided.

213

I gave Maria her blasphemous rosary and cross. 'May I borrow your chemises, for now?'

She nodded as she tied her toy about her slim waist.

Asuka got her fan back but was more excited by the lengths of silken cord I set aside, in two thicknesses and three colours – gold, green and blue. I forgave The Child for not having crimson on hand. I was sure she'd done her best. Jia Li's eyes widened when she saw the English riding crop in black leather, with a nice long loop at the whippy end. I gave it a swish, just to see gleeful anticipation light up her face. They all eyed the double-dildo, two eight-inch ivory cocks joined in a shallow 'V', but I set it aside.

'Today we will learn about the Elephant and the Sparrow,' I announced.

'Which fucks which?' Tara asked, grinning.

'They're two different positions,' I explained. 'First, the Sparrow. If a man takes you in this way, be grateful. It's strenuous.' I knelt on a cushion, sitting back on my heels.

Iola was the one who most liked to be watched, so I beckoned her, even though she wasn't the lightest. 'Sit on my cock, facing me, legs beside my hips,' I told her. She sank on to my shaft easily. To the best of my recollection, I never touched one of my girls but she was already wet. It must have been the erotic *ambience* that governed their mood.

'Fingers locked behind your head. Lean forward and rest your cheek on my shoulder.' My arms went under her splayed legs, lifting them. I gripped her sides just below her armpits. With her only supports her bottom on my thighs, my cock in her cunny and my arms under her knees, I raised and rocked her.

'Mm,' she said. 'This is nice. What do I do?'

'Absolutely nothing. Just relax and enjoy.'

Tara asked Iola, 'How does it feel, that mighty pole slow-fucking into you? Is it good? Is he stretching you deep? Look at him, the great handsome ox of a man. He's strong enough to do you like this for hours. Is that bit of gold around his cock doing lovely things to your clit? You want him deeper? You want him to fuck you so hard he bruises your cunny? Do you?'

Iola bit her lip and tossed her head. Tara's obscenities were affecting her. I bounced on my calves, lifting Iola's bottom clear off my thighs and slamming her down again.

'You're going to spend, Iola,' Tara said. 'Can you make like Hanna, a great wet gush, a fountain of it? Can your cunny clutch at Richard's cock?'

I heaved fully up on my knees, flinging Iola so high my cock almost came out of her. I dropped back as she descended so that she landed in my lap with a loud squelch. Iola might not be able to rival Hanna for wetness, but her cunny was oozing enough for any man's needs.

It was Hanna who continued Tara's obscene encouragement. 'I want to graze on her watercress when she has spent and you are done, please Richard? I'm sure she's delicious.'

I nodded. Hanna's request, that she be allowed to lick the dew from Iola's cunny, seemed to trigger the Greek girl. She let out a long moan, punctuated by grunts as my thrusts rocked her, and relaxed, sated.

I lifted her off my rigid erection and set her down, thighs spread wide for Hanna's convenience. As I climbed to my feet, I said, 'We'll get to the Elephant a little later, when my back has recovered. Asuka, pick which cords you would like me to bind you with.'

The greedy little bitch fetched them all. I was by no means a master of *nawa shibari* but all Englishmen love fooling around on boats, so I knew how to tie a knot. It's simple common sense not to cut off a girl's circulation or tie anything around her neck. I managed a fair approximation of the way Asuka had been bound when I'd met her and stepped back to admire my own work. Her breasts extruded between the cords above and below them, as they had before. The bonds that bracketed her mound weren't quite as tight so I made some adjustments. Everyone, except Hanna, Tara and Iola, watched. Those three had formed a triangle on the floor, each with her face between another's thighs.

Asuka gave me a look that told me, very politely, that she wasn't satisfied. I took the hint. A double slip-noose drew her elbows back until they touched. I wrapped her arms down from there, each turn close enough to the one before that no skin showed between them. When I reached her wrists and tied off I still had cord dangling and no means of cutting it, so I drew it down between the cheeks of her bottom, parted the lips of her cunny to run it in that soft wet slot and had just enough still left that by stretching the cord taut, I could tie it to the line that crossed her belly, three inches below her navel.

Asuka gave a little wriggle, testing her bonds to see if they were uncomfortable enough for her liking. Apparently they were, for she beamed and honoured me with a little bow.

'The Elephant?' Maria reminded me.

'I hadn't forgotten. This one is easy on the man, so if your lover is feeble or simply tired, you might want to suggest it. Traditionally it is performed on the floor, on cushions or pillows, but I'm feeling lazy. Maria, up on the table with you.'

She almost leaped on to the flat surface. Her heavy cross clunked on the polished surface. I arranged her, on her side, knees bent up to her breasts, with her bottom and cunny just projecting over the edge. With her legs tightly together, the treat between her thighs was squeezed to protrude backwards. I slid my shaft into it.

'Twist your upper body towards me and lean up on one elbow,' I instructed. 'It's important to look into your lover's eyes and show him your adoration.'

'Even if you don't adore him,' Elsa added.

'It's even more important then.' I gave Maria a couple of slow strokes. 'Maria, you may use your free hand to diddle yourself. This position is very pleasant for the man but isn't likely to take the girl to her climax.'

Fatima peered closely at where my shaft was pistoning into Maria. 'You could bugger her in this position, couldn't you, Richard?'

'Like this?' I pulled all the way out and re-entered Maria between the cheeks of her bottom.

She grunted. 'Yes. That's different. I like that, a lot. Do me hard, Richard.'

I put one hand flat on the small of her back and gripped her thigh with the other. My hips jerked, faster and faster.

'Perhaps you will come this time, Richard,' Fatima urged from close behind me. Her hand, between my parted thighs, toyed with my swaying sac and encouraged me further. 'Help him,' she called to the others.

I was touched by their response. The Sapphic triangle on the floor broke up. Hanna, standing to my left with a breast pressed to my arm, whispered, 'Please come, Richard. I so want to taste your hot cream.'

Tara, on my right, told me, 'Fill the Spanish whore! Flood the bitch's tight little bum-hole.'

Asp made a long leg and mounted the table with one lithe step. Standing astride Maria's head, she trust her pubes at me, parted her cunny's petals and finger-fucked herself. 'Come when I do, Richard! We'll spend together!'

No man could ask for more encouragement than those girls gave me, but to no avail. Maria climaxed three times, making very sure that I knew how wonderful each spasm was for her.

As I'd said, it was an easy position for a man to roger in, but even so, my back gave out before my lust was released. With a sigh, I staggered back and sank into a chair. Iola's mouth was on me almost before my rump hit the seat. My class was determined to make their tutor happy, but a gong sounded, and our day was done.

On the way back to my cell, I asked Kashk, 'In the late evening, a gong sounds and then a little after, there's another. What for?'

'You needn't worry. You're always snug in bed by then, safe behind bars. The gongs sound for us, not you. The first is a warning, to get behind closed doors. The second signals that her two cousin-wolves are loose in the corridors. Anyone they find, they eat.' He grinned. 'Would you like to take a midnight stroll, Englishman?'

I told him, 'No thank you,' although that was exactly what I intended, as soon as the time was ripe.

Thirty-two

The following day, Asuka appeared still bound as I'd left her. Someone, likely Jia Li, must have helped her with her ablutions and so on. In any case, it was the Chinese girl who fed the Japanese with bite-sized portions of the baked unidentifiable fish and spoonfuls of couscous. Asuka had refused the borsht.

I doled out Maria's chemises to Iola, Tara and Chiku to try on. 'Before you can show your lover your fantastic bedroom skills, you have to entice him into your bedroom.'

'Or entice her,' Elsa offered.

'Or her,' I agreed. 'The men, or women, that The Child sets you to seduce will be rich and powerful. They won't lack for lovers. If you are one of three, or ten, lovely girls who are subtly offering themselves, you must ensure that you're the one he chooses.'

'I'd whisper, "I can't wait to get your cock in my mouth," into his ear,' Tara said. 'That never fails.'

'I'm sure it doesn't,' I allowed, 'but first you have to get close enough to whisper. You have to draw him to you. You have to *suggest*, not shout, that you are available.'

'How?' Fatima asked.

'You are going to be attending courts, visiting great houses. Fatima, I'm afraid that you wouldn't be welcomed wearing the pretties that you are used to dancing in. Each society is different. Remember how Asp was clad when first we met her. All she could use to draw men was her eyes.'

'I had a way of moving that moulded my trousers against my thighs,' Asp said.

'Thank you, Asp. You make the point for me. You must conform to the society you are in, but tempt men with hints. For example . . .' I pulled Iola closer. 'Where I come from, for evening wear, a lady's form from her waist down is hidden by crinolines and bustles. Her dress brushes the ground. So . . .' I mimed pointing a toe and lifting a skirt. '. . . an ankle that is "accidentally" exposed for the briefest moment will draw the eyes of every man in the room. If the girl can somehow convey to one man that the display wasn't entirely an accident and was intended to be seen by him alone, that's tantamount to Tara's whisper, in effect.'

I smoothed Iola's chemise wider on her shoulders. 'In London, today, bared shoulders and half-bared breasts are perfectly acceptable. Thus, if fashion allows this much décolletage . . .' I tugged the chemise low on the lush slopes of Iola's breasts. 'And she wears her dress thus . . .' I pulled it down another two inches. '. . . then the men will gather like dogs to a bitch in heat. And *then*, if she is alone with the man she has set her cap at, and she stoops to pick up a dropped glove . . .' Iola bent without further prompting. 'Hold that pose,' I told her. 'If you look closely you can see that half of her left breast's aureole peeks over the top of her dress. In an English drawing room, that exposure, even for a fraction of a fraction of a second, will have a man fawning like a puppy.'

'In heat,' Tara added.

'Likewise,' I continued, 'the narrow but plunging neckline.' I pulled down on Chiku's chemise to plunge hers. 'Which is of particular use if the girl is less endowed. Men like fulsome breasts but in a room full of them, all modestly covered, if the girl with the smallest breasts has a deep enough neckline, it is she who will garner the greatest attention. It isn't exposure that draws, it's the promise of it.'

I turned to Tara, who was wearing the chemise with slits to her hips. 'In this chamber, at this moment, I may feast my eyes on seven pairs of naked legs, seven bottoms and seven pairs of hips. Who will I watch as she walks, in case I catch a glimpse of her lower parts? Why, Tara.' She walked for me, rolling her hips. 'Will her next step reveal the tops of her

219

thighs? Will a pace expose her bottom? What treasures will my eyes delight in next?'

'This one,' she said, lifting the skirt of her chemise at the back to bare her bum. 'We understand, Richard. We're women, remember? We all know to show an inch more than is proper and promise to show three.'

'Good,' I said, somewhat disgruntled to find that I teaching the catechism to the Pope. 'Perhaps Fatima will teach the rest of you something you don't already know. Up on this stool, Fatima.'

She hopped up with a grin. I selected a porcelain dildo that approximated a real cock in size and shape. 'Nice,' she said. Her knees bent and her mound thrust forward at me.

I set the dildo's head between the lips of her cunny and pressed a third of its length into her. Releasing it to her internal grip, I said, 'Show us what you can do, Fatima.'

She straightened and frowned in concentration. Inch by inch, the porcelain was drawn up inside her. My girls applauded. Fatima let the toy descend, then pulled it back. Her pace accelerated until it appeared that some creature, invisible except for his member, was fucking her vigorously.

The girls were suitably impressed.

'She can do the same with her back passage,' I told them. 'You won't have time to master those skills while you are here but I'd like Fatima to teach you the exercises she performs that will develop the abilities for you.'

'My pleasure,' she said. The dildo fell to the floor. Fatima stooped low enough to take Iola's hand. 'Feel how I do it,' she said, feeding three of Iola's fingers into her cunny.

My object was to teach, diligently, but to delay fucking any of them for as long as possible. Every time I used my cock without reaching my climax its ache seemed to get worse. If I could keep all the girls happily busy, I hoped that neither they nor the eunuch-spies would notice that I wasn't an active participant.

I called, 'Elsa!' Her sturdy little body hurried to my side. Her eagerness, I thought, was born of curiosity about the two-ended dildo I held. 'Try this. The ends are identical but the straps are designed for this end to go inside the user.'

With her happily busy, I turned to Asuka. 'I must release your arms,' I told her. 'I want you to show the girls your magical *Chipatama* kiss.'

'As you command, Richard.'

What a subtle little minx she was! 'As you command, Richard.' What a world of meaning she'd compressed into four simple words. Tacitly, she'd offered me anything I wished of her – her cunny – her bottom – her mouth – every delicate delectable part of her, to use or abuse at my whim. I was mightily moved to accept her offer, but resisted. Instead, I set her to demonstrating her technique, the three-finger massage and the dabbing tongue, on Adam's infallible member.

I told Maria to show off her cross's secret and use it to teach the others her swallowing skills.

Elsa mastered her straps. I beckoned Jia Li and announced, 'The Mare'. In that position the man sits up with his legs spread and his knees high. The girl sits in his lap holding his neck, with her calves up over his shoulders. As Elsa and Jia Li demonstrated, I told their audience, 'This is one way two girls can futter, even without the dildo. Can you see that?'

They nodded, thoughtful, no doubt letting their imaginations work.

'Can you suggest other ways girls can rub cunny-on-cunny, clit-on-clit?'

They could, of course, and were soon happily showing off their favourite ways. Thus, my pupils were pleasantly engaged, wandering from Asuka's little show, to Maria's to Fatima's and to the experiment in Sapphic loving class.

I talked Elsa and Jia Li through Splitting the Bamboo and then switched the Chinese girl for Asp for The Swastika and The Tripod. Iola and Tara were begging to take turns on Elsa's imitation cock. Elsa herself was positively glowing as I'd appointed her the class mistress once she'd mastered each new position. She loved to instruct and arrange limbs, which saved me from laying hands on any of the girls' more desirable parts.

My cock still ached, but not as badly as it would have if I'd been fruitlessly rogering all morning.

After lunch, Jia Li spoiled my plan. She knelt at my feet with the riding crop on her extended palms and a mute plea in her lovely eyes. Well, I'd requested the crop for a reason. That reason wasn't going to go away.

I took the crop and swished it. 'Who has felt a crop or cane or similar?'

Jia Li, Chiku and Maria responded. 'The rest of you very likely will, someday,' I warned them. 'Some of you will like it. Some won't. I can't teach you to like it but I *can* teach you not to fear it. If you were to run screaming the moment you saw a crop in your master's hand, you'd be failing in your mission.' I slapped the leather shaft on my palm. 'Girls who have never been cropped fear that half a dozen strokes will cripple or scar them. They won't. Unless the master is vicious, by the next day your bottoms will be almost healed. You might show a few proud bruises, but no more. If the man is very wicked the marks might last a week. Fear the pain, by all means, but don't be afraid of being seriously hurt.'

I smiled down at Jia Li. 'So that you may learn that a beating is bearable, I am going to give each of you three strokes, except for Jia Li. She'll get ten. Tomorrow, you will be able to look at her bottom to see how little damage she shows.'

'And kiss her bum better,' Iola said.

Maria asked, 'I want six, please, Richard.'

'Very well.'

Hanna put her hand up. 'If I want more after my three, may I ask for them?'

'By all means. Anyone who wants more may ask for them. Now, are we ready?' I took a large soft cushion and put it on the edge of the table. Jia Li bent over it without being prompted. The rest of the girls formed a giggling and chattering line. It'd never been like that when I was at prep school and we lined up for our beatings.

I had a lot of strokes to take so I laid into Jia Li's bottom steadily. I took care to land each blow squarely. If a crop 'wraps around' a hip it can leave a nasty bruise.

As I swung, the girls called out the count, 'Nine, and ten.'

Jia Li pushed herself up from the table with a polite, 'Thank you, Sir Richard.'

Asuka took her place. I drew my arm back but was given pause by Jia Li, who had dropped to her knees and had taken my cock's head into her warm loving mouth. It would have been churlish of me to stop her, so I delivered Asuka's three slaps. She took them without complaint but didn't ask for more. Hanna, next in line, took her place. What surprised me was that Asuka took Jia Li's place fellating me, as if it had been planned. Women can do that – coordinate their efforts without speaking.

Hanna asked for an extra three but yelped on the last one. Fatima bent over the table. Hanna knelt at my feet. Asuka passed her my cock as if it was a pipe they were sharing.

One by one, my pupils endured or enjoyed their beatings and one by one they applied their various techniques to pleasuring my cock. My lust grew more and more urgent. My stones had tightened and relaxed several times. The vein that ran the underside of my cock pulsed so strongly I swear I could hear it beat.

Then it was Maria's turn. My attention was so much on my cock that perhaps my swings were desultory, for she asked for six more, which I delivered with more vigour. When I was done, instead of standing, she climbed on to the table and swung round on her back to dangle her head back over the edge. Her mouth opened. My girls, clustering around me, pushed me close. Asuka took hold of my shaft between her thumb and fingers to guide it between Maria's lips.

'Fuck her face, Richard,' Tara urged.

Asuka began that massage, three fingers working on my anus, perineum and scrotum. There were hands and lips and tongues all over me. I rocked. My cock's head glided over Maria's tongue. Her lips closed around my shaft. Her mouth worked like a suckling baby. I didn't unleash my full lust. If I had done so, I am sure I'd have done Maria serious harm. Even so, the numbness and tingling that The Child had inflicted on my cock seemed to dissolve. I felt that it wasn't the physical stimuli I was enjoying that countered her evil potion. It was the incredible outpouring of loving support.

223

Whatever, my jism poured from me like liquid silk, flowing and flowing for long enough that Maria moved her head aside with her mouth full and Fatima took her place and then Chiku, till I had no more to give.

My class led me to the divan and there I rested until the gong signalled the end of classes for that day.

Kashk and Lom took me past my cell and on towards The Child's chamber. 'More chess?' I asked.

'No. You are to watch something.'

'What?'

'You'll see.'

I was taken into The Child's chamber and out the far side, adding to my map. A short corridor brought us to a heavy wooden door. Kashk unlocked it and led me in. We were on a balcony that overlooked a stone pit, perhaps fifty feet across and the same deep. There had to be two dozen wolves sprawled, stalking, licking each other, doing all the things wolves do when not otherwise occupied.

'All these prowl the corridors after curfew?' I asked.

'No. Just the two cousins. All these are their offspring. They are waiting to be sent on their missions.'

I waited to see if he'd share any more but Lom gave him a warning elbow.

I leaned on the parapet and tried to count how many beasts there were but they moved about so I achieved no more accurate a count than my initial, 'About two dozen.'

A door in the wall at the bottom of the pit opened. The Child entered, followed by the lad with gilded hair. She looked up at me and gave me a merry wave. I waved back, just as merrily.

She walked among her pets, scratching an ear here, patting a head there. Was I supposed to be impressed by her control over the ferocious beasts? If so, I was. It is a far cry from keeping two close by, as pets, to wandering among a giant pack.

She made her way back to the door and exited, leaving the youth behind. As the door closed, the first wolf bristled. Another snarled. The pack began to circle their victim.

One leaped.

I was *not* going to show my revulsion. Still leaning on the parapet, I unfocused my eyes and commanded my ears not to hear the screams and snarling and the sickening sounds of bones crunching.

I spat, to avoid vomiting, but I don't think the eunuchs noticed.

Thirty-three

On the afternoon of their last day, the girls orchestrated an orgy in my honour. It was a valiant effort. Every last one of them insisted that I pay a farewell visit to all three of her orifices. I still wasn't able to climax again.

'Perhaps your next class will do better,' Iola said.

'I doubt that. Do you know when I am to expect the new girls?'

'You have a week to rest, I'm told. We leave in the morning but they won't be here for seven days. They'll arrive with the force of Cossacks that The Child is expecting.'

As I kissed my charges goodbye I digested that intelligence. Seven days. If I was going to escape with Honey, it'd have to be soon. The arrival of my new class and the Cossacks would make it more complicated – and there'd be little point in absconding with Honey after a hundred barbaric lechers had been at her. I determined that I would make an opportunity the very next day.

So much for determination. On my first day without a class to teach, I was left abed, in chains, hungry, thirsty and horny and badly needing a pee, until early evening, as best I could judge it.

When Kashk and Lom finally allowed me up and about, the corridors felt hollow. 'Below the stairs' was likely just as populated as before, with cooks and maids and lamp-lighters and guards, hewers of wood and drawers of water, all busy about their mysterious duties, but on this level, my girls were gone. They were all off to seduce their ways into the beds and confidences of the rich and powerful. I should have wished them ill but I couldn't bring myself to. Instead, I wished them safety and comfort – but not success.

It was up to me to bring their failure about. Now was the time. My first class had graduated. My second was yet to arrive. *Carpe diem*, Richard, I told myself. Seize the day.

Kashk pranced ahead, slashing at the air with my sabre. 'There were no sweet *chattes* for you to fuck today, milord,' he jeered. 'No tight *culs* to bugger, either. Your *queue* must be in agony.' He'd been taunting me with similar witticisms from the moment my wrists had been secured to my belt. Even so, I was concerned that he didn't hold me in deep enough contempt, yet.

Lom prodded my back with the muzzle of my Dragoon while Kashk unlocked the door of bars. Lom hadn't been taught that 'touching' is too close when you have a man at gunpoint. Had my hands been free, he'd have been nursing a broken wrist and begging me not to squeeze my pistol's trigger.

The buffet was reduced in size but still odd. There were three sorts of blancmange, an aspic of some sort of shredded meats that I didn't recognise and an enormous platter of *pigeons à l'Anglais*. In lieu of bread there were potato pancakes. Everything was cold. The candles that had kept the coffee warm had guttered out long since.

I looked at the food and at my fettered right wrist, pointedly. Kashk was kind enough to return the use of one hand to me. I made myself simper my thanks.

I swigged cold coffee and chewed on an exceptionally tough pigeon. Lom spooned pink blancmange into his slobbering mouth one-handed until he found it awkward and tucked my Dragoon into his sash. Wisely, he backed twenty feet away from me before he continued his gorging.

Kashk wrapped a portion of the aspic in a pancake and ate with one hand while he idly practised his swordsmanship with the other.

'Wrist higher, point lower,' I advised. 'Like this.' I demonstrated with a pigeon's leg as my blade.

He tried to copy me. I was effusive with my praise. He hadn't learned that the more a man toadies, the greater the danger he is to your back. No doubt inspired by my admiration, Kashk 'played' at attacking me. He was as intimidating as a schoolboy with a sharp pencil but I retreated in obvious fear and contrived to topple backwards over a stool. Both eunuchs found this hilarious. I embellished my role as clown by letting the hand I was pressing down on to help me rise, slip. My face hit the floor a little harder than had been my intent. I retrieved my pigeon bone and rose with a split lip.

Rubbing my face in a suitably rueful manner, I told Kashk, 'Your attack is excellent. How is your defence?' I made a feint at him with a tiny femur.

I think what he meant to show me was a parry in *sixte* followed by a riposte. I was reminded of a stage magician I'd once seen, waving his wand.

'Very good!' I lied. 'Are you familiar with the seventh position, the parry *septime?*'

He shook his head. I tried to demonstrate with my tiny bone but threw it aside in disgust. A wooden knife from the buffet soon followed it as equally inadequate. I spread my hand and shrugged, obviously chagrined at not being able to teach him something new and valuable.

Kashk frowned, looked at me through narrowed eyes and considered. I could read his thoughts as if they were writ large upon his forehead. The walking cane he wore behind him was mere wood and tipped with a blunt brass ferule. The sabre he'd stolen from me was much longer and made of sharp steel. He'd seen for himself that I wasn't a formidable opponent. Why, he'd had to do no more than wave my sabre at me to send me sprawling.

How he reconciled my clumsiness with my reputation, I'll never know, but he made his decision. Kashk said something to Lom, who backed off further and rested his hand on the butt of my revolver. With a flourish, Kashk tossed my swordstick to me. I made to snatch it from the air but missed. He waited patiently for me to retrieve it before charging at me with a wild flurry of cuts.

Somehow, seemingly by a series of fortunate accidents, I avoided both his edge and his point. The ebony shaft of my weapon suffered a few nicks but proved strong enough to deflect his steel. My training almost tricked me into making a counter-riposte but I covered that error by tripping over my own feet.

He feinted at my wagging cock. I gasped in alarm as I took a backward leap. Lom, having finished one entire dish of blancmange, paused for a gurgling laugh at my expense before turning to the buffet for a second dessert. I watched him from the corner of my eye. Although holding both a dish and a spoon took his hand from my revolver, he made sure to keep twenty feet between me and himself.

I went into a precipitous retreat, stumbling a full circuit of the chamber. Kashk was having a fine time of it, pursuing me. Lom let me get within fifteen feet that time. After I stubbed a toe on the leg of the divan and had to hop out of Kashk's way, howling, Lom allowed me within twelve.

Panting, I lowered my weapon and gave Kashk a pleading look. He wasn't ready to grant me a rest. He advanced, waving the point of my sabre at me in what he considered a menacing way. I backed up, passing Lom but keeping ten feet from him. Kashk, striding towards me, was also about to pass Lom when I beat the sabre aside and thrust. My blunt brass ferule plunged through his throat. Without a pause, I rounded on Lom. My thumb pressed the release of my stick's spring-loaded sheath. Instead of ducking or ignoring the missile that was flying towards his face and drawing my Dragoon, he threw both arms up in defence. Belatedly, he tried to snatch them down again. My naked blade's point pierced his left eye. Not wanting to take any chances, as he was so large a man, I waggled my weapon, scrambling his tiny brain.

When I turned, Kashk was on the floor, choking up blood. It seemed a shame to cut the horrid little man's agony short, but I dispatched him swiftly for expediency's sake.

A gong sounded.

Kashk's keys released my left wrist. His clothes were blood-soaked so I took Lom's, wrapping his sash around my waist thrice to approximate a fit. The fat man proved to be a treasure trove. My two-shot Derringer had been concealed under his sash. I had no right to his razor but he had no further use for it, so I took it. My Bowie was sheathed beneath his sweaty armpit. I rinsed it with cold coffee and dried it on a red satin cushion.

For the very first time, I ventured beyond the arch at the far end of the chamber. I discovered ten luxurious cells, a water-closet and a sunken Roman bath that had been emptied, unfortunately. I craved a good soak.

There was no exit that way.

I'd just started retracing my way back to my cell when the gong sounded again. The Child's pet wolves were loose.

I'd been waiting for that signal. Now that it was after curfew, I'd be unlikely to meet up with any minions. It wasn't that I'd be reluctant to slay any I encountered. They were enemies of my Queen and so deserved to die, but a clear path would give me a better chance of finding my way out and of executing the crude plan I'd formulated.

Past my cell, I came to the door I'd managed to glimpse into when the man in black had emerged. It was latched, but only with a simple piece of wood. My second jerk snapped it.

With naked steel in each hand, I crept down the spiral staircase. It went deeper than I expected, thirty-five steep steps down. Perhaps the fortress only had three levels – the first and lowest down the sloping tunnel I'd seen Honey carried into; the second would be the 'below the stairs' entrance and armoury level; and the third was the living quarters.

The fewer the levels, the easier it would be to find my way out. On the other hand, the fewer the levels, the greater my chance of bumping into The Child's lupine pets. My ears strained for the scratch of claws on stone.

The staircase exited into a passageway that ran both right and left. I tried left and came to a vast kitchen with its oven fires still smouldering. A cupboard yielded a roast leg of lamb. I took it with me, both to gnaw on and with some vague thought of using it to distract the wolves, should I meet them.

Thus it was that when I *did* come across them, I was armed with my sabre in one hand and a large piece of meat, instead of a weapon, in the other.

Neither beast snarled nor barked. In deadly silence, they charged. The male, in the lead, leaped at me. I met it with a lunge, wrist high, point low. My sabre passed between its slavering jaws and exited through its belly. The animal's weight and momentum wrenched my weapon from my hand. The bitch was already in the air, paws extended. My two hands snatched out and caught both of its forelegs by its pasterns. Its teeth gnashed together an inch from my nose. I flung my arms out to both sides. There was a rather unpleasant sucking sound as the bitch's shoulders dislocated. Canines aren't built to spread their forelegs.

Pressing my advantage, I forced the animal's own bones inward, to pierce its brisket. The damned beast dropped atop my roast, where it'd fallen from my hand. So much for my snack!

I recovered my sabre. I am not a superstitious man but I severed both wolves' heads with my silver-inlaid blade. My sabre was sticky with gore. I wiped it on the male beast's decapitated corpse. It'd need cleaning again before I sheathed it, for all I'd achieved with my wipe was to cover it in wolf hairs.

There were a few wrong turns for me to make before my nose caught the acrid odour of gunpowder. I crouched and crept towards the smell. The broad high tunnel was dark but I have good night vision. Its far end showed a faintly paler shade of black. My nose told me when I passed the powder magazine. My ears caught a snuffling that told me that there was at least one mule tethered close by. By then, the opening was distinctly grey. Two short figures showed in silhouette. When I got closer, they resolved into a pair of guards, seated companionably on the edge of the cliff, feet dangling, their pikes set aside. They were smoking pipes that were doubtless forbidden and had a tobacco pouch and an oilskin envelope of Lucifers on the ground between them.

I set my sabre down carefully. With my swordstick's blade in my right hand and my Bowie knife in my left, I padded

231

forward. It was convenient that they sat so close together. Both of my hands struck at once. There is a pad of muscle at the base of a man's skull that if pierced vigorously and at an upwards angle, kills him so swiftly that he has no time to cry out.

My victims tumbled into the abyss. To my regret, they took their pipes with them, but they left their tobacco behind. I had the weed but no means to smoke it. My vice aside, their Lucifers were more valuable booty.

I used them to light a lamp, keeping the wick short so that it wouldn't shine too brightly. By its dim light, I led the mule I'd passed earlier towards the entrance, tethered it to the cannon and hitched it to a cart, ready. Three trips with my arms full conveyed enough hay into the cart to keep the beast fed for a day or two.

Back at the gunpowder magazine, I found a pair of felt slippers and was shod for the first time in months. My nails teased some long threads from Lom's sash. I tied one end around a bag of powder that I set against the wall. Being sure to keep it a few inches above the stone floor, I stretched the line right across the tunnel and into the magazine. Three more bags of powder served to hold my cocked Derringer firmly. It was aimed at the closest hogshead. A scattering of hay concealed my trip thread. I tied a running noose about my pistol's twin triggers and hoped that no one stumbled over it before Honey and I had escaped.

The side tunnel curved down and debouched upon a lamp-lit set of luxurious cells, similar to the ones my girls had been kept in. An old man sitting on a three-legged stool kept guard with a flintlock musket by his side. As he was facing his cells, he was easy to creep up on and dispatch.

I opened Honey's cell and shook her awake.

'Shh! It's me, Richard,' I hissed. 'I'm rescuing you. Get up!'

'I don't want to be rescued.'

'She's going to give you to a company of Cossacks, to be their toy.'

'I know.' She took a deep breath and opened her mouth.

I had no choice but to punch her silly head.

The silk rug that her cell had been furnished with was magnificent. It had to have taken a family three generations, perhaps four, to hand-knot. I rolled Honey up in it and slung her over my shoulder. Running as fast as I could, I raced to my cart, threw Honey in the back and led my mule out into the night.

A full moon was rising behind the fortress. My hackles rose at the ill-portent but I blessed the light it shone on the narrow bridge. My instinct was to race across but the surface was cracked and pitted. One good jolt could skew our path. If a wheel ran over the edge, I doubted I'd be able to drag it back.

I contented myself with a walking pace and tried not to hold my breath. We'd just achieved the secure footing of the far side when the faint sounds of distant shouting reached me. I leaped up into the seat and slapped the reins, urging my beast onward.

Fifty feet into the ravine, it stopped dead in its tracks.

I looked back. There were lights moving within the tunnel. I slapped the reins on the mule's back again. It still ignored me. There was nothing for it but to jump down and drag on the stubborn beast's harness. That achieved nothing. The shouts behind me grew louder. In desperation, I put two fingers up one of its nostrils and my thumb up the other. With a good grip on the animal's septum, I pulled. That worked. Compelled by the agony I was inflicting on its nose, it followed me.

Walking backwards, I watched the fortress. If my trap failed and someone decided to fire that great cannon before we turned a bend, we were done for. It couldn't miss the cart, which I needed. Worse, I knew that in the days of yore, flying slivers of wood had killed and maimed more sailors than cannon balls ever had. If the ball hit the cart, it'd become a grenade.

I saw a flash. The vast maw of the fortress became the crater of an erupting volcano. The ejected cannon turned end-over-end in the air. A great heat hit me and then a noise that was no noise, for it deafened me, lifted me, the mule and the cart a few inches off the ground before dropping us back in place. Staggering to keep my feet under me, I watched in awe as the cannon, falling, smashed clean through the bridge. The enormous tower of rock that housed The Child and her cohorts lurched like an arthritic and ancient priest kneeling for vespers. Slowly, shedding boulders the size of houses, it settled down and sank into the vast chasm.

The mule never balked again. Perhaps it credited me with saving its life. More likely, I'd intimidated it. Whichever, I named it Dobbin, after an old nag my parents once owned, and climbed back up into the cart's seat. A gentle slap of the reins set us moving. Our return trek across half of Asia commenced.

Epilogue

Burton dictated very little about his arduous journey West. I suspect that as it involved no more erotic encounters, he considered it not worth the telling. Honey divided her time between trying to escape him and trying to seduce him. As a result, she spent much of the journey wrapped in the rug.

The golden sovereigns from his swordstick's ram's head bought provisions wherever they were available.

Dobbin expired a dozen miles from the western edge of the Taklaman Desert. Burton carved off a hind leg to sustain himself and Honey, though she preferred to go hungry than to eat raw mule meat. He took Dobbin's place between the cart's shafts. I can't imagine the determination it took to drag that weight for two long days, one of them through burning sand, while wearing forty-odd pounds of gold.

On the third day he was attacked by three mounted bandits and thus acquired two horses. The third animal ran off before he could secure it.

He avoided Baghdad, taking a circuitous route out of caution. Before entering Kurdistan, he painted the sign of the peak and three wavy lines on the side of his cart and thus passed unmolested.

Benim welcomed Richard with open arms. Datis, Honey's father, greeted him with screamed accusations of having debauched his daughter and attacked him with a knife. Burton's defensive punch broke the man's puny neck, putting paid to the promised talent of gold. Benim took Honey into his household and hustled Burton out of Turkey with all dispatch. A week later, he was in the arms of his beloved Isabel, who insisted he delay having his golden restraints removed for at least a fortnight.

When they were, the gold proved to be only fourteen carat, but forty-two pounds three ounces still realised a tidy sum. Most of the proceeds were spent on chemists' attempts to duplicate The Child's formula. I regret to report that they failed.

nexus

The leading publisher of fetish and adult fiction

TELL US WHAT YOU THINK!

Readers' ideas and opinions matter to us so please take a few minutes to fill in the questionnaire below.

1. Sex: Are you male ☐ female ☐ a couple ☐?

2. Age: Under 21 ☐ 21–30 ☐ 31–40 ☐ 41–50 ☐ 51–60 ☐ over 60 ☐

3. Where do you buy your Nexus books from?
☐ A chain book shop. If so, which one(s)?

_____

☐ An independent book shop. If so, which one(s)?

_____

☐ A used book shop/charity shop
☐ Online book store. If so, which one(s)?

_____

4. How did you find out about Nexus books?
☐ Browsing in a book shop
☐ A review in a magazine
☐ Online
☐ Recommendation
☐ Other _____

5. In terms of settings, which do you prefer? (Tick as many as you like.)
☐ Down to earth and as realistic as possible
☐ Historical settings. If so, which period do you prefer?

_____

☐ Fantasy settings – barbarian worlds
☐ Completely escapist/surreal fantasy

☐ Institutional or secret academy
☐ Futuristic/sci fi
☐ Escapist but still believable
☐ Any settings you dislike?

_____

☐ Where would you like to see an adult novel set?

_____

6. In terms of storylines, would you prefer:

☐ Simple stories that concentrate on adult interests?
☐ More plot and character-driven stories with less explicit adult activity?
☐ We value your ideas, so give us your opinion of this book:

_____

_____

_____

7. In terms of your adult interests, what do you like to read about? (Tick as many as you like.)

☐ Traditional corporal punishment (CP)
☐ Modern corporal punishment
☐ Spanking
☐ Restraint/bondage
☐ Rope bondage
☐ Latex/rubber
☐ Leather
☐ Female domination and male submission
☐ Female domination and female submission
☐ Male domination and female submission
☐ Willing captivity
☐ Uniforms
☐ Lingerie/underwear/hosiery/footwear (boots and high heels)
☐ Sex rituals
☐ Vanilla sex
☐ Swinging

- ☐ Cross-dressing/TV
- ☐ Enforced feminisation
- ☐ Others – tell us what you don't see enough of in adult fiction:

_____

_____

_____

8. Would you prefer books with a more specialised approach to your interests, i.e. a novel specifically about uniforms? If so, which subject(s) would you like to read a Nexus novel about?

_____

_____

_____

9. Would you like to read true stories in Nexus books? For instance, the true story of a submissive woman, or a male slave? Tell us which true revelations you would most like to read about:

_____

_____

_____

10. What do you like best about Nexus books?

_____

_____

11. What do you like least about Nexus books?

_____

_____

12. Which are your favourite titles?

_____

_____

13. Who are your favourite authors?

_____

_____

14. **Which covers do you prefer? Those featuring:**
    (Tick as many as you like.)

☐ Fetish outfits
☐ More nudity
☐ Two models
☐ Unusual models or settings
☐ Classic erotic photography
☐ More contemporary images and poses
☐ A blank/non-erotic cover
☐ What would your ideal cover look like?

_____

15. **Describe your ideal Nexus novel in the space provided:**

_____
_____
_____
_____

16. **Which celebrity would feature in one of your Nexus-style fantasies?**
    We'll post the best suggestions on our website – anonymously!

_____

THANKS FOR YOUR TIME

Now simply write the title of this book in the space below and cut out the
questionnaire pages. Post to: Nexus, Marketing Dept., Thames Wharf Studios,
Rainville Rd, London W6 9HA

Book title: _____

NEXUS NEW BOOKS

NEXUS CONFESSIONS: VOLUME 5
Various

Swinging, dogging, group sex, cross-dressing, spanking, female domination, corporal punishment, and extreme fetishes . . . *Nexus Confessions* explores the length and breadth of erotic obsession, real experience and sexual fantasy. This is an encyclopaedic collection of the bizarre, the extreme, the utterly inappropriate, the daring and the shocking experiences of ordinary men and women driven by their extraordinary desires. Collected by the world's leading publisher of fetish fiction, these are true stories and shameful confessions, never-before-told or published.

£7.99   ISBN 978 0 352 34144 0

To be published in November 2008

BARE, WHITE AND ROSY
Penny Birch

Natasha Linnet has a weakness for older men, preferably those with sufficient confidence to take her across their knees. The directors of old-fashioned wine merchants Hambling and Borse seem ideal for the task, and they want her to work for them. It's an offer too good to refuse, but Natasha quickly finds that she is expected to give a great deal more than she had bargained for, to a great many more people and in a number of unexpected ways. Only the temptations being dangled in front of her make it possible for her to put up with what is being inflicted from behind.

£7.99   ISBN 978 0 352 34505 9

To be published in December 2008

GIRLFLESH CASTLE
Adriana Arden

Vanessa Buckingham has discovered strange contentment in the bizarre and secretive underworld of commercially organised slavery. Having accepted her own submissive nature, Vanessa is now happily working for the powerful Shiller Company as a 'slave reporter' for *Girlflesh News*. She has also found a lover in the form of the beautiful slavegirl Kashika. But there are forces at work that wish to destroy Shiller's carefully run 'ethical' slave business. Shiller's rival and arch enemy – the media mogul, Sir Harvey Rochester – has not given up trying to take over the operation. Having failed to use Vanessa as his unwitting pawn to expose Shiller, Sir Harvey now turns to more extreme methods.

£7.99   ISBN 978 0 352 34504 2

If you would like more information about Nexus titles, please visit our website at www.nexus-books.co.uk, or send a large stamped addressed envelope to:
  Nexus, Thames Wharf Studios,
  Rainville Road, London W6 9HA

NEXUS BOOKLIST

Information is correct at time of printing. To avoid disappointment, check availability before ordering. Go to www.nexus-books.co.uk.

All books are priced at £6.99 unless another price is given.

NEXUS

☐ ABANDONED ALICE	Adriana Arden	ISBN 978 0 352 33969 0
☐ ALICE IN CHAINS	Adriana Arden	ISBN 978 0 352 33908 9
☐ AMERICAN BLUE	Penny Birch	ISBN 978 0 352 34169 3
☐ AQUA DOMINATION	William Doughty	ISBN 978 0 352 34020 7
☐ THE ART OF CORRECTION	Tara Black	ISBN 978 0 352 33895 2
☐ THE ART OF SURRENDER	Madeline Bastinado	ISBN 978 0 352 34013 9
☐ BEASTLY BEHAVIOUR	Aishling Morgan	ISBN 978 0 352 34095 5
☐ BEING A GIRL	Chloë Thurlow	ISBN 978 0 352 34139 6
☐ BELINDA BARES UP	Yolanda Celbridge	ISBN 978 0 352 33926 3
☐ BIDDING TO SIN	Rosita Varón	ISBN 978 0 352 34063 4
☐ BLUSHING AT BOTH ENDS	Philip Kemp	ISBN 978 0 352 34107 5
☐ THE BOOK OF PUNISHMENT	Cat Scarlett	ISBN 978 0 352 33975 1
☐ BRUSH STROKES	Penny Birch	ISBN 978 0 352 34072 6
☐ CALLED TO THE WILD	Angel Blake	ISBN 978 0 352 34067 2
☐ CAPTIVES OF CHEYNER CLOSE	Adriana Arden	ISBN 978 0 352 34028 3
☐ CARNAL POSSESSION	Yvonne Strickland	ISBN 978 0 352 34062 7
☐ CITY MAID	Amelia Evangeline	ISBN 978 0 352 34096 2
☐ COLLEGE GIRLS	Cat Scarlett	ISBN 978 0 352 33942 3
☐ COMPANY OF SLAVES	Christina Shelly	ISBN 978 0 352 33887 7
☐ CONCEIT AND CONSEQUENCE	Aishling Morgan	ISBN 978 0 352 33965 2
☐ CORRECTIVE THERAPY	Jacqueline Masterson	ISBN 978 0 352 33917 1
☐ CORRUPTION	Virginia Crowley	ISBN 978 0 352 34073 3

NEXUS CONFESSIONS

NEXUS ENTHUSIAST

NEXUS NON FICTION

- - - - - - ✂ -

Please send me the books I have ticked above.

Name   ....

Address   ....

               ....

               ....

               .... Post code ....

Send to: **Virgin Books Cash Sales, Thames Wharf Studios, Rainville Road, London W6 9HA**

US customers: for prices and details of how to order books for delivery by mail, call 888-330-8477.

Please enclose a cheque or postal order, made payable to **Nexus Books Ltd**, to the value of the books you have ordered plus postage and packing costs as follows:

UK and BFPO – £1.00 for the first book, 50p for each subsequent book.

Overseas (including Republic of Ireland) – £2.00 for the first book, £1.00 for each subsequent book.

If you would prefer to pay by VISA, ACCESS/MASTERCARD, AMEX, DINERS CLUB or SWITCH, please write your card number and expiry date here:

....

Please allow up to 28 days for delivery.

Signature ....

Our privacy policy

We will not disclose information you supply us to any other parties. We will not disclose any information which identifies you personally to any person without your express consent.

From time to time we may send out information about Nexus books and special offers. Please tick here if you do *not* wish to receive Nexus information.   □

- - - - - - ✂ -